GLITTER, GLAM & CONTRABAND

HEATHER WEIDNER

Suzanne,
Watch out!
for the secrets
Heather Weidner

PRAISE FOR GLITTER, GLAM, AND CONTRABAND

"Drag queens and pawn stars and snakes! Oh my! Throw in other intriguing cases for P. I. Delanie Fitzgerald to solve, sprinkle with some old-fashioned sleuthing, toss with interesting and well-researched history on Edgar Allan Poe, and you've got yourself a recipe for an honest-to-god page turner!"

Jayne Ormerod, Author of *Goin' Coastal* and Other Cozy Mysteries set along the Shore

"Heather Weidner has once again written a must read with this work. Delanie Fitzgerald, the P. I. heroine created by Weidner, engages readers with her snappy, sassy, intelligent attitude and wicked one liners."

J. L. Canfield, Author of *What Hides Beneath* and *Icy Roads*

"*Glitter, Glam and Contraband* is fast-paced and humorous. P.I. Delanie Fitzgerald's investigation into a series of thefts at a gentlemen's club introduces her to a world of drag queens with fanciful stage names like Tara Byte and Anna Conda. But there is nothing funny about the illegal sale of exotic reptiles or antiquities that she uncovers. Delanie juggles a number of interesting cases with real world settings. Great read!"

PRAISE FOR THE TULIP SHIRT MURDERS

"Smart, sassy Delanie is back for more murder and mayhem, and readers will enjoy every twist of Weidner's cleverly plotted mystery."

LynDee Walker, Agatha Award-Nominated Author of *Lethal Lifestyles*

"Weidner's latest Delanie Fitzgerald mystery delivers everything her fans have come to expect—a spunky P.I., a fast-paced plot, and a supporting cast of deliciously sleazy characters."

Mary Miley, Author of *The Impersonator*

"The intrepid Delanie Fitzgerald once again teams up with a computer geek and an English bulldog named Margaret for a hair-raising adventure in *The Tulip Shirt Murders*. You'll be hooked from page one."

Maggie King, Author of The Hazel Rose Book Group Mysteries

"In Heather Weidner's latest mystery, *The Tulip Shirt Murders*, feisty private investigator Delanie Fitzgerald proves yet again that she can handle everything from bootleggers to murderers to strip club owners. Never shying away from dangerous situations, Delanie doggedly chases down clues until she flushes out the bad guys and solves the crime. *The Tulip Shirt Murders* is a fun read that will keep you laughing...and guessing...until the very end."

Frances Aylor, Author of *Money Grab*, A Robbie Bradford Novel

"Stakeouts, disguises, and surveys lead PI Delanie Fitzgerald on the road to catch the Tulip Shirt Murderer."

Teresa Inge, *Virginia is for Mysteries* & *50 Shades of Cabernet* Author

PRAISE FOR SECRET LIVES AND PRIVATE EYES

"Move over Kinsey, there's a new sassy PI in town – Delanie Fitzgerald. *Secret Lives and Private Eyes* is an impressive debut for Heather Weidner."

Debra H. Goldstein, Author of *Should Have Played Poker*

"If you like spunky sleuths and mysteries brimming with local color, then you'll love Heather Weidner's fun debut set in Richmond, Virginia!"

Meredith Cole, Award-winning Author of *Posed for Murder* and *Dead in the Water*

"Delanie is masterfully written. She's the strong woman readers cheer for."

Lyn Brittan, Author of The Mercenaries of Fortune Series

"Watch out Stephanie Plum. Delanie Fitzgerald has arrived. And she doesn't take 'no' for an answer."

Betsy Ashton, Author of the Mad Max Mystery Series

To Stan and my parents,
thanks for all the encouragement and love!

PROLOGUE

Delanie Fitzgerald hopped onto an empty bar stool at Federico's in Richmond's East End. The smallish room looked like it had been last decorated when disco balls and pet rocks were all the rage. The bodies, two and three deep, around the bar and two pool tables did not seem to mind the dated décor. They laughed and drank like this was a second home.

"What'll ya have?" asked the tall bartender. His tight black T-shirt stretched to accentuate his muscles.

"Ginger ale." She scanned the standing-room-only crowd.

She put a five on the bar, which he picked up when he set the drink down beside it. "A ginger ale for a ginger." The bartender smiled and left her change by the glass.

She smiled back with a little too many teeth and hoped he did not notice her scowl. Redheaded wisecracks were nothing new.

By the time he moved on to another patron, she had spotted her mark in a booth across the room. The bank executive looked younger in jeans and a teal polo shirt. The photo supplied by her client showed him in a tailored dark suit and the obligatory corporate red tie.

He sat across from a woman with long blond curls and even

longer legs that jutted out from her red party dress. They leaned in toward each other. The man smiled at whatever the woman was saying, and they continued their intimate chat. Delanie watched until the woman slid out of her side of the booth and made a beeline for the back of the bar.

Delanie waited to see if his companion would return. When it looked like the other woman was preoccupied, Delanie clicked the button for her video camera in her black clutch and picked up her drink. She eased over to the man's table. "Excuse me. Do you mind if I join you?"

"That seat's been waiting for you," he said with a smile that lingered too long.

She smiled and sat down, setting her purse on the table.

"I'm Fisher. Fisher Benson. And if you're lucky, I could be your next big mistake." He took her hand and kissed it.

Delanie batted her eyelashes and smiled again. She stifled a laugh and coughed to try to cover it. "It's nice to meet you. I'm Danielle." He didn't waste any time.

"Can I get you a refill?"

"I'm good for now," she said.

He nodded. "I bet you are."

Before Delanie could offer a retort, Fisher's earlier companion sauntered past the table. She nodded at Fisher and approached the seat she had vacated. The woman in red stilettos tripped and grabbed Delanie's shoulder. Her nails meant business. "Oh, excuse me," she said in a pouty voice. "I tripped."

"Well, hello again." Fisher slid over and patted the vinyl seat. "Danielle, this is Candi. It's good to see you again."

"My plans changed. I thought I'd swing by to see if you're still up for some fun." The woman wiggled in next to Fisher.

"I'm all about fun." Fisher scooted closer to the woman whose true age showed under the layers of makeup. The deep crow's feet made Delanie guess that the woman was in her late forties.

His smile curled into a leer. "Danielle, are you up for some fun?"

"Always." She hoped she could keep her poker face during Fisher Benson's trite come-ons.

"Let's blow this popsicle stand. My place is around the corner. You can come too if you feel adventurous." Candi looked down her nose at the woman who introduced herself as Danielle.

Fisher signaled the waiter for the check. "Well, Danielle. What do you say? You up for a private party?"

"Sure. I'm game. Let's go have some fun." Delanie licked her lips and stared at Fisher, who dropped a handful of cash on the table. Candi grabbed Fisher's hand and led him through the throngs. Delanie followed the couple and made sure to capture their exit on her hidden camera.

After some banal chatter on the curb in the cool, late fall evening, the plan was for Delanie to follow Fisher, who would follow Candi to her place. Delanie climbed in her black Mustang, kicked off her heels, and set her clutch purse on the dashboard. The camera rolled to capture whatever happened.

The caravan pulled into an apartment complex after a short ride behind Fisher's black Mercedes GLS. They drove around the club-house and pool and parked near a building at the back of the neigh-borhood near the dumpster.

Delanie watched the couple walk up the stairs to Candi's place, and she turned her purse to make sure she captured their entrance to the second-floor apartment. Fisher paused and looked over his shoul-der. Then he followed the older woman inside. Delanie clicked the button on the camera and pulled slowly out of the lot. Fisher's escapades with two dates would be plenty of fodder for Mrs. Benson's divorce attorney. Another successful night of pretend dating for the private investigator who just wanted to go home to a hot bath and a good book.

1

Delanie Fitzgerald's phone rang as the woman at the drive-thru handed her an iced mocha. "Thanks." She looked at the caller ID and took a deep breath before she clicked the button on her Mustang's steering wheel. "Hi, Chaz. What's new with you?"

Chaz or Charles Wellington Smith, III, the owner of The Treasure Chest, a local gentlemen's club in downtown Richmond, turned out to be Delanie's best cash-paying client. She had spent last summer helping him clear his name when he was accused of murdering the mayor. And somehow, he always thought of her when something new popped up in his orbit.

"Hey, long time no speak. How are you? Thanks for getting me that information for my campaign so quickly."

After Delanie had cleared Chaz of the former mayor's murder, he decided to throw his hat in the ring for the special election. Delanie was not sure how this would turn out, but she would assist if he wanted to keep her firm on the payroll.

"No problem. What can Falcon Investigations do for you?"

"The first mayoral meet and greet went as I expected. This town's not ready for me, but that doesn't mean that I'm not going to turn it on its ear. There's a debate coming up, and I need more info on the competition. Do you have time to do some digging?"

"Sure. Duncan and I will be glad to work on it. Send me the names. When do you need it?" She would have to break the news to tell her partner, Duncan Reynolds, that Chaz, the T&A king, was still one of their clients.

"You're a peach. The next couple of days will be fine. If you're downtown, stop by the club. We'd love to see you. You'd be surprised as some of our recent changes."

"What happened at the meet and greet?" she asked.

"You know. What always happens. The self-righteous ones got on their high horses and acted like I didn't belong there. They don't realize how much my club generates in taxes for the city." After a pause, he continued, "And I probably shot my mouth off too much. But now they know I'm a force to be reckoned with, and I'm running for mayor. Thanks for being on Team Chaz."

"Okeydoke. Send me the names, and we'll get right on it. See ya soon." Delanie clicked the button to disconnect the call and headed to the office. She wondered if Chaz's mayoral run was a publicity stunt. Shrugging off the thought, the private investigator decided to help him with the opposition research. It would be interesting to see what the unconventional Chaz would do when surrounded by Richmond politicos. He came from a wealthy family, but his antics always seemed to put him at odds with polite society.

She parked in front of her office, next to her partner's Tweetie bird yellow Camaro and hip checked her car's door. Unlocking the front door to the empty reception area, she said, "Duncan. Hey, Duncan, you here?" Falcon Investigations inhabited a small suite in the middle of a strip mall.

"We're back here," he yelled.

Wandering past the kitchenette and her office, she noticed Duncan's office was empty, too. Her computer geek partner sat with his feet on the conference room table, and the TV was tuned to a local news station. His sidekick, Margaret, the wonder dog, snored loudly from the corner of the room. The English bulldog had sinus problems, so she sounded like a cross between a lovesick moose and an angry water buffalo when she snored or snorted.

"Whatcha doing?" Delanie sidled up next to her partner's chair.

"Watching the local news. I saw your boy Chaz doing an interview. He's on TV every chance he can get." Duncan took his feet off the table.

"Speaking of our dear friend, Chaz, he called me this morning. He has more campaign research he wants us to do."

"At least he pays in cash." Duncan sighed. "What does he need?" He grabbed the remote and muted the volume on the TV.

"Dirt on his competitors. He'll send the list of names over later. I know you'll get the scoop for him in a snap." She smiled.

"It shouldn't take long. Easy money. Speaking of drama, we had some excitement around here this morning. When Margaret and I rolled in, there were police and emergency vehicles all around Snakes and Scales."

"The pet shop? What happened?" Delanie asked.

"Not sure. By the time Margaret and I walked down there, the emergency crews had left, and there was a closed sign on the door. I couldn't find anything on social media about the incident, and nobody was at the store. That's why I had the local news on."

Distracted by her phone's alert, Delanie paused to check her screen. When she realized it was a news alert about a nearby county, she pocketed her phone. Duncan stared at her with his best puppy dog imitation.

"What?" she asked.

"I thought maybe you could call your brother. Aren't you a little curious about what happened across from your office? What if it was a murder or an armed robbery or something?"

"I haven't talked to him in a while. Let's see what he can tell us." She thumbed through her contacts, and clicked on the one for Lieutenant Steve Fitzgerald, the oldest of her two brothers.

When the call connected, she heard his voice mail message. At the beep she said, "Hey, Steve. This is Delanie. When I got to the office this morning, Duncan said that we had some police action

going on across the street. I wanted to check in to make sure everything's okay and whether or not I needed to worry about it. Call me
when you can."

Delanie disconnected as the local lunchtime news flashed across
the screen. Duncan scrambled to unmute the television.

The second story was about Snakes and Scales. Duncan turned
up the volume, and Margaret raised her head to see if there were
snacks. When nothing caught her fancy, she returned to her nap.

The local reporter, standing in front of the closed exotic pet store
said that the owner, Ken Montgomery, had died at the scene. An
investigation was pending, and police had no more details at this
time."

"How sad," Delanie said. "Now I'm curious. I'll let you know what
Steve says when he calls me."

"There was no scuttlebutt from the other store owners. And I
didn't see anyone from the pet store. Usually his son or daughter is
around."

Her phone rang. "That's odd." She clicked the button and said,
"Falcon Investigations. This is Delanie Fitzgerald."

"Hi, Delanie. This is Deke Jennings, owner of Freeda's. You
stopped by here a while back to talk to me about the mayor's murder.
Anyway, I have a job I'd like to talk to you about. Do you have time to
stop by the club this week to chat?"

"Hi, Deke. It's good to hear from you again. What's your schedule
tomorrow?"

"How does ten-thirty tomorrow work for you?"

"Perfect. See you then," she said.

Duncan looked at her quizzically when she disconnected. "That
was Deke Jennings from Freeda's. He wants to talk to us about a
job."

"I remember, you dragged me to his club last summer. And you
were the only female there." Freeda's, well known for its infamous
weekend drag show brunches and exotic pink cocktails, had been a
fixture in downtown for years.

"And we had a nice night. But even better, we solved the crime. I'll see what he wants tomorrow. I'm going to catch up on some email. Holler if you need me."

"I'm going to see if I can find anything else about Ken Montgomery or his pet shop. Margaret and I will be heading out in a little while. I have some stuff to do before tonight. We've got a date with Evie. It's game night." Duncan clicked the remote to turn off the TV.

Delanie smiled when she thought of Duncan and his steady of late, Evie Hachey. The diminutive brunette with the tortoise shell glasses shared Duncan's love for comics, gaming, and superheroes. They seemed to be the perfect match – inseparable since their meeting earlier in the year at a comicon.

Delanie followed Duncan down the hall to her office. She immersed herself in two hundred unanswered emails. A sound made her look up. The strange noise sounded like someone scooting something across the floor. Straining to listen, she paused. Not hearing anything else, she returned to her computer.

About ten minutes later, Delanie heard the noise again, and this time it was louder. It sounded like it was coming from the hallway. Jumping up, she walked toward the doorway at the same time Duncan traipsed down the hall. His dog shadow waddled behind him.

"Did you hear that?"

"No. I guess not. What are we listening for?" he asked.

"It sounded like someone was moving something. I heard some creaky sounds like something was being dragged. It was weird. I heard it twice, and it got louder."

They paused and listened.

After a few minutes, Duncan said, "I didn't hear anything. We're outta here. See you tomorrow."

"Sure," she said, half-listening for that sound again. "Have fun at game night and say hi to Evie for me."

The front door shut and clicked. Delanie returned to her laptop. About twenty minutes later, she heard the noise again, and it sounded like it was above her desk.

Delanie pushed the papers to the side and climbed up on the

desk. Pushing the drop ceiling panel up, she peered into the shadows. Nothing seemed to move, but it was too dark to tell for sure. She climbed down and brushed the dust off.

Deciding that she was at a good stopping point, Delanie packed up her laptop, grabbed her purse, and decided to head to the gym. She had better things to do than share her office with a creepy noise.

2

DELANIE SMILED AT HER GOOD FORTUNE AS SHE PULLED INTO A PARKING spot in front of Freeda's in Richmond's Fan District. Parking in this trendy neighborhood was usually at a premium. She clicked the key fob to lock the Mustang.

Staring into the darkened lobby, she hoped Deke would answer her knock. At about the time she decided to try the door by the alley, she heard shuffling. The large man who looked like he had played linebacker in a former life unlocked the door and held it for her.

"Hi there. Thanks for coming over." When she stepped in, he relocked the door and motioned toward the interior of the restaurant. "Can I get you something to drink? Espresso?"

"That would be great." Delanie looked around the bar. It had not changed since she had been there trying to clear Chaz's name last summer. The warm grays and aquas enveloped the black bar accented with pendant lights. The furniture had a Scandinavian look to it. The last time she was here, the lights had been a lot dimmer. The bar looked different in the daylight.

"Grab a seat. Any table that's open. I'll join you in a minute," the tall, bald man said as he set two clear glass mugs on the counter.

Delanie chose the table closest to the bar. She watched Deke in the long mirror as he prepared the coffee.

When the machine stopped whirring, he joined her. "It's good to see you again."

"You, too. What can my partner and I help you with?"

"Half of my business comes from the bar, and the other half comes from the weekend drag shows in the dining room next door. They've grown in popularity over the years. We have special events on certain weekends and brunch on Sundays." Delanie leaned forward about ready to ask some questions when Deke continued, "We've had some things disappear lately from the dressing room. I was hoping that you could do some investigative work."

"What's missing?" she asked.

"We've had several wigs and some jewelry go missing. The wigs and the costumes are crazy expensive."

"Did you call the police?"

"Not yet. I was hoping you could help first," he said.

"Who has access to the dressing room?" Delanie fished through her purse and pulled out a small notebook and pen to jot down what he had to say.

"The talent. There are usually about five to eight performers each weekend. It's secluded from the public areas, but the waitstaff and other employees can get back there. On any given weekend, there are probably eighteen to twenty people on duty on both sides of the house."

"Any cameras?" she asked.

"No. Only in the parking lot. I don't want to make the talent uncomfortable."

"So, more than likely, this is an inside job. What can I use as a cover to get in and poke around?"

Deke laughed. "You're not tall enough to pass for a queen. Can you wait tables?"

"Sure. No sweat." That was what Delanie had said about roller derby last summer, and she got a few bruises for her efforts. How hard could waiting tables at a drag show be? She had only worked the snack bar at the neighborhood pool for a couple of summers in high school. It could not be that much different. Could it?

"I can introduce you to the team as a weekend waitress. I'll say that you were in a jam, and you needed a job," the man said, draining his coffee.

"When should I be here?"

"Brunch starts at eleven on Sunday. Be here by eight-thirty to get oriented. Black pants, black shirt, and non-skid shoes."

"Here's a copy of our contract and standard fees." Delanie passed several pages to Deke.

He flipped through it and signed the last page. "I'll mail you a check if that's okay."

She nodded.

"We'll see what you find and then figure out if you need to come back," he said.

"Can you send me a list of your employees and your talent?" Delanie pushed her business card across the table.

He nodded. "I want to find this person. I don't like knowing someone here is a thief. I let them into my circle, and someone betrayed me." His voice drifted off.

"Thanks for your business." She rose and extended her hand that disappeared when Deke enveloped it in his. After goodbyes at the door, Delanie made her way back to the Mustang. She would call Duncan with the good news about a new client as soon as she had done a little shopping for her new waitressing outfit.

DELANIE DROPPED her shopping bags and purse on her desk and hollered, "Hey, Dunc."

"We're in the kitchen."

She rounded the corner, and Duncan said, "We took a break for lunch. I was engrossed in a website project for a dentist."

Delanie smiled. Duncan did web design as his legitimate

computer work when he was not hacking to help her find information for her clients.

She wrinkled her nose and asked, "What are you fixing?"

"It's fish sticks and brussels sprouts. Evie said we need to eat more veggies." Duncan stirred the glass container he took out of the microwave.

Delanie took a step back when she got a whiff of his lunch. Before she could tell him about the new client, her phone rang. "Be right back." She hoped that he would be done with his lunch by the time she returned. The odor would probably linger much longer.

"Hi, Steve." She plopped in her office chair.

"Hey, D. Sorry it took me so long to get back with you. It's been a crazy week so far," her brother said.

"I called about the Snakes and Scales pet shop incident. Duncan said he saw a crowd of emergency vehicles when he arrived at work."

"Yep." It sounded like he was chewing on something. "We got a call from the son who opened the shop and found his dad dead on the floor. It looked like he fell into one of the glass cases and hit his head. We're waiting for the ME's report, but my guess would be a heart attack or some kind of medical issue."

"Oh, how sad. I didn't know them that well, but they've had a store here for years. I was curious if it was a break in."

"You should be okay. It's an isolated incident. Plus, your partner has enough cameras around your place. Nobody's ever going to sneak in. Everything good with you?"

"It's been busy. You, Liz, and the kids need to come by some time. Your cuties are growing up too fast." Delanie smiled when she thought about Steve's kids. The two boys, Aiden and Ethan, were seven and five, and Charlotte had turned three a few months back.

"I know. They're not little any more. We'll do dinner soon."

"Sounds good. See ya." Delanie stuck her head around the corner into the kitchen. "Safe to come in there?"

"We're done." Duncan wiped his hands on his jeans. "And what's wrong with brussels sprouts? They're good for you."

"Nothing." She held her nose. "Steve said that the son called 9-1-1 when he found Mr. Montgomery dead. He doesn't think it was foul play, so there's no mad man on the loose. On a lighter note, Deke also hired us to find who's been pilfering stuff at his place."

"Good for the new client. Not good for the Montgomery family. I mean I'm glad he wasn't whacked in his own store." Duncan made his way to his office, and Margaret toddled down the hall after him.

"Stop. Do you hear that?" Delanie waved her arms around. "It's that noise that's been driving me crazy. I noticed it yesterday. It's back. And I hear it up there." They both looked at the ceiling.

"Sorry. I missed it." He paused and turned his head.

"It sounds like it's on the roof. I'm going to record it next time to prove it to you. Do you have a drone? We should check the roof."

"I'll bring the drone in if it'll make you feel better." Duncan yelled as he and his dog shadow disappeared into his office.

3

On Sunday morning, Delanie parked in the alley next to Freeda's and hurried in through the back door. Men in black aprons buzzed around the bar and the kitchen. After her eyes adjusted to the darkened interior, she spotted Deke hauling three plastic crates of glasses. He set them down behind the bar, and she stepped between two barstools.

"Hi, boss. What would you like me to do today?" she asked.

"Hey. Let me show you around. I changed my mind about the waitressing. I thought up a job where'd you'd be backstage the entire time. I'm going to have you act as concierge for the gals in the show. You'll be my runner today. Nonskid shoes?"

"Yup. I'm ready."

"Sounds good. Follow me," he said.

In the kitchen, two men in black sliced fruit and placed the chunks in aluminum pans. "Hey, Nicco, Alejandro. This is Delanie. She's going to be working here for a little while. Give her any help she needs." Both men nodded.

A young guy in white wandered through with a pan of dishes. "Donnie, this is Delanie. She's going to be joining us. Help her out if she needs it."

"Welcome," said the young guy with the big toothy smile. He zipped through the swinging doors before Delanie could reply.

She increased her pace to keep up with Deke as he moved from the kitchen to the dishwashing area. He pushed on a swinging door and exited to a hallway. The brick interior walls of the hallway looked original to the building. The drag show dining room and stage area must have been added later. She hurried to stay in step with Deke as he rounded a corner.

"Our main dining room is over there. This hallway leads to the backstage area." Deke pointed in the opposite direction. He turned and pushed the thick oak door in front of him.

They stepped inside a dressing room where mirrors and vanities lined the walls. Shoes, glitter, boas, wigs, and dresses covered each vanity station – every little girl's dream room for dress up. She looked in awe at the rainbow of wigs and matching outfits. Everything sparkled.

Deke interrupted her thoughts, "Grab a stool. The ladies are rolling in. They're usually here by nine or nine-thirty. There are a coupla prima donnas who roll in at the last minute." He put two fingers in his mouth and let out a whistle that echoed throughout the long, narrow room.

"Ladies, may I have your attention for a minute. This is Delanie, and she's new to my team. Today, she's going to be your concierge to make sure everything runs smoothly in the dressing room and backstage. If you need something, Delanie's your gal. I'll let the ladies introduce themselves."

"Welcome, Delanie. We need a housemother back here to keep these slobs in order. I'm Tara Byte," said the tall guy who hung up a black garment bag next to his station. "You can come sit by me, and I'll give you the scoop on everyone." He was about six foot four by her guess and bald. He looked like he would fit in a junior size with legs that were longer than Delanie was tall.

Someone in the back mumbled something as Deke left. Delanie did not catch the comment. She sat on the stool next to Tara Byte. "Thanks. I'm learning the ropes today. Can I get you anything?"

"I'm good for now. Girl, what are you doing here? You don't want to be a queen, do you? Here, sit down. You need to have your colors done."

Before Delanie could say anything, he whipped out a makeup case the size of a tackle box and redid her foundation.

"I needed a job, and Deke's helping me out."

He dabbed makeup on her face. "Sit still. You've got great hair. These witches here would kill for your red curls. But you need to cover up those dark circles. We'll work on a night-time beauty regime for you later. You have fabulous eyes. You need to highlight them with liner and mascara. And glitter is always good. At first, I thought you were trying to get in on the act. Sister, you're too short. Can you dance?"

"I guess. Deke didn't say anything about me performing. It was kind of him to help me out in a pinch," she said.

"He's good like that. He's an old soul who looks out for folks. Quite a few people here owe Deke a lot."

Delanie smiled. "I'm not sure I'm cut out for the show, but I like hanging out back here and looking at all the costumes. It's like my Barbie collection came to life."

Tara Byte laughed. "So, you're not a drag queen wannabe? Okay, here's the quick lay of the land. That's Amber Alert." He pointed to the Rubenesque blond who looked like a cross between Marilyn Monroe and Mae West. She nodded, and Tara continued, "The tall redhead over there is Ginger Snap. She does a movie star glamour schtick like the gal on Gilligan's Island. And the one over there with the black wig is Paige Turner. She's the naughty librarian."

Before Tara could continue, a tall African-American guy rushed in and dropped his bags and makeup case on the chair next to Delanie. He took a deep breath and looked at her like she was an interloper.

Tara said, "And Delanie, this is Kiki Jubilee. Kiki, Deke said Delanie is our housemother until further notice. Need anything? You look like you have the vapors."

"Huh," the tall guy in jeans and tennis shoes said. "Uh, no. I just overslept. And it takes me at least two hours to perfect Kiki. I could use a coffee, lots of cream and sugar, Sugar," he said with a wink.

"Sure. I'll be right back. Does anyone else need anything?" Delanie exited to a chorus of no and un-huhs.

When she returned, Tara Byte had transformed into a Cher look-alike, complete with a waist-length black, blue, and sparkling wig that matched her cobalt blue and silver gown. She slid on bracelets and a necklace with an aquamarine surrounded by rhinestones the size of a doorknob.

Delanie handed Kiki the coffee. "Just set it there, Honey." Kiki pulled a roll of duct tape from her bag. "It's for the wig, Sweetie," she said in response to Delanie's puzzled look. "It keeps the wig on when I dance. It's hot under all those stage lights, and I don't want to have a wardrobe malfunction and lose my coif." Kiki slipped on a red bathrobe and sat down for makeup.

"Who's that hag?" asked a pale guy who sauntered in with two suit bags and a makeup case.

"She's not a hag. Deke hired her to help out around backstage. That's Delanie. She's at our beck and call." Tara turned toward Delanie. "Don't mind her. She's always in a mood. Diva," Tara whispered, waving a finger at the guy. Then in a louder voice, she said, "Delanie, that's Anna Conda," as she waved her hand over her shoulder at the guy who poured himself into the easy chair in the corner. He carefully took off his sneakers and socks, put them under the counter of his vanity, and disappeared into the back room.

"She's very fussy. And she'll turn on you just like her namesake," Tara said, winking.

"At least she doesn't bring that monster snake with her any more. It did nothing for the act except terrify everyone in the front row. That live boa gave me the willies. I was glad when Deke banned it from the premises." Kiki fanned her face with her hand.

Delanie busied herself with straightening the work areas. The flat surfaces looked like a makeup counter in an old department store after a group of thirteen-year olds came in for the free samples.

A few minutes later, a fully transformed Anna Conda waltzed

back in the room. "I heard that," she said to Tara. "And welcome," she said to Delanie. "Stay out of my stuff. Don't get in my way, and we'll get along just fine."

"It's nice to meet you. Is everyone doing okay? Let me know if you need anything." When no one replied, she sat back on the seat next to Tara. Delanie watched Kiki apply false eyelashes and spackle enough pancake makeup on to fill in every line and crease.

"Excuse me," Amber Alert said. "Could you get me a glass of water?"

Delanie nodded and headed for the kitchen. When she returned, Donnie the dishwasher walked through the dressing room, greeting the talent.

"Oh, hi," he said when Delanie set Amber's glass on the counter by her makeup kit. "I was checking to see if anyone needed anything."

"That's her job." Anna Conda said, spitting out the words like they were sour.

The young busboy stuffed his hands in his black jeans and shuffled out the door.

Tara Byte made a tsk, tsk sound and waggled her finger at Anna. "Don't break the little boy's spirit." She turned and walked toward the door. Her long blackish blue hair swayed in time to her sashay.

Before anyone could comment, Deke came in with a headset and clipboard. "Ladies, five minutes until show time. We need to get a move on. It's a full house. There are two bridal parties and a fortieth birthday bash, so let's make it good."

"See ya later, Sweets," Tara sent air kisses Delanie's way. Kiki Jubilee and Anna Conda trailed Tara out into the hallway.

"Places, everyone," Deke disappeared as quickly as he had arrived.

The music pounded though the walls, and Delanie settled in the side chair in the corner. After the Kool and the Gang medley, Donnie, the busboy, slipped in the doorway. He jumped when Delanie said, "May I help you?"

"Oh, hi," he said as he grinned. "I didn't see you there. I'm here to pick up any glasses or dishes the ladies left."

She grabbed several glasses and a cup and saucer from the vanities. Delanie handed them to Donnie, who balanced them in the crook of his elbow. "Thanks." He retreated to the kitchen.

Delanie yawned and returned to her seat. As much as she loved her job, stakeouts made her crazy. To ward off the drowsy feeling, she stood up, stretched, and decided to check out the backstage.

The hallway dead-ended into an area that looked like a maze with floor-to-ceiling black curtains. She navigated through the curtains and peeked around. Deke stood on the opposite side, looking like a stage manager with his clipboard and headset. Kiki Jubilee and Amber Alert waited in the wings next to Delanie. She could see the back of Tara Byte on stage, lip-syncing to a Cher medley. When the music ended, Tara took a deep bow and blew kisses to the crowd. She exited near Delanie to the crowd's roar of applause. Anna Conda took the stage and did a routine to a Celine Dion medley. After three or four bows, Anna waved to the audience. Amber and Kiki took the stage next and chatted with the audience about celebrations. Amber did a fairly good impersonation of Marilyn Monroe's famous "Happy Birthday" song.

Deke waved his arms from backstage. All the entertainers lined up on both sides. When "It's Raining Men," blared through the speakers, they paraded out onto the stage like beauty pageant contestants.

The crowd went wild, making it difficult to hear anything. It was standing room only at the edge of the stage, and all the women waved dollar bills at the entertainers. The ladies took their final bows and exited the stage as Deke called each name to rounds of applause and whistles. Instead of an encore, the queens moved to the edge of the stage, and Deke started calling tables forward for group pictures.

Delanie watched for a while and then headed to the dressing room. Sure that the entertainers would need her after their photo sessions, she busied herself with straightening things dropped on chairs and the floor.

The queens trickled back into the dressing room and kicked off their stilettos. Delanie assisted with zippers, drink orders, and any other tasks the talent could think of. Most of the entertainers changed into street clothes and removed the makeup and glamour. A few left in full face paint.

Tara Byte, Ginger Snap, and Kiki Jubilee were the last to leave. "Thanks, Delanie," Tara said. "See you next weekend. You're a good addition back here. You kept things humming."

Delanie smiled as she picked up towels and trash left on the counters. Deke came in as she straightened items left on the vanities.

"How was your first time?" Deke leaned on the door jamb and crossed his legs.

"Not bad. I didn't notice anything out of the ordinary."

"Nobody reported any issues. We haven't had anything pilfered in about a week. Most carry their belongings with them and are careful with their tips. But some do leave shoes, boas, and other stuff here. They get a little sloppy and leave things out. How about you come back next week? Oh, and Friday, we have a special event from eight to midnight. Rehearsal starts at six. And then we do a repeat of today on Sunday. If you don't get any leads next weekend, we'll chat and work on a new strategy."

"Sounds like a plan. See you next weekend." She followed him to the alley exit.

Autumn had arrived, a relief from the sweltering Richmond summer. Delanie rolled down the windows and cranked up the tunes as she headed home for an afternoon to catch up on laundry and housecleaning.

Before she got to the toll booth after the Powhite Bridge, her phone rang. "Hey, Chaz. What are you up to on this gorgeous day?"

"Howdy. I emailed you the list of names I need some oppo research on. The debate is Thursday evening. Possible to get it by then?" He slurped something loudly in the background.

"Not a problem. Duncan's a whiz at finding stuff."

"Good. In other news, I bought that property in Goochland that you did some reconnaissance on for me. I'm going to move forward on an all-male revue and restaurant in the burbs. The timeline will depend on how the mayor thing works out. I think it's time to diversify my income streams."

"Congratulations. Business is good." Delanie zipped through the express lane at the toll booth.

"I'll be looking forward to what you and your partner find on my opponents. I need all the help I can for Team Chaz. See ya."

"Go Team!" She clicked the phone off and headed home to check out his list. Chaz wanted to stir up something with the other candidates. Knowing him, the dirtier the information, the better. She wondered what Duncan could find in the dark places of the internet.

4

THE NEXT MORNING, DELANIE PARKED IN THE LOT IN FRONT OF THE office. A short woman with henna-colored hair stood on the sidewalk, tapping on the glass front door with her key. Duncan's car was nowhere to be seen.

"Hi, may I help you?" Delanie asked.

"Oh, hi. I'm Tina Montgomery. My dad owns, well, owned Snakes and Scales, the pet shop over there. I wanted to know if I could talk to you and Duncan. I thought maybe you could help us."

"I'm Delanie Fitzgerald. I'm so sorry to hear about your dad." She unlocked the door and held it for the woman who wiped her cheeks with her hands. "Come on back. Can I get you some coffee?" The woman in the oversized, gray cat sweater nodded as she looked around the office space.

Delanie started the coffeemaker as Tina sat at the table in the kitchenette. "What can we do for you?"

"I'm sure you've heard by now that my dad passed away at the store this week. It's been terrible. I still can't believe it," Tina said, sniffing.

"I'm so sorry for your loss," Delanie said.

"When my brother came in that morning, he discovered my dad.

They covered the shifts at the store. I stop by once a week or so to do the books." She sniffed and looked around the kitchenette like she was waiting for someone. Before Delanie could comment, Tina continued, "We haven't heard back from any of the officials yet, but they're guessing that he had a heart attack. He had had some issues in the past and had a stint put in last summer. The store was a mess when we arrived. It looked like he fell and broke a couple of the aquariums."

"How can Duncan and I help you?" The coffeemaker chugged and let out a burst of steam. When Delanie rose to get the mugs, she heard Duncan and Margaret come through the back door.

"Hey, Delanie. You here?" he called out.

"Tina and I are in the kitchen." Delanie grabbed another mug. She moved the creamer and sugar to the table.

Tina rose as Duncan entered with Margaret bringing up the rear.

"Hi, Tina," he said. "I'm sorry to hear about what happened."

She leaned forward and hugged the surprised Duncan.

The woman with the heart-shaped face and rosy cheeks, looked down at her shoes. "I was hoping you and Delanie can help me with something." Tina returned to her seat at the table and stirred cream and lots of sugar in her mug.

Delanie handed Duncan his usual, black coffee.

"Thanks. Why don't we go to the conference room where there's space to spread out, and you can tell us what you had in mind." Duncan picked up his "There's No Place like 127.0.0.1" mug.

After everyone had found a chair and settled in, Margaret circled the table three times until she located the perfect space to park for a nap.

"Like I told Delanie. I do the books for my dad. I can't quite pinpoint it, but something doesn't feel right. There are some withdrawals and then a deposit from some business accounts recently that I can't reconcile. My brother didn't know what they were for either, but each one caught my attention. There was only an account number, no name for the entries. It looked odd. Normally, there's some detail for each transaction line. I may be letting my thoughts run wild because I don't want to believe my dad's gone. I was hoping you two could do some searching and let me know if I'm imagining things."

"If you're suspicious, we can check into it for you. Let me go get our contract and fee information for you." Delanie stepped out of the room.

When she returned from her office, Tina said, "My dad and brother, well, half-brother, Glen, are all the family I have. My mom died when I was little, and Glen's mom, Elsie, died a few years back. I'm not sure what we'll do with the store. Glen and I need to get with the attorney and the CPA to figure things out. The copy of the will that I have leaves everything to me and Glen."

"The store's been there for a while," Duncan said. "It's a fixture in the neighborhood."

"It used to be a traditional pet store with dogs, cats, birds, and fish. My mom loved cats. Then after she died, dad married Glen's mom, and they had him. When Glen was in middle school, he got interested in reptiles. My dad thought it was good for him because it gave him something to focus on since school wasn't his strong point. So, through the years, it turned into a fish, reptile, and amphibian shop, and they made it quite lucrative with their regulars and the shows they did. They changed the name a few years back," Tina said with a sigh.

Delanie put the papers on the table, and Tina pulled them closer to her. The bookkeeper rummaged through her purse for a pen. After signing the contract, she continued, "Here's a deposit to start. We'll see what you find. Maybe we could meet sometime this week or next and go over what you uncover?"

"Not a problem," Duncan said. "Accounting entries are what caused some suspicion? Can you send me copies of them, so I can dig around?"

She reached into her purse and pulled out several photocopied sheets, folded in half. "Here. These are the ones I've noticed. I'm going to go back over the accounts tonight to see if I can find anything else. You can start with these."

Duncan looked over the sheets as Delanie said, "Is there anything else that seemed odd to you?"

"Well, my brother was acting weird. Weirder than normal. I thought it was because of my dad's sudden death, but he's been out of kilter all this week. He acts stressed, and when I ask him about it, he either clams up or gets short with me."

"Tell us about your brother," Duncan said.

"Glen is almost twelve years younger than me. We get along okay for half-siblings with a big age gap. We never really had a lot in common. His mom always babied him. I was in high school or college when he was little and pretty much on my own. I moved out before he was a teenager. Glen finished high school and did a couple of years at the community college. When he decided school wasn't his thing, he moved back in with my dad and worked in the store full-time. Glen lives in the basement at dad's place."

"No spats or disagreements?"

"With me or my dad?" Tina asked.

"Either," Duncan replied.

"No, I don't think so. The shop was doing well, and Glen has a good thing going with his online sales. He'd even started doing talks and reptile demonstrations for groups. And that's pretty good for him because he's normally shy. He likes his snakes and lizards better than he likes most people."

"Is there anything else you can tell us?" Delanie asked. "Any unusual clients? Any problem ones?"

Tina hesitated.

"You can tell us," Duncan said. "We'll respect your privacy."

"Glen has some interesting clients. They're into snakes and creepy spiders, and they're not very sociable when I'm around." Tina's voice trailed off as she looked down at her hands. "I think they're mostly weird guys who like reptiles. They seem harmless. I'm more concerned about the unexplained money."

Duncan said. "Give us a couple of days, and we'll report back on what we find. If you uncover anything else or think of something, call or text us."

Delanie pushed their business cards to Tina's side of the table.

"Thank you both. This is a relief. And I hope it's a big nothing." Tina stood. "It feels like something is going on, and I'd like to put the whole mess behind me and figure out what to do with the store. I don't like having a cloud hanging over my head, and I really want to get back to my normal life, if that's possible."

Duncan walked Tina out to the front door as Delanie picked up the mugs and retreated to the kitchen to tidy up.

"We'll see what we can uncover for her. If she's curious about some of the payments, then maybe there's something there." Duncan rummaged through the refrigerator. When he didn't find what he was looking for, he closed the door.

She dried the mugs and returned them to the cabinet. "It's nice having a few cases at the same time. I wonder if Tina and Glen will keep the store open."

"Dunno. Tina doesn't seem to be real enthusiastic about it. By the way, I found some stuff for Chaz today. I sent you the file. One of his competitors owns a lot of rental houses in downtown Richmond, but he hasn't paid his taxes in a while. And another one's mother has a construction company that was awarded a huge contract for work in the district that he represents. Oh, and one of the guys doesn't technically live in the city. He has a house in the Church Hill neighborhood, but he had the toilets removed, so he could label it uninhabitable and not have to live there."

"Where do you find stuff like this?" Delanie asked with a smile.

"I have my sources. Right, Margaret?" The English bulldog raised her head and yawned. "Chaz should be able to stir up some stink at his next campaign event with this. It's enough to throw shade on his opponents. Hey, I brought the drone in. Have you heard the noise recently?"

"No. But, let's check the roof if you have time. The other day, it sounded like it was right above my desk."

"Gimme a minute," he said. "And I'll meet you in the alley."

By the time Delanie poured a second cup of coffee and headed out the back door, Duncan was readying his drone. She sat next to Margaret on the steps.

"If there's anything unusual up there, we should see it." Duncan put the drone on the asphalt and clicked a button on the controller. The contraption whirred to life and rose to roof level. Duncan monitored its progress on a small screen as he guided it up and down their section of building. He hovered near the air conditioning unit. After several more passes, he had the drone linger over them. Delanie waved, and Margaret woofed at what sounded like a big bug.

After it landed, and the propellers stopped spinning, he picked it up. "Come on. "Let's go look at the footage."

"This is so cool. We can use this for stakeouts."

"Maybe for getting the lay of the land. You can't use them to sneak up on people. You don't want it to get shot down by the bad guys," he said.

Delanie settled in the conference room chair as Duncan plugged in his laptop and turned on the large TV. They watched the drone make several passes over the roof. Duncan played it again.

"Nothing looks weird to me," he said.

"I guess I'll call maintenance if I hear it again. It was the strangest thing. I can't even really describe it well. It was like a scooting sound, but then sometimes, it was louder. And sometimes, it sounded creaky."

"Margaret, you're on guard duty," he said. "High alert." She raised one eyebrow from her napping location. When she didn't hear any references to food, she closed her eyes.

"Good job, Margaret." Delanie patted the bulldog's head. "Maybe it was the wind or the building settling. Who knows? Thanks for checking it out from the air. Oh, I have something else for you, the list of folks who work for Deke Jennings either in food prep or the entertainment. If you have time, could you see what your magical searches turn up?"

"No problem. I'll be in my office working on some web pages."

"I'm particularly interested in anyone with a police record." Delanie followed the dynamic duo down the hall. She woke up her laptop, emailed the list to her partner, and made a spreadsheet with all the names and information she knew about Deke's crew.

There it was again. That noise. After a pause, she heard it again. She looked up and saw a couple of the ceiling tiles move. "Duncan! Duncan! It's in the ceiling. It's here again! Did you hear it?"

Duncan rushed in with a barking Margaret hot on his heels.

"Shhhhh!" Delanie said. "I heard it again. And the ceiling tiles moved."

They stood there for a few moments. "I don't hear anything," he said as Delanie continued to stare at the ceiling.

"There's dust on my desk. See! Something moved up there. I'm calling maintenance." Delanie picked up her cell, but before she could dial, Margaret let out with a deep guttural growl and raced off barking down the hall.

The bulldog stopped in the kitchen and raised a ruckus.

Duncan jumped into protector mode and tried to soothe Margaret. After the dog finally calmed down, she slurped water from her bowl and sat panting near the doorway. Everyone once in a while, she'd glance at the ceiling and growl.

When the barking died down, Delanie left a message for maintenance.

Mystified, all three waited in the hallway listening again for the unusual sound.

5

DELANIE SAT IN THE MUSTANG, FLIPPING THROUGH DUNCAN'S FINDINGS on the employees at Freeda's. Three of the queens, Ginger Snap, Anna Conda, and Kiki Jubilee, had arrest records for selling or possessing marijuana and drunk and disorderly. They had either served their time or had their sentences reduced for good behavior. The kitchen staff had several with records, including Donnie the dishwasher, who was twenty-five. His age surprised Delanie. She thought he was still in his teens with his slight build and baby face. His juvenile record had been expunged, but he had had several petty arrests in his twenties and served time for drugs and fencing stolen goods. Now she had a targeted list of candidates to watch tonight.

She put the papers in her briefcase in the front seat and grabbed her phone and keys. It was time for Freeda's Freaky Fridaypalooza. Delanie walked around to the back of the building and slipped in though the open alley door. She was on high alert for any odd or unusual behavior.

Inside, Deke restocked the bar while the kitchen staff moved around like ants on a mission – everyone in constant motion.

"Good evening." Her eyes adjusted to the darkness of the room.

"You ready for a wild night?" Deke emptied a wooden crate of liquor bottles. He arranged them on the glass shelves. All labels faced forward.

"I'm game. What would you like me to do?" Delanie watched Donnie peek through the kitchen door. She waved, and he smiled and retreated to the back.

"Let's keep it the same as last Sunday. Be my liaison for the talent. The show is longer today, and there are more costume changes. And more opportunities for something to go missing. We'll see what happens. You may want to pop in and out of the dressing rooms at random intervals to check on things."

"Sounds like a plan." Delanie wandered through the kitchen and down the hallway to the dressing room.

Amber Alert sat at the vanity mirror and glued on false eyelashes as a guy plopped behind her in the overstuffed chair. He took off his sneakers and socks.

"Hi, Amber," Delanie said.

"You back for some more glam?" the drag queen asked without turning around.

"I am. Deke said this show was longer than Sundays." She turned to the guy who put his things in a blue gym bag. "Hi, I'm Delanie. Deke hired me to make sure you all have everything you need between acts. Please let me know what I can help with."

"Hi. I'm Tod, but I'll be Nova Cain in a few minutes. I could use a glass of water. I'm parched." He moved to the vanity next to Amber. "Oh, and I'll probably need a zip by the time you get back." He winked and threw his suit bag over his shoulder.

"No problem. Amber, do you need anything?" After Amber shook her head, Delanie hurried to the kitchen.

Several others had arrived and set up after she returned from her errand. They filled most of the vanities that surrounded the perimeter of the room. Gowns, props, boas, and wigs hung from hooks or wherever there was space. Delanie had not seen this much glitter since Christmas.

"Here, you go." Delanie put a glass next to Nova Cain. "Hi, ladies. I'm Delanie. Please let me know if I can help with anything."

"Hey, Dee-lay-nee," Tara Byte said from across the room. "Come over here and chat." She patted the empty stool next to her station.

The private investigator sat on the stool next to Tara who brushed a glitter powder over her makeup.

"I'm glad you're here. You're a good stage mother for us, but I wasn't kidding about your colors. That lipstick looks washed out with your skin tone." Tara grabbed an applicator and layered foundation on Delanie. Next, she pulled out mulberry lipstick. "Sit still. You wiggle too much. I'm almost done with your lips. Pucker, so I can blot it. Good. Now, just a few more minutes. I want your eyes to pop. Your baby blues are one of your best features. You need to show 'em off with that gorgeous red hair."

Delanie sat obediently on the stool. "So, what do you do when you're not on stage here?" she asked.

"I'm a computer programmer downtown. That pays the bills, but this is what I do for fun. There. Much better." She dabbed the kohl black eyeliner along her bottom lids.

Delanie admired her new look in the mirror. "Thanks." Her face felt heavy with all the layers of makeup. "What's your look tonight?"

"I like to mix it up. I usually do Cher. But I go blond from time to time. I do a mean Marilyn Monroe when Amber isn't around," Tara said with a wink. "Tonight, it's Cher, and then I do a lip sync to Kermit the Frog's, 'It's Not Easy Being Green,'" with my lime sparkles and wig. That's when I put on my ostrich feathered headdress. Go big or go home. It's my showgirl number."

"I need to come back one day and watch the whole show. I miss a lot from backstage."

"Plus, I'm sure these queens keep you hopping." Tara winked again and flashed her one hundred-watt smile.

"Hey, Debbie. I need a zip over here," Nova said.

"It's Delanie, you chucklehead," Tara yelled.

"Whoops. Delanie, I could use some assistance over here." Nova put her hands on her hips and tapped her foot.

Delanie zipped Nova's white nurse's uniform. "There you go." She had to stretch to reach the top of her collar.

"Thanks, Dear." Nova returned to her seat to position her nurse's cap on top of her blond wig.

Anna Conda dropped her bags on the counter next to Tara and started unpacking her makeup and jewelry. Before Delanie could greet her, Kiki Jubilee burst through the door with enough waves and air kisses for everyone. She grabbed Delanie and gave her a bear hug that lifted the private investigator off the floor.

"Hey, baby," Kiki said. "It's good to see you again. Could you get me a rum with a little splash of Coke in it and two lime wedges?"

"I'll be right back with your drink. "Can I get anyone else anything?"

When Delanie returned with the drink, Anna Conda, Ginger Snap, Paige Turner, and Amber Alert decided they wanted drinks. Delanie spent most of the next half hour fetching drinks, wiping up spills, and finding lost earrings. Ginger Snap had the most interesting request. She wanted Delanie to research hotels and concerts for her next month in Miami.

Deke stepped through the doorway and bellowed, "Ladies, five minutes until showtime. Tara, Kiki, and Nova, you're up. Ginger, Paige, and Anna, you're in the next set."

The ladies filed out, and Delanie followed close behind to make sure they didn't have any last-minute needs. She slipped behind one of the tall black curtains as Cher blasted through the speakers. Tara Byte took to the stage for her song and dance number.

Delanie jumped when someone tapped her hard on her shoulder. "Excuse me," a stagehand whispered. "One of the ladies needs some assistance in the dressing room."

"Thanks," Delanie said as she hurried down the hall.

Paige Turner, partially hidden by the vanity, searched through bags and tossed clothes behind her.

"Can I help?"

The entertainer jumped and bumped her head on the vanity's counter. "Dern that hurt. Even with this Dolly Parton wig on," she said, rubbing the top of her head.

"Sorry. I didn't mean to startle you. Can I help you with something?" Delanie repeated.

"My earrings are missing. I have a set of faux garnet ones covered in rhinestones. I use these hoops for the first set. The red ones go with my ruby dress and cowgirl boots. I'm the little bit of country for the show. Then I do my naughty librarian schtick for the finale."

"Where did you last see them?" Delanie poked at balled up tissues and empty diet soft drink cans on the nearby vanity.

"They were in my jewelry holder. I put this pair on and went to the bathroom. When I came back, the case was empty."

"I'll help you look. Where have you been besides the restroom?"

"Just in this room. I threw my stuff in that chair and set up shop here," Paige said.

Delanie pulled the cushions out of the chair. Then she scooted it forward. The only thing she found was a quarter. Returning the chair to its original spot, she asked, "Did you go through all your bags?"

"Yes." Paige dumped her black gym bag out on the counter. Next, she checked the pockets and then emptied her suit bag.

"What about your street clothes?" Delanie asked.

Paige pulled out a pair of skinny jeans and checked all the pockets. "Nope. They're gone. And there's no telling who's been back here," she said, her shoulders slumping. "Even though they were gawdy as sin, they're still expensive. This is the second pair of dangles I've lost here in a month."

"I'll keep looking, and I'll let Deke know. Can you go on with your hoops?"

The drag queen sighed loudly. "Yes, but it won't be the same. This pair doesn't complete my outfit."

Delanie patted her shoulder. "I'll keep a look out for them."

"Thanks. If I find the witch who lifted them, we're going to have a chat in the alley." Paige frowned and returned to touching up her makeup. "I may look sweet, but I can be a tornado when I want to be," she drawled.

Delanie moved the discarded clothes and bags, looking for the missing earrings. She wandered over to the other vanities when Paige stood, grabbed her guitar, and headed toward the stage.

The private eye followed to see if she could find Deke. Spotting him on the far side of the stage, she picked her way over cables and wires that crisscrossed backstage along the path behind the stage to the other side.

She waved to Deke who stepped closer to her. She whispered, touching both her earlobes, "Paige is missing a pair of earrings. Garnet and rhinestones dangles."

"Hmmmmm. Everything else going okay?"

Delanie nodded. She watched Kiki Jubilee do a medley of Aretha Franklin songs. After "R-E-S-P-E-C-T," Delanie tiptoed to the other side and made her way back to the dressing room.

Tara Byte, Anna Conda, and Nova Cain changed costumes and adjusted wigs.

"Everything okay in here. Anybody need something to drink?" Delanie asked.

"Nope, we're good. That cute little boy from the kitchen popped in and brought ice water," Nova said.

Delanie raised an eyebrow. She would definitely have to keep an eye on Donnie.

There was a changing of the guard when Kiki Jubilee and Amber Alert swooped in. The other three entertainers hurried backstage.

"My goodness." Kiki waved her hand as a fan. "This wig is H-O-T, hot. Sugar, can you get me a big sweet tea? And if Sven is bartending, tell him to add my special juice." Kiki winked and laughed.

"Sure. I'll be right back. Oh, Paige lost a pair of rhinestone and garnet earrings. If you see them, let me know."

"I swear," Kiki said as Delanie headed toward the door. "More stuff disappears from back here. I'm going to start bringing a suitcase that locks."

Delanie approached Alejandro in the kitchen for the tea, and he returned with a to-go cup and a lid. She hoped to get a glimpse of Donnie, but he was nowhere in sight.

"Thanks a bunch," she said as Alejandro nodded and returned to his prep tasks.

She scurried to the dressing room in time to help Kiki out of her gown. The beaded and sequenced sunburst dress weighed a ton. Kiki handed her a reinforced hanger.

"Okay, last wardrobe change," Kiki said, removing her wig and wiping her brow. "This is for the big finale. Hand me that aquamarine dress over there." The mini dress sparkled under the vanity's lights. Kiki, in her Spanx, shimmied into the dress. Delanie zipped her up as Tara Byte walked in.

"Hey, baby. How'd it go?" Tara asked.

"Great. You warmed them up for me. It's a full house tonight, and they're pretty well liquored up and pretty loose with the dollar bills. We'll be swimming in tips tonight."

"Hey, D. How's it going? These witches running you ragged?" Tara asked.

Delanie smiled. "It's been fun. But I'll sleep well tonight. I'm giving my Fitbit a workout."

"When you're done with the Queen Bee over there, come help me get out of this dress. It's time for my big number."

"Hold your horses. I need her to help me with my showgirl topper. Delanie, grab that headpiece there with all the feathers," Kiki said.

Delanie picked up the heavy headpiece. The teal, pink, and purple ostrich feathers tickled her nose. Some fluttered to the floor and left a trail behind Kiki.

"Hold it steady, and I'll slide under it. It has some Velcro on the collar, and then I have hairpins for the top. There's an art to getting in and out of this."

Delanie secured the collar as Kiki put a handful of bobby pins in her mouth. "I got it from here. Thanks. Go help her before she pops a vein," she mumbled as she stuck pins in the headpiece and her pink wig.

After getting Tara and her ombre wig situated, Delanie sunk down in the easy chair, the ladies sashayed backstage. She did not have time to rest because the remainder of the crew flooded in to put on the finishing touches before they joined the big finale.

Delanie got a short break when entertainers took the stage for the last time. She picked up all the trash and discarded plates and cups, a good cover for checking out all the vanities and workstations. Still no sign of Paige's earrings.

The music faded, and the gals made their way back to the dressing area where they returned to their street looks and waved goodbyes.

"How'd it go?" Deke asked, standing in the doorway.

"Just the earring issue tonight," she replied. "I have a couple of ideas."

"Call me tomorrow, and we can chat. Lunch time is a good time to catch me."

"She nodded. "Thanks," as Paige Turner waltzed out of the restroom, grabbed her oversized Gucci bag, and waved over her shoulder.

6

DELANIE JUGGLED AN ICED TEA, A PAPER PLATE WITH HER BBQ sandwich, and her laptop as she padded down the hall to her office. After getting situated and digging into the North Carolina-style sandwich that served as her breakfast and lunch, she fished her phone out of her purse.

"Hi, there. May I speak to Deke Jennings? This is Delanie Fitzgerald."

"Just a moment," said the voice with the slight Caribbean accent.

Before Delanie had time to multitask, he said, "Deke here. What's going on?"

"Hey, I was calling about the pair of sparkly earrings that went missing from the dressing room. A lot of folks were in and out of that room. I'd like to bring a hidden camera in my bag next time to see what we can see on Sunday. Are you okay with that?"

"I guess. It's probably the only way we're going to catch whoever's doing this," he said.

"Do you know what was previously stolen and when? That might help me see some patterns."

"I'll send it to you when we hang up. I've been keeping a list."

"It would be helpful if you had work schedules for those days, too.

I'll go through them to see if we can rule anyone out," Delanie said.

"Or determine if there are any suspects. Next weekend, we have a Saturday night show and brunch on Sunday at the normal time. Let's see what you find. Anything else I can do?"

"No. I'll look over the dates and the staff to see if I can piece together anything. See you at brunch," she said as she disconnected.

Her phone dinged about an hour later with Deke's email. According to his notes, a Queen Bee coffee mug, a rainbow boa, a pair of red-sequined stilettos, a man's wallet with four hundred dollars, a chandelier zircon necklace, a pair of zircon-encrusted dangle earrings, three specialty wigs, and Paige's earrings had disappeared from the dressing room in the last four months. From the dates, it looked like the crook had gotten braver as time passed. The lifted items' values had also increased over time.

Delanie recorded the thefts in a spreadsheet and started plotting the dates that staff worked. She hoped this would at least give her a narrower list of suspects. She heard the weird noise again. Delanie sat up in her chair. It was hard to pinpoint what it was. Sometimes it sounded like something sliding. Then other times, there were creaks like something was pushing on metal.

She listened intently for several minutes, and then the creaking started again. It sounded like it was right overhead, and then the sound moved out into the hallway. She kicked off her shoes and climbed on the desk. Easing the ceiling tile up, she peered inside. Nothing moved. And no weird noises. When she tired of holding her arms above her head, she climbed down and gathered her things. She'd finish her research in her kitchen at home, where it was quieter.

When the car started, she told the radio to "Call Duncan." After listening to his quirky message, she continued, "Hey Dunc. I was in the office today, and I heard the noise again in my office. It's creeping me out not knowing what it is. Have you heard anything from the maintenance guys?"

Once at home, she set up shop on her kitchen table and opened her spreadsheet of missing items. Delanie created a pivot table that she graphed in Excel. Out of entertainers, waiters, and kitchen staff, three were no longer employed and six of the people were not present on the day things were pilfered. From the entertainment side, Ginger Snap, Nova Cain, Kiki Jubilee, Anna Conda, Paige Turner, and Amber Alert were all scheduled on days something went missing. Ginger, Kiki, Paige, and Amber also had items stolen from them.

Delanie stared at her list. None of the wait or kitchen staff reported anything missing. And their schedules were all over the place. She rubbed her eyes and stretched.

Duncan's ringtone interrupted her stretching exercises. "Hey, there," she said.

"I called maintenance the other day, but I haven't heard back from them. I'll call them back when we hang up."

"Something's not right on the other side of those ceiling tiles. I keep hearing that noise. It's driving me nuts, so I went home where I could concentrate. On a less scary note, Deke sent me a list of stolen items and the work schedules for his staff for those dates. I'm looking for patterns. I need to borrow one of your magic cameras tomorrow for the drag brunch. Do you have one handy?"

"I do. Margaret and I are going over to get Evie soon for a movie marathon. I can drop it off if you're going to be home. I have the purse one you normally use. I also have another one that is motion activated if you want that one. I usually slip it in a backpack or a gym bag."

"Let's try both. I'll be here all afternoon. Thanks for bringing it over."

Delanie returned to her graphs to see if anything else popped out at her. There had to be something in the wait and kitchen staff schedules.

THE NEXT MORNING, Delanie scooted into the last parking space near Freeda's front entrance. She grabbed her purse, keys, and a backpack with Duncan's new camera in it and jogged around to the alley to find a locked back door. Delanie knocked until her knuckles turned red. Alejandro opened the door and peeked outside.

"Thanks," she said as he held the door for her. He glared at her and returned to the kitchen prep area.

Delanie brushed off the cool reception and waved to the staff she passed on her way through the kitchen to the back hallway. Not seeing Deke, she headed to the dressing room, hoping to have it all to herself.

Anna Conda's bag sat on the counter across from Tara's usual spot. Delanie put her camera-purse on the vanity next to Tara's station. She added a water bottle, hairbrush, and a pair of dangle earrings as bait. Clicking the on button, she set the black backpack with the motion-sensor camera in the corner, facing the door.

Delanie jumped when Anna Conda said, "What are you doing here so early? Trying to score bonus points with the boss?" The drag queen wore an orange sunburst sequined gown and bouffant wig, reminiscent of the 1950s.

Delanie smiled. "I want to do a good job for Deke. He was kind to me."

The tall entertainer sat in the chair near Tara's vanity. "He's a good guy. He watches out for people."

When she did not continue, Delanie said, "Can I get you anything?"

"I'm good for now." Anna adjusted her blond wig and touched up her eyeliner.

Delanie busied herself arranging items around the counters. She picked up two pairs of discarded stilettos.

"Where do you get your shoes?" she asked, looking at the size fourteen shoes covered in sequins.

"Online. You can get anything on the internet, including large-sized, glamorous shoes. I do all my shopping there."

Before Delanie could comment further, Tara Byte breezed in and dropped a gym bag and two garment bags on the chair. "Hey, y'all! Miss me?"

Anna Conda mumbled something under her breath.

"Of course," Delanie said. "It's good to see you."

"Help me get my stuff together. It has been a morning. I couldn't find my wig. And I was out of coffee. And then my car wouldn't start. I had to Uber over here."

"How do you take your coffee?" Delanie asked.

"Dark, like me. Though, if you walk by the bar, tell him I'd like some Baileys in it."

Delanie smiled and retreated down the hall.

When she returned with an Irish coffee, Kiki, Nova, and Amber had joined the party. All were in various stages of dress. Delanie fetched drinks, held wigs, found makeup bags, and zipped up gowns for the next hour. When the gals finally took the stage, she slumped in the chair in the corner.

Delanie had not worked this hard since her part-time college jobs. The brief respite gave her a few minutes to think about what else she needed to do. She should call Duncan to follow up about his call to the maintenance guys and stop by Chaz's to drop off Duncan's findings. She did not want to email the sensitive content about his political competitors, and it was a good opportunity to check in with her client.

Her quiet did not last long. The talent returned to pack up. On the way out, she noticed that several of the ladies had left bags at their stations.

After everyone had cleared out, she grabbed her props and the cameras, anxious to see what they had captured. The video reveal would have to wait until after a quick stop at Chaz's club.

DELANIE KNOCKED on the front glass door of the Treasure Chest. She peered in the darkened lobby. Nothing moved in the dim light. She could see a lobby area and a doorway to the club. About the time she pulled out her phone, a giant man appeared and flipped the lock. He held the door for her.

"Hey, Delanie," he said with a wide smile that showed his gold tooth.

"Marco, how are you? Is Chaz around?"

"He's back in the war room. It's campaign central around here. Follow me," he said.

Delanie had to pick up her pace to match the strip club's security director's stride through the darkened lobby to the main stage bar area with an elevated stage. The gentlemen's club looked tame without all the flashing lights. In a few hours, the entire atmosphere would change when the doors opened to the public. Chaz had installed different crow's nests on all the dance poles since her visit last summer. She wondered if they were new platforms for the exotic dancers. Delanie always suppressed the urge to do her pirate imper-sonations when she was in Chaz's club.

Marco led her past Chaz's office to a conference room at the end of the hall.

"Delanie!" Chaz yelled. "Welcome to where it all began for Team Chaz." He jumped up, grabbing a red ballcap and T-shirt. "Here, you need some swag. Here's one for your partner. And one for his dog. And a couple for your friends."

"Thanks." She held up the 'Chaz for Mayor' T-shirt. Margaret would look fabulous in it.

"I have something for you, too." Delanie handed him the thick folder containing the opposition research. "I didn't want to email this to you."

"I need this." He grabbed it from her hand. He flipped through the pages about his fellow candidates. "This is good. Really good. A strip club owner doesn't look so bad when compared to a slumlord and a chiseler. Thanks. I'll go through this and be ready for the next showdown. Speaking of that, the debate is tomorrow night. Are you free? I'd love for you to be there. I need as many friendly faces in the crowd as I can get."

Chaz caught Delanie off guard. "Yes, I can be there," she said.

"Super. Seven-thirty at the City Hall building." He flipped through more of the pages. He sneezed and wiped his nose on the back of his hand.

Delanie cringed. She had the urge to fish through her purse for her hand sanitizer or a tissue for Chaz.

"Pull up a chair. We're brainstorming. You know Marco and Steve, my surveillance guy. This is Petra, my publicist." He waved at the brunette with the bob cut in the tailored pink suit. He waved his arm at the white board behind him. "We're doing a phone bank next weekend. Everyone here at the Treasure Chest will be making calls for the cause. And Petra got me gigs on all the local morning news shows."

Delanie smiled again. Before she could comment, the animated Chaz continued, "I rented an office on Broad Street for a real campaign headquarters. I'm all in for this. I'm a legitimate candidate. I am ready to take on Richmond."

Delanie hadn't seen Chaz this excited before. "Duncan and I are pleased we can help."

"And I want you all to come to my election night party. Hopefully, it'll be a victory celebration, but if not, it will still be an epic party."

"Where will it be?" she asked, thinking about all the swanky hotels in Shockoe Slip in the Bottom.

"Here, of course." He waved his arms. "Old money Richmond will die that the new mayor's victory party is at a strip club. This is a new era. And I'm bringing change whether they like it or not."

Delanie hoped he did not see her roll her eyes. "Let me know if you need anything else. I've got to be getting back."

"I'll send you invites to the big bash. Tell your friends who live in the city to vote. I have big plans. The people of Richmond won't know what hit 'em," he said.

Delanie, secretly glad that she lived in the county, was not eligible to vote in the mayoral election.

Marco walked her back to the front door. As Delanie turned to leave, he asked, "Think he's got a chance?"

"Anything's possible." She winked.

"It might be kinda cool being security for the mayor." Marco winked back. "Who knows what challenges that'll bring."

7

DELANIE HAD AN IDEA ON HER WAY TO THE OFFICE. IT WOULD BE FUN TO host a "Friends-giving" before everyone's traditional Thanksgiving with their families. If she put several six-foot tables together, she could stretch them from her dining room to her living room, and there would be plenty of space for guests in her bungalow, a 1939 Sears Catalog mail-order house.

She loved her quirky house that had history. When it was new, the materials had been shipped by railroad and assembled on the owner's lot. She loved that many of the boards still had the part numbers stamped on them.

By the time she had parked in front of the office, the plans were materializing for most of the menu and the guest list. She would call her best friend, Paisley, later and enlist her help. Delanie and Paisley Ford had been besties since elementary school. Her social-butterfly friend would help her pull off a dinner party, even when neither of them was known for their culinary skills.

"Duncan, hey Duncan. What do you think of this?" she yelled from the hallway. She followed the voices she heard into the conference room where Tina Montgomery and Duncan sat in front of an open box of doughnuts.

"Oh, hey," Duncan said. "Tina stopped by with doughnuts. She's catching me up on life at the reptile store."

Delanie dropped her purse in the seat across from Tina and slid into the chair. "Oops, sorry, Margaret. I didn't see you down there." She bumped the bulldog with her foot. Margaret raised her head and gave her the evil eye before returning to her nap.

"So, like I told Duncan, I spent most of yesterday at the store. Glen and I have been putting things back in order. There was a lot of glass to clean up. The police suspect that the aquariums broke when my dad had a heart attack and fell into them. Anyway, when I was in the backroom, I found two dead tarantulas, so that's how my day started. Creepy, huh?"

Delanie scrunched up her nose at the thought of big, hairy spiders skulking about. She hoped Tina did not notice.

"I know. It spooked me too," Tina said. "You'd think after being around all the slithery, crawly things for so long that I'd be used to them by now. But I'm not. It gives me the heebie jeebies to go in there in the dark. The terrariums and aquariums have a weird purply glow when the big florescent lights aren't on." After a long pause, Tina continued, "Glen was pretty broken up about the spiders. They were probably in one of the glass containers that broke. They're fragile creatures. A fall or a squeeze can be fatal to them. Anyway, as we were cleaning up, I tried to pry information out of my brother, but I wasn't very successful. I was hoping Duncan could come by later and talk to him. He might open up more to him."

"Did you find any other accounting anomalies?" Delanie asked.

"No, just the ones I told you about. They're odd. They don't appear at any regular interval. You know, like our monthly electric or phone bills. Even purchases for our inventory tend to be on a regular cycle. These are random, and there is no additional information that I can find about them."

"You do the books for the store and the internet sales?" Duncan asked, helping himself to another cream-filled doughnut.

"Yes. It's all under the same company," Tina said.

"Do you ship the online purchases?" Duncan asked.

"Of course. There are several shippers that transport live reptiles. They have to be nonpoisonous and in special containers. We get shipments all the time from breeders. You'd be surprised what gets sent through delivery companies. Glen also ships out a lot of online orders, but some of his clients come into the store. They tend to buy supplies, too, and a bunch of them hang out and play with the snakes."

Delanie wrinkled her nose again.

"Can you get me a list of Glen's major sellers and the regular buyers?" Duncan asked.

"Sure. Why?" Tina asked.

"It's a hunch," he said. "I was hoping to spot some connection."

"I need to be heading back. I'll email you the list. Thanks again for helping me." Tina rose and picked up her oversized purse.

"Thanks for the doughnuts." Duncan rose to show Tina to the door. Margaret woke up a few minutes later. When she did not see her favorite guy, she trotted off down the hall.

Delanie grabbed a chocolate glazed doughnut and headed to her office.

"What's the plan?" Duncan asked, stopping in her doorway.

"I'm going to go through the camera footage again from the drag show. Nothing jumped out at me the first time. And I promised Chaz I'd go to his debate tonight."

Duncan snickered. "I'm going to dig around on the internet to see what I can find about Snakes and Scales and the accounting questions. I'm curious about Glen's web presence. I have a hunch I want to check out on some special internet browsers."

"Hey, I'm thinking about having a Friends-giving in November. Would you, Evie, and Margaret come?"

"Sure. Sounds fun. But I'll pass on Chaz's debate," he said, winking. He and Margaret disappeared down the hall before Delanie could ask any more questions.

Duncan appeared in her doorway a few minutes later. "I forgot to tell you. Maintenance came by yesterday. They didn't find anything in the ceiling. The supervisor said that you probably heard vibrations from the pipes or the heating unit. There's a lot of open space behind our drop ceiling, and the sound echoes. He said there's nothing to worry about."

Delanie made a face. "Not sure if I buy that. I know what I heard. I even saw the ceiling tiles move. My house is old, and it makes noise from time to time, but nothing like that."

Duncan shrugged his shoulders. "Let me know if you hear it again. Maybe I could rig a camera up there."

"Plus, the weather's still nice. The heat's not on yet," she said to Duncan's back, as he headed back toward his office.

Delanie pulled out the staffing spreadsheets and the theft list from Freeda's. She spent hours looking for common denominators. Disappointed at not finding a smoking gun, she settled for a few leads to pursue. It was difficult because work schedules varied from week to week, and none of the clues pointed to any one person. Perusing the camera feeds did not yield anything of value either.

She stood and stretched and then did some yoga poses to ward off the kinks in her back. In the middle of her downward dog, she heard the sound again. Today, it sounded like a soft scrape. It lasted for a few seconds, and then she heard it again. It sounded quieter the second time.

Delanie tiptoed out of the office into Duncan's office. "I heard it again," she whispered. "It's not the pipes."

He followed her back to her office. They stood in the hallway in silence for a long time. Duncan closed one eye and made a face.

"I know what I heard," she said.

"I'll bring in some cameras that work in low light and put them in the ceiling if it will make you feel better."

"Thank you. It's driving me crazy. And the drag show thefts are bothering me, too. I'm at a standstill. I need to rethink my strategy for catching the culprit in the act. Nothing's worked so far."

"Sorry. Let me know if I can help," he said.

"At least I've picked up some good makeup tips," she said as she shrugged her shoulders. "After I make a few calls, I'm heading out."

"Say hi to Chaz for me." Duncan retreated to his office.

DELANIE FOUND PARKING on a side street in the middle of the government district. She locked her Mustang and walked a couple of blocks to the Richmond City Hall building. Maybe if the debate became boring, she could sneak out and view the city's skyline from the observation deck. It would be cool to snap some sunset pictures of the city. She turned the corner onto Broad Street and smiled when she saw Chaz's gold Hummer parked at the curb. Normally, an advertising wrap of bikini-clad women covered the vehicle. Today it had been updated for Chaz's campaign. Hashtag Team Chaz and his web address appeared in red across all the bikini tops. He was definitely going to make a splash in staid Richmond politics.

It was standing room only in the debate hall. Delanie claimed a spot against the wall between two doors. Was the debate this popular or were people curious about the T&A king's foray into politics?

The moderator took the stage and explained the rules for the evening, stressing there would not be time for audience questions. He repeated that point and then introduced each of the candidates to a mix of applause and some boos. Delanie spotted Chaz's contingent across the room. She recognized Marco and Steve and some of the other staff from the Treasure Chest. Noticeably overdressed women filled two rows behind the guys. The women's tight outfits looked club ready, and their makeup would make the drag queens jealous. They stood and hooted when the moderator introduced Charles Wellington Smith, III. Petra the publicist, sat stoically where she could be seen from the stage. Nothing seemed to escape her gaze.

Six candidates filled the small stage area. The moderator provided a question and a few minutes for each to answer and some time for rebuttals. The constant discussion of taxes and the condition of the schools and roads gave Delanie a dull headache. She wished she had changed her shoes to something practical or at least had a chair to sink into. She was not equipped for hours of standing in her boots with three-inch heels.

Chaz surprised Delanie this evening. All of his answers were on point, and he did not do his usual attack-dog schtick with his fellow candidates. He was polite in his responses and minded his manners for a change. Chaz sounded almost professional, like he really wanted this job. She wondered if the audience was disappointed. Some probably came for a raucous evening.

At about the time Delanie was considering sneaking out, the moderator posed the last question of the evening. "Why should we elect you mayor?"

Each of the candidates listed a litany of reasons why he or she was the best choice. Chaz was the last to answer.

Delanie caught a glimpse of Chaz's publicist, Petra, staring down Chaz with her dark eyes. Her eyebrows crinkled into a scowl, and she pointed her index finger with its perfectly manicured pale pink nail at him. Chaz seemed to soften at the warning she was telegraphing to him.

Chaz took a deep breath, grabbed the lectern with both hands and said, "I am a disrupter. If you want Richmond politics to be the same old same old, then I'm not your candidate. I've lived in Richmond my entire life. And I think it's time to try some new, radical tactics. We can't continue to do things the same way we've always done them and expect different results. If you want to move forward, then I'm your candidate. And right after we finish here, I'll be holding a press conference out front, and I have some things you may want to hear about. You may be shocked. Some of these people who told you what great elected officials they would be have some skeletons in their closets. Come outside. I'll tell you the truth. I have all the dirt." His contingent let out squeals, whoops, and whistles, much to the chagrin of the moderator.

Delanie stretched. Yep, Chaz was back even with perfect Petra's warning. He could not help himself.

Slipping through the front doors, Delanie made her way outside. The observation deck would have to wait for another day. On the sidewalk, the press and the TV cameras made an arc around Chaz's Hummer. Delanie found a spot on the curb by the vehicle's front passenger bumper where she could get a good view and stay out of the fracas. She scanned the diverse audience, and she did a double take when she thought she caught a glimpse of Anna Conda in the back row. Before Delanie could move closer for a better look, the drag queen had disappeared into the crowd.

A few minutes later, Chaz appeared at the front doors, followed by his entourage. The crowd had doubled in size and spilled out onto the street. Chaz took center stage on the curb with the gold Hummer as his background. He raised both arms as shushing sounds rippled through the throngs. People kept streaming out of the building. They covered every inch of space on the steps and sidewalk up and down Broad Street. Steve, from the Treasure Chest, handed Chaz a microphone. Petra stood quietly on the outskirts within eye contact of the candidate.

"Ladies and gentlemen, I am Chaz Smith, and I'm running for mayor. It's time this city had someone who's not afraid to tell it like it is. There's more to your slate of candidates than you probably know about. They look down their collective noses at me because I own Richmond's finest gentlemen's club. And somehow, that doesn't jive with their definition of respectable. But they didn't do any introspection. Let's start with Calvin Mullins. Mr. Mullins's mother, Deedra, is the primary owner of DEM Construction, and over the past ten years, while he has been serving as your councilman, his mother's company has secured not one, but three contracts with the city with a street value of over sixteen million dollars. How does this happen? Is no one looking at conflicts of interest? But wait, I have more. Mr. Ron Jenkins over there. Yes, Ron, we see you slinking away." He stared at a man in the back of the crowd. "He owns rental houses in the city. I won't pass judgement, but I bet if we ask his tenants, the term slumlord would come up in the conversation, and if that's not bad enough, he doesn't pay his fair share in taxes. Do you want a tax dodger for mayor? That's just not right. I pay my taxes."

The crowd muttered and rumbled. Delanie heard a few boos emanating from Chaz's contingent of exotic dancers.

"And finally, I want to talk about George Peters. He's represented the good people of the first district in the West End for close to four years as their councilman. Well, Mr. Peters is a homeowner in that district, but he doesn't actually live there. He claims he's refurbishing the property. Well, I think he needs to get some new contractors. The project has been going on for three and a half years, and in that time, he's been residing in a lovely McMansion in Goochland County. I call upon you to demand answers from your City Council. And I challenge the press to investigate my allegations. They'll validate me. I may own a gentlemen's club, but I pay my fair share, and I live in the city that I love. I tell the truth, and I'd be honored to be your candidate for mayor. Vote Team Chaz! Thank you." The crowd erupted in applause.

The crowd hollered a chorus of "Team Chaz" chants, and the candidate waved to the crowds as he climbed in the passenger seat of the Hummer. His dancers passed out bumper stickers and paper pirate hats to the crowd.

Delanie waded through the crowd to get to her car. Chaz did not disappoint. She could hardly wait to see tomorrow's headlines.

8

DELANIE SAT ACROSS FROM DUNCAN IN THEIR CONFERENCE ROOM, watching the three local newscasts. Duncan had worked his techno magic, so they could see all three on the same screen.

"Your boy caused quite a stir yesterday," he said.

"He was subdued during the onstage event, but he let loose at his press conference with all of your research, I might add. The cheering crowd yesterday on the street was impressive. I'm not sure if that translates into votes or not. But he's definitely a showman."

"He's had some effect. As of this morning, Calvin Mullins and George Peters have dropped out of the race. That leaves Chaz, Ron Jenkins, Elrod Meekins, and Christine Addison."

"The field's getting smaller, and Chaz is still in it. I thought this was a publicity stunt when he first mentioned it. I'm surprised he's taking it seriously. Let's see if he can go the distance."

"I couldn't find anything on Meekins or Addison. They're relatively newcomers and look squeaky clean. Meekins is a Baptist minister, and Addison has served on several high-profile committees and the school board for two terms," Duncan said.

"Hang on. It's going to be a wild ride. Chaz surprised me during the debate. We'll see if he can pull off this campaign thing."

Duncan leaned over and put a Team Chaz red ballcap on Margaret and smiled. "I'm getting hungry. I'm going to walk over to Gotham Pizza. Wanna go?" Margaret raised an eyebrow.

Delanie nodded. Duncan turned off the TV feed, and they headed down the hall, followed by Margaret who was bringing up the rear flank.

"Stay here, girl, and guard the office from the weird noise," Duncan said.

"Did you hear it?" Delanie asked. She followed him out through the reception area and the front door.

"No. I've never heard it. And I forgot the cameras. I'll bring them tomorrow. Did you hear it today?"

She shook her head. As they walked across the parking lot to the restaurant, Delanie glanced at Snakes and Scales. The store looked dark. No closed sign on the door.

They ordered at the counter of the small pizzeria and found seats in a booth in the corner.

"Any luck with the account research for Tina?" Delanie asked.

"I haven't been able to find out anything on the accounts on the other side of the payments she highlighted. But I did some investigating in the land of snakes, spiders, and exotic fish on the dark web. It's quite the industry. You can get almost anything you want. I learned a lot about the backrooms."

"Huh?" she said as the clerk called their number at the counter.

After getting drinks and settling back in the booth, Duncan continued, "Backrooms. A lot of these stores have a place where they have items for sale that you're not supposed to have. There are all kinds of federal, state, and local regulations about what can be kept or sold legally. Some breeds are illegal to import but can be raised locally. Other vendors are dodgier and sell stuff they shouldn't. You're supposed to have paperwork and other documentation if you're allowed to own or sell certain species." Duncan stopped talking and dug into his lunch.

"What does that have to do with Ken Montgomery?" she asked, taking a bite of her slice of cheese pizza.

"I found Glen's advertising on some of these collector sites. And he's got a following. He posts advice on feeding and care of exotic reptiles. He seems to be quite the expert. And in the past, he's offered some species that are banned in Virginia."

"I wonder if Tina is aware?"

"Doubtful. I'm going to keep digging. I'm going to post some inquiries to see if I can chat up Glen online. He might be freer with his responses if he thinks I'm a prospective buyer. Why don't you meet Tina for lunch or something? See if you can figure out what she knows about her brother's inventory and clientele."

"Sounds like a plan. At least this case is moving forward. I'm at a brick wall on the Freeda's case. Only one pair of earrings has gone missing since I've been there. And nothing but normal backstage stuff showed up on the hidden cameras," she said with a sigh. "It's been a snoozefest."

After they finished their lunch in silence, Duncan picked up the trash.

"I'm going to have to call Deke today to see what our new plan is," Delanie said.

"'Bout ready?" She nodded and followed him through the glass doors.

"That's interesting," she said, pointing to the pet store. "It looked dark before, and now there are five or six cars parked out front."

"Snake club?"

She laughed. "Let me know what you find on your forays into the dark web. I'm headed back into the world of glitter and glam."

"In both cases, everything is not what it seems," Duncan said, holding the office door for her.

Delanie settled in her office and fished her phone out of her purse. After the third ring, she heard, "Freeda's."

"Hi. This is Delanie. May I speak to Deke?"

After a minute or so of upbeat instrumentals, Delanie heard, "Deke here."

"Do you have a few minutes to talk?"

"What's up?" he asked.

"Nothing showed up on the cameras last week. Since I've been hanging out, there's only been one item missing, and that wasn't on a Sunday. Are you okay if I set up again next weekend?"

"Let's try it for one more weekend and then regroup. We have a large event on Saturday evening and brunch on Sunday. Can you cover both?"

"Sounds like a plan. See you soon," Delanie said, pulling up her spreadsheet to see if she had missed any connections.

Hours later, Duncan stuck his head in her office. "It's game night, and I've got to get the food. Need anything before I leave?"

"No, I'm good. Oh, don't forget the cameras for the office," she said.

"Yup. See ya later." He disappeared down the hallway with Margaret following behind.

"There has to be some connection," Delanie said to herself. "Stuff just doesn't disappear." She printed the spreadsheet and grabbed several fluorescent highlighters. She color coded the cells to show who had missing items and who was scheduled on what dates. The rainbow-colored cells jumped out at her. Anna Conda, Alejandro, Nova Cain, Donnie, Kiki Jubilee, Brett a bartender, and Deke were all present when items were lifted. With the exception of the owner, these would be her targets this weekend. It had to be one of them unless it was some random person, but that did not make sense with multiple thefts.

Delanie's phone rang and distracted her from her strategizing. "Falcon Investigations," she said.

"Hey, girl. This is Kathy from Lion Insurance. I'd like to talk to you about a work opportunity."

"It's great to hear from you. What can I do for you?" Delanie asked.

"I have a workman's comp claim that I need you to investigate for me. We had someone call in an anonymous tip that a guy who's out with an injury claim is coaching and playing football."

"Send me over the file, and I'll be happy to check it out for you."

"Great," Kathy said. "I knew I could count on you. Sending the file over now. It's for a Phillip Bell. He hurt his back when he was moving some equipment at his job with a financial company downtown. He's also a coach for the local arena football team. Let me know what you find."

"Thanks for thinking of us," Delanie said as she disconnected. While she waited for Kathy to email the file, she woke up her laptop. "Let's see what we have on Phillip Bell." "Interesting," she mused to herself.

Kathy's company was always a steady supply of quick workman's comp cases.

Delanie read several online articles about Assistant Coach Phillip Bell. By day, he worked as a financial specialist with a firm in one of the skyscrapers downtown. On weekends, he coached defense for the arena football team, the Richmond Rowdies. It was off-season for the sport that usually played at the Richmond Coliseum in the spring. But with a few clicks, she found out the team practiced at different times during the year at the Redskins Training Camp field. The team's website detailed practice times and locations, including today. Good for a nosey private eye. She would swing by this evening to see what she could find out about Mr. Bell who, according to Kathy's file, injured his back moving furniture in his new office.

Checking her watch, Delanie had an hour or so before the Rowdies practiced. Enough time to get a latte and a good parking space. Before she could gather her things, she heard a crack and a shuffling noise in the kitchen area.

She grabbed her purse and laptop and tiptoed to the kitchen. Listening for the sound again, she held her breath and her heart pounded. When she was about ready to give up, she heard it again. This time it was louder, and it sounded like something scooting across a surface.

Investigating the noise would make her late for football practice. She gathered her things and headed to the car. Once inside, she texted Duncan. *Heard the noise again in the kitchen. Please bring cameras.*

Her phone dinged a few minutes later with a smiley emoji.

Delanie scored a prime parking spot on DMV Drive, close to the practice field's entrance. She drained the last few drops of her coffee and grabbed a clipboard and Duncan's magic hat that had a hidden camera behind the embroidered logo on the front.

She hiked through the open gates to the fencing that encircled the field. There was no security check like there was when the Washington Redskins were in town. Guys in T-shirts and sweats practiced drills on the main field. Rowdies staff surrounded the field's perimeter. When a large guy in a ballcap blew a whistle, the players hustled over to the sidelines.

Delanie pulled out her phone to see Coach Bell's photo. It did not take long to find a match on the sidelines. He was a middle-aged guy in a golf shirt and khakis. Delanie clicked the button on the brim of her hat and held her head steady to get a good shot of the coach.

He waved his arms around and blew his whistle. The players formed two facing lines. Something did not please the coach. Coach Bell waded into the opposing lines. He adjusted stances and yelled at one of the players on the defensive side. He stepped out of the way and blew the whistle.

The guys practiced the play, and when the quarterback on the opposite side threw the ball down the field, Coach Bell erupted. Delanie made sure to capture all the dramatic arm waves and finger jabs on camera. Then Coach Bell grabbed the middle linebacker and pulled him out of formation. Jumping in his spot, the coach blew the whistle and lunged toward the center. The coach knocked the younger man over and headed straight for the quarterback. A whistle blew, and the players returned to their spots. He repeated the demonstration with several other plays.

Delanie switched off her hat camera and walked toward the entrance. She left Coach Bell waving his arms and yelling at the defensive line. Easy day of investigating. It surprised Delanie that Coach Bell was out in public and participating in lots of physical activity when he was supposed to be on medical leave. Kathy's company should be pleased with the football footage of the injured financial analyst. Now, if she could just solve the mystery of the creepy ceiling sound and figure out who was swiping items from the drag queens...

9

It was a busy Saturday evening in the Fan District. Delanie had to drive around the block several times before she found parking near Freeda's. She grabbed her backpack and clutch purse with the hidden camera and hurried to the alley behind the club.

Someone had propped the back door open, so Delanie stepped inside and looked around. She wanted to get to the dressing room before the entertainers arrived. Passing Alejandro in the hall, she waved, but he turned his head. Delanie shrugged and picked up her pace. He was definitely on her watch list.

She breezed into the dressing room. Kiki's bags were draped over the overstuffed chair and two vanities. Hearing advancing steps in the bathroom area, Delanie put her clutch in the corner. Then she staged two pair of sparkly earrings and a tube of Yves St. Laurent lipstick with the Saks Fifth Avenue logo on it next to the purse. She hoped the blood red Bourgogne Alternatif would be irresistible for the thief. She clicked on the cameras and set the backpack in the corner on a stool, an inconspicuous place with a good view of the room.

"Hey, baby," Kiki said, blowing air kisses at Delanie. "What's shakin'?"

"You look lovely in that red sequined dress. Can I get you anything?"

"Hmmm. You could help me hang up my other outfits. We do at least three wardrobe changes on Saturdays. I had to bring a ton of things with me. Tonight's is a naughtier bunch than our brunch crowd, and the tips are better," she said with a wink.

Delanie spent the next fifteen minutes helping Kiki hang up her dresses, boas, and headpieces. She must drive an SUV to transport all of this.

"Hey, hey, hey!" Tara Byte announced as she entered the room in a turquoise, beaded dress that clicked as she walked. "Delanie, I'm glad you're here. Please get me a Greyhound. And tell the bartender more vodka than grapefruit juice, please."

"And I'll have a Diet Coke," Kiki said, without looking up from her makeup case.

By the time she returned, Nova Cain, Amber Alert, Anna Conda, and Paige Turner had arrived. Garment bags and suitcases littered the dressing room floor. Delanie dodged bags and powder dust storms, ran errands for drink orders, and zipped ball gowns for the next hour. She even had to lead a search for Kiki's red and zirconia stilettos, size fifteen. She found the missing shoes in a stack of discarded clothes.

When Deke called for the entertainer introductions, Delanie slumped in the puffy chair to catch her breath. Too many more nights like these and she would not need to go to the gym. Before she could plan her next steps, Donnie wandered into the dressing room. Delanie sat still. He visited a few vanity stations and applied some eyeliner from Kiki's makeup bag.

He jumped when Delanie said, "May I help you?"

He slid both hands into his apron pockets. "Uh, no. The chef sent me back here for dirty cups and plates."

Delanie's pulse raced. Could he be her guy? He did hang around backstage a lot, and he had a record. He was very interested in the ladies.

"What did you put in your pocket?" Delanie demanded, standing.

She stepped closer to the young guy. She drew up to her full height, and he took a step backwards.

He paused and stared at her while she glared down at him. Seconds ticked by.

Worry flashed across Donnie's face, and he pulled both hands out of his pockets. He turned his hand over and showed her a wrapped piece of peppermint candy and an empty palm.

Disappointed that she only caught a candy pilferer, Delanie smiled at the younger guy. "Here, let me help you." She picked up empty glasses, aluminum cans, and foam take-out containers.

Donnie balanced all the items and scurried toward the kitchen. Leaving the cameras on guard duty, Delanie strolled backstage. Anna, Kiki, and Tara, all clad in brightly colored dresses, lip synched to a medley of Harry Belafonte songs. They reminded Delanie of exotic, rain forest birds in all their finery.

When the medley ended, they took a bow to roaring applause. Deke stepped on stage and said, "It's time for a little bit country and a little bit rock 'n roll." The crowd erupted again in applause as Paige Turner and Nova Cain took the stage. Paige had her Dolly Parton wig and her pink guitar, while Nova looked like a doppelganger for the 1980s Joan Jett. Both performed to Donnie and Marie's country and rock classic from the 1970s TV show. Afterwards, they had a combo lip synch dance off. Paige represented the country side of the house, while Nova grinded and thrusted for the rockers.

Delanie jumped when Deke put his hand on her shoulder.

"Sorry. I didn't mean to scare you," he whispered. "How are things?"

"Fine. I brought my cameras again. These two are really good." She nodded her head toward the stage.

Deke smiled. "Let me know if you need anything." He disappeared into the black curtains.

Delanie watched until the end of the set. After rounds of applause, Paige and Nova sashayed offstage. Kiki and Anna appeared next in their showgirl costumes. They performed to a montage of Barry Manilow hits.

Picking her way over cables and wires backstage, Delanie peeked at the stage from behind the curtains. Nothing held her interest, so she wandered back to the dressing room.

Nova sat at her station where she wiped her face and neck with a plush towel. She had pulled off her jet-black wig and toweled her short, spiked hair. Taping a dark pageboy wig on, she reapplied her makeup. "Delanie, could you get me a glass of ice water?"

"Me, too," Paige said, as she touched up her makeup.

When Delanie returned, Paige had disappeared. Delanie handed Nova her drink and set the other on the counter across the room.

Nova did not say anything, so Delanie straightened up the abandoned articles on the floor.

Paige returned in a full-length silver sequenced gown with a slit up the side that was taller than Delanie. The material underneath was blood red. "Zip, please," she said.

Delanie stood on her tippy toes to reach the top of Paige's collar.

"Thanks. I'm going to do my Gypsy Rose Lee act." She grabbed a sparkly white and silver boa off her chair and slung it low over her shoulders. "Ciao, dah-lings."

"Could you hand me my stethoscope?" Nova asked. "And my medical bag."

Delanie rummaged around for the requests.

"Thanks. This is my big finale. I do a medley of songs about doctors. It's always a hit. Who doesn't love a nurse?" Nova reapplied the blood red lipstick and blew a kiss at the mirror. "It's hot out there. Can you get me a gin and tonic after this number? Tell the bartender that Nova wants her bad medicine."

"Will do," Delanie said as the drag queen stood and sauntered out with all her props.

When she returned with the drink order, Tara, Anna, and Kiki were back with their requests. After several trips to the bar, Delanie finally got everyone situated.

Anna paraded out in a short cave woman dress. She touched up her makeup and put on a red wig. She looked like the Ann-Margaret character on an old episode of "The Flintstones."

Before Delanie could comment, Kiki came out of the restroom in a silver and purple sequenced jumpsuit. That and the matching cape, reminded Delanie of the 1970s daredevil, Evel Knievel.

"Like it?" Kiki asked, extending the cape to show the purple interior. She twirled around and said, "The cape and the pants part come off. They're tear-aways for my big finale."

"Love it," Delanie said. "I'll try to slip out to catch your last number. One day, I'm going to watch the entire show from the other side of the curtain."

AFTER THE LAST bow and lots of photos, most of the queens changed into street clothes, removed their makeup, and strolled out. Nova and Anna put on club-scene dresses and heels. They packed their gear and headed out to continue their Saturday night.

Delanie rechecked the vanities. She made sure all the clutter was off the floor and that the trash actually made it to the garbage can. This job was a combination of room mother, babysitter, and maid. She needed to resolve this case soon.

Grabbing her backpack and picking up the clutch that had tipped over, she pocketed her prop earrings. Delanie smiled when she realized the lipstick was missing. She hoped she had the thief dead to rights on the recording.

On her way out, she waved to Donnie. The busboy smiled as he cleared a nearby table next to where Deke and a tall Scandinavian-looking bartender chatted.

"Good night," Delanie said to the two men.

"Everything go okay?" Deke asked. "Are you coming in tomorrow?"

She nodded.

"Okay. See you then. Where are you parked?" Deke asked.

"A couple blocks down."

"I'll walk you out," he said. When they were a few yards from the club, he asked, "So what's up?"

"I set up a little sting operation. My Saks Fifth Avenue lipstick disappeared. I couldn't check the cameras in there without blowing my cover, so I can't wait to get home to see what I caught."

"I hope we wrap this up soon. I don't like having a thief in our midst. Let me know what you find."

"Will do. This is me." She pointed to the black Mustang.

"Thanks for your help," he said as she closed the car door behind her.

She revved the engine and drove home with purpose. Traffic was light at this hour. Delanie whizzed through all the toll plazas with no delays and pulled in her driveway about thirty-five minutes later.

Delanie rushed inside and dropped everything on the kitchen table. She poured a glass of milk while she waited for her laptop to wake up. After a few clicks, she logged into Duncan's server to view the hidden camera footage.

At twelve-thirty-six by the camera's timestamp, she saw a hand with royal blue nails bump the clutch purse. It wobbled and fell on its side. The rest of the footage appeared sideways from a tipped over purse. Someone picked up the earrings and quickly replaced them. Then the hand scooped up the lipstick. And much to Delanie's disappointment, the thief stood outside of the camera shot. Delanie's pulse quickened. Who had blue nails tonight? Tara's were aqua to match her Cher outfit. It couldn't be her. Someone had darker blue nails. Who was it? Delanie wracked her brain, trying to remember.

She watched the wonky camera angle until it ended about one-fifteen. Okay, maybe the other camera captured something. She clicked around until she located the backpack footage.

The footage for the same timeframe was black. Delanie backed it up. The screen was dark for most of the evening. Either it malfunctioned, or something blocked it.

Puzzled, Delanie zipped to the beginning of the evening. She saw her arm adjust the backpack, and then she saw herself back out of the picture. The lens caught a good swath of the dressing room. The talent came in and out of the room, getting ready for the evening's show. For about fifteen minutes, the room looked empty. Nova Cain and Anna Conda walked into the frame and then disappeared in the back.

Then an arm appeared and the camera jolted. The picture looked like an earthquake struck. Someone picked up the bag and unzipped it. After rummaging inside, the hand set the bag on the table, facing down. The nosy person must not have opened the small front pocket with the camera.

That was a bust. Some mystery person stole Delanie's lipstick. And the bag camera caught only an arm, navy blue nails, and the top of the table.

10

DELANIE PARKED IN FRONT OF FREEDA'S AND DRAINED THE LAST FEW drops of her high-test coffee. It felt like she had just left here. Grabbing her bags, she walked around to the alley entrance. Deke and a guy who Delanie did not recognize stood near the kitchen. Delanie nodded to the men as she made her way to the dressing room. Taking advantage of being alone, she set the clutch purse back on the small table with a hairbrush and a bottle of burgundy Givenchy Le Vernis nail polish. Maybe, like the lipstick, this would be tempting to the thief.

Hurrying across the room, she set the backpack on the cabinet against the wall and angled it to capture the room. For good measure, she draped a scarf and a boa over it to make it look like it was part of the discarded wardrobe pile. There were several already in the room, so it would not look odd.

Before Delanie could relax, the talent arrived with lots of bags and noise.

Kiki and Anna plopped down at their mirrors with their backs to the door. They each applied a heavy layer of stage makeup. Anna created a blush dust storm.

"Hey, baby," Kiki said. "How're things? You look exhausted."

"I haven't worked a back-to-back late night and then a Sunday brunch before," Delanie said.

"You'll get used to it," Anna said, blotting her lips. Nova Cain sashayed in and dropped her bags on the counter next to Kiki.

"Delanie, come here and see me. You need a touch up," Kiki said.

Delanie sat on the stool next to her. Kiki applied foundation under Delanie's eyes. Then she whipped out an oversized brush to cover her face in a sparkly powder.

"Sit still," Kiki said. "You're a little wiggle worm. I'm getting ready to line your eyelids." She applied a black liquid liner. "Don't blink for a second. There are two secrets to good stage presence. One is big eyes, and the other is voluptuous lips. Always overline the lips." She pulled out a brownish liner and colored around Delanie's mouth.

"Wow," Delanie said when she looked in the mirror. "Too bad I don't have a date tonight." She had been dating FBI agent Eric Ellington off and on, but he had been assigned to a case in Kansas, so she had not heard from him in a couple of weeks. Delanie let out a heavy sigh. Her stomach fluttered when she thought of the tall agent from last summer's counterfeit case. Delanie liked her freedom, but sometimes, she wished there was someone special.

"You okay?" Kiki asked. "You look stunning, but a little sad. Too bad you won't pick up any guys around here." She winked at Delanie and smiled.

Tara Byte walked in and dropped her bags on the vanity next to Anna. "Hey, you look good. Could I bother you for an iced tea or a Coke? It has been a morning."

"Not a problem. Anybody else want anything?" Delanie scanned the room.

"Irish coffee," Kiki said, and Anna shook her head.

A shriek jolted her out of her daydream. Kiki squealed again and reached over to Nova's station. "I just love Saks." She grabbed the box. "Oooooh, and a lovely shade. Can I borrow it?"

"It was a gift," Nova said.

Kiki grabbed the lipstick – the hot lipstick – and waved it around like a wand. She tried the shade on her wrist. When it passed inspection, she layered it on her lips "Thanks," Kiki said, setting the tube on Nova's counter.

Delanie's eyes kept landing on the tube of red lipstick. She hoped the thief would get too comfortable and slip up. And that she would have proof on the recording. The clock's hands crawled all morning. This show could not end soon enough for Delanie, who felt unusually jumpy. She tried to keep busy.

Deke called for the first two acts. Delanie picked up the discarded clothes on the floor and draped them over the chairs and then wandered to the restaurant to kill time. She ordered a Coke from Brett, the tall blond bartender. Maybe the caffeine or the sugar would improve her mood. She shook off the melancholic feeling and reminded herself of what her purpose was here. She had to focus.

Delanie hurried back to the dressing room. A few moments later, the ladies started traipsing in and dropping articles of clothing on the floor. Delanie assisted with a few zippers.

With no pressing tasks and no one demanding her help, she walked backstage to catch a glimpse of Paige Turner's country medley. After taking several bows to whistles and applause, Paige exited and headed straight for the dressing room, passing Nova Cain rushing to find her mark on the stage for the next act.

Delanie returned to the dressing room to check on the gals. Anna Conda bumped into her when she rushed out.

"Ooops. Sorry," Anna Conda said, hastily on her way down the hall. The large queen elbowed Delanie in the ribs.

Before Delanie could comment, Tara Byte let out a shriek and then an ear-piercing squeal. "Shut up! Where is my fabulous necklace? I have to have it for my Cher number. It matches the dress and wig perfectly. Which one of you witches has it? Freeze! Nobody move."

"Where did you have it last?" Delanie asked.

"I keep my jewelry in my gym bag." Tara dumped her the bag out on the counter. Then she rummaged through her makeup bag. "Check that bag," she said to Delanie.

Delanie looked through every pocket. "Sorry. No necklace."

"How am I supposed to do Cher with no necklace? This is a disaster. It ruins the entire ensemble. And if one of you took it, I want it back. That sucker was expensive. Glamor does not come cheap," Tara said, waving her hands around. "Hand me my wig. I guess, I will just have to rise above this calamity and do my best. It won't be the same without my signature necklace."

Tara taped on her black and blue wig and slipped on her silver stilettos. She muttered curses all the way to the stage area. Delanie moved a towel and washcloth at Nova's station. She folded both and stacked them neatly next to the queen's makeup case. She moved on to the rest of the stations along that wall. No necklace. She wanted to search bags, but she was afraid someone would pop in while she was rummaging.

After she checked all the vanities in the room, Delanie heard booming applause. As it died down, the queens made their way one by one to the dressing room. The ladies dumped boas, shoes, and wigs on every flat surface. It did not pay for Delanie to clean up until after they left.

Delanie glanced over at the small table. The clutch and the hairbrush sat alone where she left them, but somebody had swiped the nail polish. Delanie took several deep breaths to calm the jitters. She grabbed her phone to access Duncan's server, but a shrill squeal interrupted her. Delanie looked up to see Kiki and Nova tugging on a long strand of beads.

"Give me that back." Nova yanked on the necklace.

"I was just looking at it. The pink pearls would go well with my black evening dress," Kiki growled, pulling harder on her end. The necklace snapped and beads flew everywhere.

"Now you've done it. You clumsy oaf. I expect you to pay for that." Nova put both hands on her hips. "It was very expensive."

Kiki rolled her eyes and waved her arms in the air. "I'll do no such thing. I will not pay for my own necklace. Mine went missing last week." Nova stepped closer to Kiki who took several steps backwards.

"It wasn't yours. I bought it last week at a place in Short Pump."

"Do you have the receipt?" Kiki asked, raising both eyebrows and staring down Nova.

"Yes. From a real boutique and not one of those guys selling hot jewelry on the sidewalk where you usually get your stuff," Nova hissed.

"You lying sack of..." Kiki yelled as she lunged at Nova, knocking her down. Kiki landed with a thump on the other queen's back and the brawl began.

Nova pulled off Kiki's wig and threw it on the floor. That led to shrieks and scrapping. Kiki got in several good blows before Anna Conda pulled her off Nova who curled in a ball to protect her face.

"Enough!" Anna Conda yelled. "Knock it off. It was a cheap necklace. Go to your separate corners. Kiki, if she produces a receipt, pay her for it. If not, let it go. Both of you, stop it."

Nova slowly got up and slinked to her station.

Kiki grabbed her wig and marched toward the restrooms.

No one else said anything, and the onlookers leisurely returned to whatever they were doing before the ruckus. The dressing room fell eerily silent.

Delanie picked up her phone and logged into Duncan's website. Hopefully today's camera placement caught the thief in action. After multiple clicks, she located the footage from the clutch purse. And like yesterday, a manicured hand came into the camera's range. This time the nails glimmered a ruby red. The hand grabbed the polish and disappeared.

Disappointed, Delanie navigated to the backpack's feed. After several clicks, she moved forward. The bewitching hour was half-past twelve. The backpack camera caught Anna Conda in her ruby red nails walking over to the vanities and rummaging through a bag on the floor. Delanie caught her breath. Did the drag queen pocket anything?

Then Anna Conda adjusted her wig and wiped something from the corner of her mouth with her pinkie. She walked out of the frame as Nova Cain entered the room. Delanie stopped the footage and reversed it.

She picked up the feed again at the point where Nova Cain looked over her shoulder and paused. Then she made a beeline for Tara's station. The tall queen looked over her shoulder several times and paused. Then she rummaged through Tara's black gym bag and pulled out the aquamarine necklace. She held it up to the light and then secreted it in her medical bag. Delanie gasped. Kiki was probably right about the pink pearl necklace, too.

Delanie pocketed her phone and walked with purpose to the backstage area. She tapped Deke on the shoulder and leaned in. "I know who did it. I caught her on camera," she whispered. "It's Nova Cain."

His face looked crestfallen. "Keep it to yourself for now. I'll come and get you right after the show."

Delanie nodded and made her way to the backroom, trying to look cool and collected.

The show finally ended, and the talent wandered in to pack up. Delanie took several deep breaths to calm the anticipation that tingled in the pit of her stomach.

Deke stuck his head in the doorway. He cut his eyes toward the private investigator. "Great show, ladies. Hey, Nova, could you stop by my office? I need your signature on some papers."

"Ooooh," Kiki said, glaring at the other queen.

Deke stared at her and stepped in the hallway.

"Sure. I'm always eager to give autographs." Nova Cain rose and followed him to his office.

Delanie hung back outside the big oak door. Before Deke closed it, he said, "Delanie, could you join us?"

Deke shut the door behind her. Delanie's eyes darted around his tasteful office. The dark cherry furniture highlighted the burgundies and beige tones in the room. His executive desk held only a pen set and a phone. It did not surprise her that Deke was a minimalist.

He pointed to the guest chair beside Nova, still in her nurse's costume. She sat with her long legs crossed. Her red stilettos matched her shiny red lips and nails. Probably the stolen Saks lipstick.

"Nova, something's come to my attention that I would like you to explain." Deke glared at her.

She squirmed and put on her best pouty look. "What?"

Delanie pulled out her phone and tapped to queue up the video. She held it so Nova could see. As the clip played, the drag queen fidgeted in her seat, tapping her foot like a metronome on the floor.

"What?" she repeated. "I don't know where that video came from."

"It's from today," Deke said. "I want those things returned, Tod."

"I don't know what you're talking about. And I prefer to be called Nova. Someone obviously doctored that video to frame me. First Kiki and her accusations, and now this. And what are you doing with it? You're just the maid," she hissed at Delanie.

Before she could provide a retort, Deke interrupted. "Things have gone missing around here for quite a while now. So, I hired a private investigator to get to the bottom of this. I want the stuff returned."

"I don't know what you're talking about," she said with a sneer. Nova leaned forward and picked up Deke's silver pen.

"Put that down now," he growled. Nova returned the pen and sank into her chair.

"The wigs, costumes, earrings, necklace. Do you want me to go on?" Deke asked.

Nova turned her head without replying.

"Last chance. I want the stuff returned."

"Or what?" she asked without looking at the owner of Freeda's. "I don't have to take this." She stood and stormed out of the office. Delanie looked at Deke, and they followed the queen back to the dressing room.

"Did you sign enough autographs?" Kiki asked Nova as Deke and Delanie entered the dressing room.

"Shut up," Nova hissed. "I've had enough of this place and all your attitudes." The queen started throwing her things in her gym bag.

"I still want my money for those pearls," Kiki muttered.

Nova picked up her prop medical bag and swung it at Kiki's head, making contact with her ear and cheek.

Kiki screamed and lunged at Nova, and round two started. Deke seized Kiki's shoulders and pulled her back, while Anna grabbed the bag that Nova was swinging around. When Ana and Nova tugged on the bag, it flew open, and a bottle of nail polish, Tara's aquamarine necklace, and a gold compact flew across the room.

"You witch," Tara yelled, scrambling for the necklace.

Before the cage match could continue, Deke yelled, "Call the police."

Delanie dialed 9-1-1 and stepped into the hallway.

Kiki landed on Nova's back with a thud and pinned her to the floor. The smaller queen in the nurse's uniform ducked and shrieked. She covered her head with her arms and tried to curl up in a tight ball.

"Enough!" Deke bellowed. "This has gone on way too long. The police will be here soon. Kiki, let her up. You go cool off at the bar."

Kiki rose reluctantly. "Nobody gets away with stealing from Kiki," she said. Tara took her by the elbow and escorted her out.

"Get up," Deke commanded.

Nova rose slowly and collapsed into the chair. "I'm going to need an ambulance." The disheveled queen adjusted her skirt that was covered in dust and makeup smears. She had lost her nurse's cap and wig in the melee.

Deke glared at her.

"Don't think I won't press charges against all y'all." Nova turned her head toward the wall.

A few minutes later, Tara and Kiki escorted two Richmond police officers in the dressing room.

"That's her," Kiki yelled, pointing to Nova. "That's the one who attacked my person and stole from me."

"I'm injured, Officer," Nova replied. "I was unjustly attacked. I think it was a hate crime. That beast hit me for no reason."

Kiki made a hrummpf noise. "I hate that she stole from me. And now she's being downright nasty."

The female police officer said, "I'm Sergeant Downing, and this is Officer Ruiz. Okay, we're going to get to the bottom of all this. Call an ambulance," she said to her partner. "In the meantime, sit tight until we sort this out." All the queens started talking at once, and someone let out with a long, shrill whistle. Everyone froze.

"You can use my office if you need it," Deke said.

Sergeant Downing looked at her partner and said, "Why don't you use the office to interview these folks, and I'll get her story here." She stared at Nova, who put on a show of being injured. She held her midsection with one arm and cradled her head in the other hand. She moaned every few minutes for good measure.

Deke led the queens and Officer Ruiz to his office.

Sergeant Downing asked, "So what's going on here?" as Deke returned and stood in the doorway next to Delanie.

"I'm Deke Jenkins, the owner. I hired her," he said, pointing to Delanie. "She's a private eye. We've had quite a few things stolen around here, and I wanted to get to the bottom of it."

The sergeant jotted notes and looked up at Delanie. "I'm with Falcon Investigations. I caught Nova Cain on camera taking a neck-lace that belonged to one of the other queens," she said, waving her phone. Delanie tapped a few buttons and showed the footage to the officer.

"You can't prove it's me. The video could have been doctored." Nova paused when everyone looked at her. Then she grabbed her arm and moaned.

Sergeant Downing handed Delanie her card. "Please email the video to me."

"This is her bag with some of the stolen items in it." Deke indicated the discarded medical bag. The officer took pictures as two EMTs entered.

"She got in a brawl with one of the other ladies," Sergeant Downing said. "Check her out and let me know her status."

By the time Officer Ruiz returned to the dressing room, the EMTs had decided to transport Nova to the hospital.

"Finished in there?" Sergeant Downing asked.

Officer Ruiz nodded.

"Do you mind accompanying her to the hospital? I'll meet you there as soon as I finish here."

"Gotcha," Officer Ruiz said.

The EMTs strapped Nova to a gurney, and the officer followed the procession out.

"What's next?" Deke asked.

"After she gets checked out, she'll be arrested. Ruiz let the others know they could press charges for the stolen items. And the person involved in the scrap wants to press charges for assault. I think I have all I need here." Sergeant Downing put the stolen items and Nova's prop bag in evidence bags. "Anything else?"

"No, I think that's enough for today. Thank you," Deke said.

"I'll send you the footage and a copy of my report," Delanie said.

Deke and Delanie followed the sergeant to the restaurant side of the building. Sergeant Downing nodded and disappeared into the lobby.

"Do you want something to drink?" Deke asked, as he poured a drink for himself.

"A Coke is fine," Delanie replied.

"I was hoping for a quieter resolution, but at least it's over," he said.

"You did the right thing."

"I appreciate all of your help." He handed her the glass. "Gimme a minute, and I'll write you a check for what I owe you."

"Thanks. I need to get my stuff. I'll be back," she said.

In the dressing room, Tara Byte sat quietly, removing layers of stage makeup. "Well, that was exciting. We didn't ever have that much action in here. You heading out?"

"Yep. I have to do stuff at home that's not as exciting as life here," Delanie said. "And it's nowhere near as glamorous."

"I hope I get my necklace back soon," Tara said. "I need it for my act."

"I'm sure you will after the police are done with it."

Tara grinned.

"I'm definitely coming back one Sunday to see the show from the other side of the stage. I want to see all of your act." Delanie straightened hair and makeup brushes on the counter.

"So, what's your story?" Tara asked, raising her perfectly shaped eyebrows.

"I'm Delanie Fitzgerald. I'm a private investigator."

"A grownup Nancy Drew. I knew there was something special about you when I met you." Tara passed her a business card. "In case you want to keep in touch."

The glossy black card advertised RightTech Computing. Tara's daytime gig was as Lamar Davis, Information Technology Application Manager.

Delanie smiled. "There's always more than what meets the eye," she said with a wink.

11

THE NEXT DAY, DELANIE PULLED INTO THE LOT IN FRONT OF SAMMIES, A sub and pizza place downtown, near the VCU campus. With a few minutes to kill before her appointment with Tina Montgomery, she thought about what she wanted to cover in the conversation. Her goal was to get more information on Glen's banned creatures and whether it was common knowledge with everyone at Snakes and Scales.

When she did not see the bookkeeper in the restaurant, she asked for a table for two in the corner. After the waitress took her drink order, Tina entered through the glass doors. Delanie waved as her client looked around and hurried over. She plopped in the wooden chair across from Delanie and let out a deep breath.

"Been here long?" Tina asked. "I had to drive around the block twice to find parking."

"Just got here. How are you?" Delanie asked.

Before Tina could answer, the waitress with pink hair returned with Delanie's iced tea. "What can I get you to drink?"

"A Diet Coke, and I know what I want for lunch if you're ready. I'll have two slices of pepperoni pizza."

The waitress looked at Delanie. "I'll have the house salad with no tomatoes or onions with Italian dressing, please."

After the waitress returned to the kitchen, Tina asked, "How are things going with the search?"

"We should have a report for you later this week. Duncan is still researching a couple of things. I know this is hard for you," Delanie said. Tina dabbed her eyes.

Tina sniffed and rummaged through her purse for a tissue. She wiped her eyes and nose. "Thank you. It happened so suddenly. I didn't get to say goodbye to my dad. I'd been busy at work lately and hadn't been by the store in a while. Now the store seems so empty without him. And Glen's no emotional support. He's acting weirder than usual since Dad's death."

"How often do you usually go by the pet store?" Delanie asked.

"At least once a week, but I've been involved with a big project at work for the past two months. We're implementing a new accounting system, and I've been staying late every evening. I haven't been to the store much in the last month because of my day job. I usually go on Saturdays to pay bills and check on the accounts. Plus, it was a way to see my dad regularly, and we'd usually have lunch together."

"What can you tell me about Snakes and Scales's inventory? I'm curious about where you get your stock."

Tina looked puzzled. "Different places. The majority of it comes from a couple of distributors. We get most of the fish from a distributor in San Diego. The reptiles usually come from one in Washington, D. C. But my brother does get some specialty snakes and lizards from local breeders."

"Could you get me a list of the names and addresses?" Tina furrowed her brow. "I think it will help with Duncan's research. How does your stock get to the store?" Delanie asked.

"Sometimes the guy in D. C. sends someone if Glen has a huge order. And Glen's been known to drive up there to pick up special orders. But you can ship some animals."

"What if he buys from a breeder?"

"They either come to the store, or he picks up the animals from their place. There are a few breeders in Virginia and North Carolina that we do business with. There used to be one in Florida, but I think it closed up shop after one of the big hurricanes. I can check on those for you when I'm at the store."

"Any advantage to using a breeder versus a distributor?" Delanie asked.

"I think both have their pros and cons. Some breeders can have species that you can't import. They're bred here in the states, so there are exceptions to some of the bans. That's attractive to some customers. Most of the distributors are located on the coasts. You know, for easier shipping. They usually deal in volume, so the prices can be better. Snakes and Scales has used both to get inventory."

"What can you tell me about backrooms in pet shops?" Delanie asked as she speared a cucumber.

"We have a workroom. Glen keeps extra stock back there or animals he wants to watch. He does seminars there sometimes." Tina took a bite of her pizza. The cheese stretched, and she twirled it with her finger.

"He does a lot of presentations?"

Tina nodded. "He goes to schools and other groups to talk about exotic snakes. And he posts regularly on our website and a couple of blogs. People come to him with questions. People know him as the snake guy."

Delanie decided to try another tactic in her line of questioning. "What happens if someone comes in and wants to buy a poisonous snake or something that is so exotic that it's banned?"

"It happens probably more than you'd think. It's usually teenaged boys who don't know the rules of what you can and can't have in a residential area. But there are adult collectors out there who pay top dollar for exotics. My dad tried to educate folks about their purchases or about having pets that require a lot of care. Glen's more focused on sales. It's good for the business, but I think he sells snakes to people who don't know much about what they're getting into. It's different than a puppy or a kitten. I wish he was more like my dad," she said, her voice drifting off.

Delanie looked puzzled, and Tina continued, "Reptiles need special care and specific diets. You can't run to the grocery store for

their main food supply. They typically eat rodents. If you don't keep
live or frozen ones on hand, then you have to buy these things called
snake sausages. Glen said that they're for the squeamish who don't
want to do the rat thing. The habitats need to be maintained, and
some need special lamps or heaters. Plus, their cages need to grow
with the animal. Some reptiles get to be rather long. Their care can
be rather pricy."

Eww, Delanie thought. She tried to keep a straight face and not
wrinkle her nose. "Do you keep any reptiles?"

"Oh, no. I have three cats, Winkin', Blinkin', and Nod. They're
good company, and better for snuggling." She showed Delanie
pictures of her cats on her phone. "Do you have pets?"

"No, I work crazy hours. It wouldn't be fair to leave a pet alone so
much. Margaret, the bulldog, rules our office. She's Duncan's sidekick.... And I'm her godmother," Delanie said, disappointed that she
didn't have any photos to show.

"She's cute. I've seen them riding round in his yellow car." Tina
finished a slice of her pizza.

"So, what happens if someone calls asking for a cobra or something else that's dangerous?"

"We explain what can and can't be sold. Nobody needs a cobra. I
don't understand those people who want to keep dangerous snakes."

"Me either." Delanie finished her salad.

The waitress stopped by and asked, "Could I get you anything
else?"

"Just the check," Tina said. "I need to get back to work."

"Do you ever get any weird or unusual requests at the store?"
Delanie asked.

Tina laughed. "Sometimes. They want exotic animals. One time,
someone with an exotic snake called and asked Glen to come and
get it."

"Did he?"

Tina nodded and continued, "We get two or three calls a month
from people who think we're exterminators. We don't remove snakes
or bats from your attic. But the county does call Glen from time to

time if animal control ends up with a pet snake or lizard that's been abandoned, and they can't care for it."

"That's interesting," Delanie said. "What does he do with them?" Delanie asked.

"Sometimes they stay at the store. Others he takes home. He keeps a menagerie in Dad's basement. Some he adopts and others he finds homes for. He's had a couple of big ones go to zoos."

The waitress put the check on the table, and Delanie grabbed it.

"Let me pay my half," Tina said.

"I've got it. I appreciate you spending your lunch time talking to me." Delanie placed her credit card on the little black tray.

After goodbyes on the sidewalk, Delanie crossed the street and retrieved her car from an honor pay lot. On the way back to the office, she clicked the button on her steering wheel. "Call Duncan."

After a few rings, she heard, "What's happening? Still working on the drag queen thefts?"

"Nope. Wrapped that up yesterday. The police took the bad queen away after she got in a fight with her accuser. Deke's another satisfied client. And I had lunch with Tina Montgomery today. She didn't seem to know much about backroom reptile sales. She explained at length that her father always made sure to educate people who asked for banned animals. She mentioned that Glen is more motivated by money. I did find out something interesting. She said that the local animal control offices call her brother if a snake or lizard gets abandoned."

"Interesting. So, he's definitely known in the lizard and snake world." It sounded like Duncan was chewing something. "I remembered to bring the cameras. I put one in the ceiling by your desk. I put another one in the hallway. We'll see what we can see."

"Thanks. That noise is driving me nuts. Did you hear it today?" Delanie asked.

"Nope. It likes you better."

"Wow. I feel special."

"Hey, if there's something up there. We'll find it just in time for Halloween," he said.

"And then the election. There's always something exciting going on," she said.

"Speaking of excitement. Have you heard back from Chaz?"

"No. His last request was for the oppo research. I guess he's good to go for a while. But you know Chaz. He has us on speed dial. And he won't hesitate to call," she said.

"He likes you better, too. You should invite him to your Friends-giving. It'd be cool to have the mayor there."

"Good idea." She laughed. "I'm on my way in. Have you found anything else for Tina on those transactions?"

"I was able to track one of the numbers that appeared several times. It belongs to a distributor, Little Arnie, in a suburb of Washington, D. C. Snakes and Scales made the payments, but I have no idea what was purchased."

"Tina mentioned a guy in D. C. Maybe, you and I should take a road trip?"

"I call shotgun," he said. "I've got some work I can do during the drive."

"Tomorrow then." Delanie disconnected and rolled down the windows in the Mustang. Maybe their trip to the nation's capital would provide some of the missing puzzle pieces or at least a reptile adventure.

12

THE NEXT AFTERNOON, DELANIE AND DUNCAN PULLED OFF INTERSTATE 495 in Maryland onto a side street in a business park in the suburbs of the nation's capital. Delanie glanced at her GPS. "I'm looking for EEK Distributors," she said.

"It looks like an industrial park." Duncan looked up from his laptop. "I thought the animal distributors would be on a farm or something."

"The address has it on 46th Avenue and Lafayette Place. Wait, that's 46th, and it's a dead-end." She made a quick right turn that caused Duncan to slide around in his seat. He glared at her. "Sorry. What did you tell this guy when you talked to him?"

"I'm a collector looking for some exotics, and some friends recommended him to me. I have a couple of names from the dark web if he's looking for references. That should give me enough street cred to gain entry. Plus, I went over to Snakes and Scales yesterday and talked to Glen about reptiles. I know enough to be dangerous. So, I'm hoping I look like a wannabe collector."

"And who am I?"

"My friend," he said with a shoulder shrug.

"That sounds like a wimpy story. I need something better. And I'm not staying in the car."

"Suit yourself. You could be my girlfriend who's into lizards."

"Sure. I can pull that off. It's better than Bat Girl." Delanie looked for the building number.

Duncan wrinkled his nose. "You made a good female sidekick to the dynamic duo at RVACon. And may I remind you that we won first place in the costume contest. We looked good."

Delanie rolled her eyes as she spotted the address and pulled into a parking lot next to a long brick building. She pocketed her phone and keys and picked up Duncan's magic camera hat. She put it on and pulled her ponytail through the opening at the back.

Not finding any doors on that side of the building, they trekked around to the front. A small, faded sign announced that they had arrived at EEK Distributors. Duncan pulled on the glass door, but it was locked. He whipped out his phone and sent a text.

A few minutes later, they heard shuffling, and a man who filled almost the entire door frame, opened the door. "Duncan?"

Delanie reached up and pushed the button on the bill of her ballcap to capture the interview.

"Yes. Hi. This is my girlfriend Delanie. She came along for the ride. My peeps, Snake Eyes and Black Mamba, said I should reach out to you. They said you had the best collection of exotics in the mid-Atlantic region."

The man looked the newcomers over and finally held the door for them. "Come in. I'm Arnold Adimari, but my friends call me Little Arnie."

Delanie elbowed Duncan before he could comment on the irony of the man's nickname.

"Follow me," the olive-skinned man with dark, curly hair said. He locked the front door and led them down a dark hallway past an empty reception area. The hallway opened up into a long white room with glass cases filled with every imaginable kind of snake. Delanie was fascinated by the colorful markings on some. But she was not curious enough to get too close to the containers. She spotted rows and rows of frogs, spiders, and lizards in terrariums.

"So, what can I do for you?" Little Arnie asked.

"You came highly recommended. My friend, Snake Eyes, said you can get almost anything, and you were the guy I needed to talk to. We drove all the way up from Virginia," Duncan said.

"Like Noah, I've just about got two of everything. Whatcha looking for?"

"I collect snakes. I have a couple of corn snakes, a rosy boa, a couple of California kingsnakes, and a ball python. Frosty, my python, is an albino," Duncan said.

"You forgot the alligator," Delanie added with a smirk.

Duncan gave her a dirty look.

"It's okay," Little Arnie said. "We all have things in our collections that we probably shouldn't. What is said here, stays here. Don't worry. And some alligators are legal in Florida if you have a permit. I have been known to be able to get my hands on all kinds of species. My clients have lots of unique requests."

"I have a small alligator in my basement," Duncan said. "But right now, I'm looking for something that none of my friends have to add to my menagerie."

"It's for his fortieth birthday," Delanie added. Duncan smirked at her.

"Happy birthday. We have lots of unique animals here. You want a snake? I have a salmon corn snake with pink eyes, an awesome green tree python, some blue iguanas, some veiled chameleons, and a really cool dragon."

"Oh, dragons," Delanie cooed, grabbing Duncan's arm. "Let's get a dragon."

"I've only got one. I acquired it for this guy who changed his mind when he saw the size of it. You'll need a space big enough for him. And this is one that needs a lot of care and feeding. And, you probably won't want to post his picture on Facebook if you get my drift," he said with a wink.

"Oh, he's awesome," Duncan said when they stopped in front of a huge glass case with a five-foot Komodo dragon.

"What a beautiful creature." Delanie put her hand up to the glass enclosure. The dragon with the smooth head stared at them without turning. "You could name him Godzilla." The Komodo dragon stuck out his forked tongue on cue.

Little Arnie glared at her. "This is a huge investment. Of both time and money. You need to be sure you can take care of him all the time. Do not make this decision lightly. They can grow up to eight feet and weigh upwards of two hundred pounds. Plus, they need to be able to move around in their enclosures. He needs space. This is just a holding tank until I figure out what to do with him."

"Uh, I guess you're right," Duncan said, dejectedly. "Hey, big fella. You look like you're high maintenance. How long do I have to think about it? Could I call you later in the week? And if I bought him, would you deliver it, or do I need to come and get him?"

"We could work something out. But you're going to need the right enclosure for him. Do you have the space at home?"

Duncan nodded. "My guys live in the basement at my house."

"Before you leave, let's look at the salmon corn snake and the green tree python. They may be more up your alley." Little Arnie steered them toward another row of glass cases. "This is the corn snake."

"It's pink!" Delanie squealed. "And look at those pink eyes."

"Maybe you should get it for her for her birthday." Little Arnie poked Duncan in his rib cage. "You'll be a hero. And if you don't like pink, this one is a little more manly."

Duncan rubbed his side.

"That's beautiful, too." Delanie looked at the fluorescent green and yellow reptile. It had wrapped itself around a tree branch in the enclosure. Its only movement was the occasional flick of its tongue. The snake's vibrant colors matched the colors on Tara Byte's showgirl headdress.

"As much as I like the Komodo and would be honored to have it, I probably should stick with snakes. I'm going to think about it and text you tomorrow if that's okay."

"Sure. Sure. Take your time." Arnie checked his phone. "I'll walk you out. Call me when you make your decision. And whatever it is, if I don't have it in stock, I can get it."

Duncan and Delanie trailed Little Arnie down the hallway. He locked the front door behind them.

Delanie clicked off the camera in her ballcap and put it in the backseat. She fluffed her bangs with her fingers. After looking at her reflection in the rearview mirror, she retrieved the cap and put it back on. Delanie started the car and revved the engine.

Duncan said, "Well, Little Arnie didn't question my dark web contacts, and he didn't hide anything."

"It's nice to get special treatment," she said with a smile.

"I'll check your video feed in a minute, but I'm pretty sure there were a lot of contraband critters there. He showed us all kinds of species, most of which aren't legal in the Commonwealth based on the Virginia Game and Inland Fisheries website." Duncan opened his laptop and tapped on the keys.

"I tried to walk up and down all the aisles. Hopefully, it'll give you what you need."

"I'm with Indiana Jones on this one. Snake world creeped me out. I'm taking a shower as soon as I get home." Duncan squirmed in his seat and opened his laptop.

"They were colorful and fun to watch, as long as they were in the cages." Delanie looked for the entrance to I-495. "I'm not sure how I'd feel if I came face to face with one of them outside of an enclosure."

"It makes me love Margaret even more." Duncan pulled up the undercover footage of all the inhabitants at Little Arnie's. "You did a good job. You even got the names of each species on the labels. That'll help. I'll do some more research on his inventory. Now we need to find out what Glen Montgomery was buying from Little Arnie."

13

DELANIE DROPPED HER MESSENGER BAG ON HER DESK AND FISHED OUT her laptop. Stepping around the chord dangling from the ceiling near her desk, she hoped Duncan was able to capture the source of the noise on camera. It was time to put this mystery to rest.

Halfway through updating her notes on the Montgomery case, Duncan and Margaret popped in. "You're here early."

"I needed to catch up on some paperwork. Uncover anything interesting?" She pointed to the dangling chord.

"No. Nothing. I'll leave them up for a couple more days. I wonder if it's the air ducts or the building settling. That's what the mainte-nance guy suggested. Sometimes, I think I hear music at my house, but it's air blowing through the ducts."

"It wasn't the ducts. It's too random. Plus, it's nice outside. The air and heat aren't on."

"Well, if you keep hearing it, we could get some paranormal specialists in here to check it out. I know some guys."

"The Ghostbusters?"

"Funny. But, no. These guys are pretty serious about their work. They've even been on TV."

"Let's try the cameras first. If I were a betting girl, I'd go with an earthly explanation first." She tried not to do an eyeroll. Sometimes, it was hard to tell when Duncan was being serious.

Duncan shook his head and headed for his office with the brown log with legs bringing up the rear.

A few seconds later, a low, guttural growl came from the hallway. Margaret ran by Delanie's doorway barking and snarling. And Duncan chased behind her. Delanie had never heard the English bulldog that upset before. She followed the chaos down the hall. The barks echoed through the narrow corridor, and Duncan started yelling.

Delanie stopped dead in her tracks near the doorway to the kitchenette. Delanie screamed.

Margaret charged a huge snake that lay under the table and across most of the small room's floor. The bright yellow and white snake had coiled itself around the center post of the small table. The rest of it stretched across the vinyl floor.

"We need to get out of here." Delanie scrambled back in the hallway.

"Margaret, heel! Down girl, now!" Duncan yelled. He dove into the room after his dog.

The agitated snake hissed and looked like it was trying to strike at Margaret. Duncan grabbed the chubby bulldog by the middle. He pulled the dog, who was in full attack mode, out in the hall. Duncan snatched her by the collar and dragged her to the foyer. Margaret struggled to free herself to return to the intruder in the kitchen.

"Stop it, Margaret. Calm down," Duncan commanded. "Good girl. You're great security. I don't want you to become his lunch."

Delanie pulled out her cell phone, unsure of whether to call the police or animal control. She searched for the number for the latter until Duncan interrupted. "Call Snakes and Scales. Tell Glen to get over here now."

She searched for the number and connected to the store. After three rings that seemed to take an eternity, a male voice answered, "Snakes and Scales."

"Glen. This is Delanie Fitzgerald from Falcon Investigations. We have a problem and could use your help now."

"I can hardly hear you with all the noise. Is that barking?" Glen asked.

She raised her voice. "Sorry. This is Delanie, Duncan Reynolds's partner. There is a huge, yellow snake in our kitchen, and we could use your help."

"Where are you?"

"Across the strip mall from you. I'm headed to the front door now, so you'll see me waving frantically," Delanie said.

"I'll be right over," Glen said as the phone went dead.

"He's on his way," Delanie said.

Duncan grasped Margaret's collar with both hands.

"Let's take her outside to calm her down. Glen will know what to do." He pulled Margaret toward the door that Delanie held open.

They stood on the curb. The only sound was Margaret's panting.

Glen and another guy ran across the parking lot. The second guy looked like he was holding a bottle of mouthwash. "Where is she?" Glen asked.

"In the kitchen." Delanie waved them inside the office.

The two men rushed inside, and Duncan leaned over to calm Margaret. "Good girl. You warned us. And saved us from that intruder. You're our new Director of Security." He patted her on the head. She made a huffing sound and plopped down on the sidewalk.

"Stay here," Delanie said. "I'm going to go see what they're doing in there. I can't believe that creepy snake has taken over our kitchen."

Delanie tiptoed toward the kitchen. She pulled out her phone and recorded the scene. Glen had the snake in what looked like a headlock while the other guy had the middle and the tail. He was trying not to let the snake wrap around him. Delanie got a whiff of mouthwash and spotted several small puddles on the floor. The snake writhed and twisted, trying to free itself.

"Got her, Justin?" Glen asked.

"Yup. She's agitated, but she'll calm down," Justin said.

"Ma'am, if you'll hold the door, we'll take her back to the store." Glen moved forward with the front of the snake.

Delanie stepped outside and opened the glass door as wide as it would go. She ducked behind it like a shield.

The two men carried the protracted snake across the parking long. Delanie guessed it was about eleven foot long. It wiggled, but they had it under control. Delanie looked around and was surprised the activity did not draw more of a crowd. It was not every day two guys parade a giant, yellow snake across a strip mall. Delanie wondered if she should report this to anyone.

She closed the door and followed the men and their captive to Snakes and Scales. The men placed the snake in an oversized terrarium and clamped down the locks on the top.

"Whew. She was in a mood," Justin said. "I'm glad you got that tic back without any harm."

"Tic?" Delanie asked.

"Reticulated python. Sometimes it's called a retic or a tic." Glen wiped his hands on his jeans. "We wondered where she had gotten to."

"How long had she been missing? And did you tell anyone?" Delanie glared at the two men.

"I didn't want to cause a scare. Lucy went missing the day my dad died. With all the commotion with finding him, I didn't realize she was gone until later. I thought she'd turn up in the store," Glen said.

Delanie frowned. "I'm Delanie Fitzgerald. I'm Duncan's partner. For the last week or so, there was a noise in the ceiling that I couldn't explain. Now I think I know what it was."

"She probably crawled up in the ceiling and traveled from store to store." Glen looked down at his scuffed boots. "I'm glad she's back. We'll check her over to make sure she's okay. There's no telling what or if she's been eating on her adventure. She's probably hungry if she couldn't find anything."

"I almost had a heart attack. My pulse is still racing. She wasn't what I expected to find at work this morning. And what was with the mouthwash?"

"Oh, I left that at your place. It helps with the big snakes," Justin said.

Delanie looked puzzled.

"We use it when we're acclimating big snakes to humans. If they act aggressive when you enter their lair, a splash or two in the mouth lets them know that you're not food. This breed is always interested in eating." Justin leaned on the front counter.

"Good to know. She's beautiful. But I like her better over there. I've never heard Duncan's dog go that crazy before." Delanie put her hands on her hips.

"It'll take Lucy a little while to recover, too. Today was more excitement than she's had in her life. She'll be fine now that she's safe and sound." Glen looked down at his shoes.

The extended silence felt awkward. The two men stared at the snake that lay coiled in the terrarium. Delanie decided to leave. She waved and backed out of the store and trotted across the parking lot. Duncan and Margaret sat in the kitchen. The spills had been cleaned up and the chairs righted.

"Wow. That was something," Delanie looked under the table just to be sure before she sank in one of the chairs at the small table. "Margaret's my hero."

"I guess I can take the cameras down," he said with a smirk.

"I told you I heard something weird. Next time, you'll believe me." Delanie winked at her partner.

"I'm exhausted. Margaret and I may need to go home after lunch. I'm sure she's worn out and ready for a nap. I hope we're done with snakes for a long time."

Delanie laughed. "I know. I'm still jumpy. But on a serious note, Glen knew that snake wasn't accounted for. He said it went missing the day his dad died. I'm not sure that I buy his story that they didn't realize she was gone in all the commotion."

"You'd think he'd warn people." Duncan scavenged through the refrigerator for something to eat.

"He said that he didn't want to cause a scare. But finding that thing in here almost gave me heart failure. And I've never seen Margaret move that fast."

"She saves her energy for when she really needs it." Duncan pulled out several take-out containers.

"How long has that been in the fridge?" she asked.

"Dunno." He tossed them into the trash. "Should we report the snake to somebody?"

"Probably. I'm going to call Steve later to get some big brother, cop advice. My spidey sense is on high alert. I looked up reticulated pythons on my phone. They're banned in Virginia. And so is the green tree python that Little Arnie was pushing," she said with a smirk. "And Tina said they found two dead tarantulas after her dad's death. When her dad fell and broke the glass cases, what else escaped?" Delanie shivered at the thought.

"I'd rather not think about it. But this pretty much confirms what the mysterious payments were for." Duncan pulled the bag out of the trashcan and headed for the back door and the dumpster.

Delanie picked up her phone and texted her brother. *Free for lunch this week?*

She heard the back-door slam twice.

"I forgot to tell you," Duncan yelled. "I can trace two of the four mysterious payments on Tina's log to Little Arnie's establishment. The third entry was a payment some mysterious account made to the store. I'm still working on that one, but it looks like they sold some contraband." Duncan returned to the kitchenette and stood behind Margaret.

Delanie's phone dinged with a response from Steve. *How about one today? Jersey Mike's at Brandermill?*

See you there, she texted.

"I'm going to meet my brother. Maybe he'll have some insight or at least a contact I can talk to about our great snake adventure. I hope you and Margaret recover quickly. I'm a little creeped out about all of it." She shuddered at thoughts of snakes and tarantula running loose.

∾

A FEW MINUTES before her lunch meeting, Delanie parked in front of the sub shop next to Steve's police cruiser. An arctic blast of air conditioning greeted her when she opened the door. It was too late in the fall to have the AC running at full tilt. She spotted her tall brother in his Chesterfield County PD uniform at the counter. She slid in next to him. "How's life?"

"The kids are doing well in school, and Liz is working part-time in a doctor's office. Work's work. It's always a little nutty when there's a full moon," he said.

"I hope she likes her new job. Is that table okay." Delanie indicated the one by the glass window. "I'll order and be back in a minute." Her brother nodded and sat in the red, metal chair, facing the front door.

Delanie returned a few minutes later and pulled the chair out across from her brother.

"Something interesting happened this week, and I need some advice."

"Why does when you say something interesting, it means so much more?" he asked.

"I dunno. I'm just lucky, I guess. Anyway, I kept hearing a strange noise in the office, and we couldn't figure out what it was. It sounded like sliding or scraping in the ceiling. I heard it multiple times over several days."

Her brother looked up at her and stared.

"What?"

"I'm just trying to see where this is going," he said.

A youngish guy interrupted when he brought over their lunches.

After opening sandwich wrappers and chip bags, her brother asked, "So what was it?"

"Margaret found a huge yellow python in my office kitchen."

"Who's Margaret?" he asked, taking a bite of his Italian sub.

"I told you that there was a giant reticulated python in my office, and you want to know about Margaret?" She stared at her brother. "She's Duncan's English bulldog, and my favorite guard dog."

"Was the snake alive?"

"The snake escaped from Snakes and Scales when Mr. Montgomery died. She must have crawled through the ceiling to my place. At least now we know what the noise was."

Steve nodded.

"What's the status of Mr. Montgomery's death investigation?"

"I can check, but I think the ME ruled it as a heart attack." He took a giant bite of his sandwich.

"The sister, Tina, does the books for the store. She asked Duncan and me to look into some odd payments she uncovered. Duncan was able to trace a couple of them to a reptile distributor in Maryland."

"Okay," Steve had a puzzled look on his face.

"The accounting entries were suspicious because they had no detail information like the other purchases. Duncan and I took a road trip up there yesterday. The guy has lots of snakes, lizards, and spiders. I looked up some of the more exotic ones. They, like the yellow snake in my kitchen, are banned in Virginia."

That got Steve's attention. "I know someone at Game and Inland Fisheries. Can you and your partner meet with him if I set something up?"

"Sure. Let me know when. I have a funny feeling about this. The two guys at the pet store didn't seem the slightest bit concerned that a giant, banned snake was missing. Plus, they didn't tell anyone."

He raised his eyebrows. "Probably didn't want to draw any more attention to it. They figured it would turn up."

"Oh, it turned up, and they paraded it across the parking lot this morning. They weren't trying to hide it. He called her Lucy. And what if that wasn't the only thing that got loose? I'm already creeped out by the python. Maybe it's time to find new office space. Prior to this, I only had a couple of problems with cars in the back. A giant snake is a whole new ballgame."

He laughed. "I'll call my contact and let you know when we can set something up. I'm sure he'll want to hear about Lucy."

"Thanks. You always know the right thing to do." She smiled and lightly punched him in the arm.

"We're having Thanksgiving at our house this year. Liz's dad and stepmom are coming. I'd like you and Robbie to be there."

"That'd be nice," she said. She hadn't seen the younger of her two older brothers in a while. Robbie, a bouncer in a trendy club in Shockoe Bottom in downtown Richmond, worked nights and slept most days. It would be nice to have her family together again. Ever since her dad died, the three siblings tended to be wrapped up in their lives and did not hang out much. Delanie shook off the nostalgic feeling and picked up their trash. The holidays would be a nice time to reconnect.

"I've got to get back. I'll call you later."

She trailed him out to the parking lot. Not a bad week for Falcon Investigations. They had uncovered a jewelry thief and some contraband reptiles. She wondered what additional surprises Halloween and the upcoming mayoral election would bring.

14

Tired of sitting at her desk, Delanie pulled out Duncan's magic cap from the closet and adjusted it to fit. She wanted to see Glen's backroom for herself, and she thought the clutch purse camera would look a little overdressed for a pet shop visit in the middle of the afternoon.

Delanie locked the office and trotted across the parking lot. A few cars sat in front of Glen's store. She had hoped to catch Glen during a quiet moment to chat him up about his reptile collection.

A shrill alarm startled her when she opened the glass door. Glen stopped talking to the guy at the counter as she entered. He nodded and bagged the man's purchase. The door alarm sounded again when the man left. Delanie scanned the store that appeared empty of humans. The only movement came from the cages and terrariums.

"Hi, Glen. I wanted to stop by and check on Lucy." Delanie browsed through the pet supply racks near the counter.

"She's fine. She's resting in the back, so I can keep an eye on her. I have no idea what or if she ate. So far, she's been doing okay. I don't think her adventure will have any adverse effects."

Delanie nodded. She hoped her face did not reveal her sarcastic thoughts. This guy was so wrapped up in his snakes that he did not even think about how anyone else felt. "Can I see her? I didn't get a good look at her yesterday. I was kinda in shock. I didn't expect to find her in my kitchen."

"Uh, sure. This way." He lumbered down the aisle past terrariums filled with spiders and lizards. Glen pushed the swinging wooden door open and flipped on the overhead lights that buzzed as they warmed up.

Delanie reached up and turned on her hat camera to capture the contents. Boxes, crates, and cages lined the walls. Her eyes darted from them to two long rows of terrariums, the focal point of the workroom.

Glen stopped midway down the first row. "Here, she is. Resting comfortably."

"She's beautiful," Delanie said.

The yellow and white snake lay coiled around a piece of drift-wood. Lucy's tongue flicked every once in a while, the only movement from the giant snake.

Distracted by a scratching sound, Delanie looked around the room. The noise got louder.

She turned around and gasped.

What looked like hundreds of rats wriggled and moved in an oversized cage behind her. The inhabitants were in constant motion in the small cage. Delanie backed slowly down the aisle. She tried to will her heart rate to return to normal. Trying to compose herself, "I didn't expect to see that."

"You woke up Lucy's dinner." Glen looked around the room. "You don't have pets, do you?"

"No. We had a cat when I was a kid. Duncan's dog, Margaret, keeps us company in the office."

Getting the sense that Glen wanted to end the conversation, she turned to the other row of containers and peered through the glass. "What's in here?" Delanie pointed to a long glass case that was the size of a large, upright piano.

"I'm holding two alligators for someone who's moving." Glen looked down at his feet.

"Wow. I almost didn't see him. He looks camouflaged with all the plants and rocks in there. How big does he get? And where's the other one?" She stepped closer to the container.

"Look there. At the back of the cage. You can see one of his eyes." Glen lightly touched the terrarium with his index finger. Glen shifted his weight to his other foot and looked around the room again. "They're caimans. They're smaller than the alligators you see on TV and usually grow to be between fifteen and thirty pounds. But they can get as large as eighty pounds. They both fit now in this tight space, but they'll quickly outgrow that cage."

Delanie leaned toward the terrarium. She moved her head slowly to capture the room and all its inhabitants. "This is fascinating." She stepped back and toured the room before Glen could stop her.

She walked down both rows, sidestepping Glen who approached her. "I know you're busy, so I won't take up any more of your time. Thanks for showing me around and letting me see Lucy. I hope she's fully recovered." I know it took me a little while to get over the fright, Delanie thought.

Glen looked relieved when she headed out of the store. She thought she heard a sigh from him when she stopped by a rack of reptile supplies. "If I were to get a pet for my nephews, what would you recommend?"

Glen definitely sighed again.

"How old are they?" He slid his hands in the pockets of his jeans.

"Five and seven."

"I'd start with fish or a turtle at that age. What do they like?"

"Superheroes and Legos. I thought a pet might make a nice gift." She browsed through racks full of aquarium equipment and knickknacks.

"It's a lot of responsibility. I'd think about it." Glen looked down at his sneakers.

"You're probably right. And I don't know if my sister-in-law would appreciate the new addition to the family. Let me talk to her first, and I'll come back."

Delanie turned to leave. A "ghost fish" sign on a bubbling

aquarium caused her to pause. She stepped closer for a better view. Staring at the water for a while, the only thing she spotted in the tank were different sized castles and treasure chests with lids that opened and closed. Occasionally, bubbles drifted to the top of the tank.

Before she could ask about the inhabitants of the tank, Glen snickered. "Did you spot them? They're elusive, but many have claimed to have seen them."

Her brow furrowed after a second look. She leaned forward and stared.

Glen laughed. "It's a good conversation piece. You'd be surprised at the people who are convinced they spotted one. It was just a boring display of tank ornaments until I added the sign."

Delanie snapped a picture and smiled. "Maybe ghost fish would be perfect for my nephews or my house. Low maintenance. My kind of pet. Thanks again," she said as she exited.

She texted Duncan about the new video footage of Lucy and Glen's backroom. Delanie added a picture of the ghost fish for fun.

Delanie felt out of sorts. She grew up with two older brothers who always brought all kinds of creepy crawlers home, but the snake encounter and the cage full of rats gave her a hair-raising feeling that was hard to shake. Maybe some shopping therapy would counteract all the slithering, hissing, and scratching.

15

RELIVED THAT THE EERIE NOISE AND THE GIANT SNAKE HAD BEEN removed from her office, Delanie sat at her desk finishing her lunch and watching funny, dog videos on the internet.

Duncan stuck his head in her doorway, and she jumped. Margaret poked her head in too between his legs.

"Hey, sorry. Didn't mean to scare you. I think I cracked the identity of the other mystery account on Tina's list."

She stared at him and raised her eyebrows. After a pause, she said, "Well?"

"It belongs to a distributor in Belize."

"Huh?"

"A small country in Central America," he replied.

She smirked at him.

"The guy in Belize specializes in exotics that no one else owns. If you have the money, you can buy almost anything. Snakes and Scales did a wire transfer of $11,658 for whatever was purchased," he said with a smug look. "It took some doing, but I finally found it."

"I wonder if Tina can help us link receipts and purchases to inventory," Delanie mused. "My brother, Steve, has a contact at Game and Inland Fisheries. We're going to meet with his guy at three today. Wanna go?"

"Tempting, but I don't like hanging around that much law enforcement. You can represent us."

"Can you send me any video you have on the snake stuff. I have the link for what we took at Little Arnie's," she said.

"Check the server. I added the snake parade across the parking lot and your tour of Glen's backroom. I also put everything on this thumb drive in case you want to share."

"You're the best. That should be enough to prove what's going on. Glen had alligators, too."

A steady banging behind the building interrupted their conversation. At first, Delanie thought it was the dumpster being emptied. Then they heard more clanging against the side of the metal container.

They paused a moment, and the noise continued.

Delanie rushed behind Duncan to the back door. Margaret woofed several times and stood ready to make an exit as soon as the door opened. Duncan reached for the doorknob and the dog's collar to keep Margaret from charging.

Two shots rang out.

Duncan hit the floor, barely missing Margaret.

Delanie froze. After a few seconds with no other sounds, she opened the door a crack and peeked outside.

A man in dingy jeans and a smudged T-shirt stood with his gun drawn. A fat, black snake, with a chunk missing in the middle, twitched on the asphalt.

Delanie eased out onto the back steps for a closer look.

"That is the fattest snake I've ever seen," the man drawled, bending over to catch his breath. He had longish brown hair and a reddish beard that had not been trimmed in a while.

"Where did you find him," Delanie leaned over for a better look. Black and green designs covered the entire snake that continued to convulse. She guessed the snake was about five feet long.

"I, uh, was in the dumpster. I pulled out a cardboard box, and that thing moved and scared the tar out of me. He struck the side of the dumpster, and I hightailed it out of there faster than you can say chicken lips. When I turned around, he slithered on out and chased me. He's an aggressive critter."

"I'm glad you're okay. Can I get you anything?" she asked the man. Delanie turned to find Duncan recording the dead snake with his phone.

"A drink would be good." The man wiped his forehead with a dirty, red bandana and then jammed it in his back pocket.

Delanie retreated inside to grab a Coke. She spotted a large, plastic storage bin with a lid next to the refrigerator. She dumped out the contents on the table and took it with her outside.

"Here." She handed the man his drink.

He put the gun in the back of his jeans and took the can. "I was hoping for something stronger, but I guess this'll be okay." He popped the top to a fizzy reception, took a few gulps, and wiped his mouth with the back of his hand.

"Mind if I keep the snake? Our friend is a collector, and he may be able to tell us more about it," she said.

"I don't want it. Can't sell it. I found a bear once in a dumpster. This is my first fat snake. Thanks for the drink. I'll be heading out. I've had enough for today." He nodded and walked to the end of the alley and climbed in a beat up pickup truck, the bed filled with an assortment of junk and boxes. He started it, and the motor belched. The truck made a grinding sound before the motor started. He backed out in a cloud of gray smoke.

"I've had my fill of snakes for a while. How much do you wanna bet that this is one of Glen's, too?" Delanie looked at Duncan, who stopped filming.

"Probably. I took a picture of its head and asked Google what it was. Pictures of Gaboon vipers popped up."

"Sounds dangerous." Delanie took a step backward.

"According to this site, it's highly venomous with two-inch fangs. Oooh, look at these pictures. They have intricate black and green designs – diamonds and stripes. And it's got horn-things on its nose.

Don't touch it. It's still twitching. I'm going to get some gloves and a stick."

Delanie scanned her phone for Gaboon viper information. Duncan interrupted her search when he returned with his arms full of trash bags, gloves, a broom, and Clorox. The snake jerked and then seemed to collapse on the asphalt. Duncan managed to get the snake in a trash bag with the help of the broomstick. He dropped the bag of snake in the plastic bin and clamped the lid on tightly. Then he scoured the spot on the asphalt. When he finished, he tossed the broom and gloves in the dumpster.

"I'll replace the broom. I don't think we should take any chances if it's truly that venomous. Hopefully, the Clorox will dilute anything on the pavement."

Duncan ran inside and returned a few minutes later with a roll of duct tape. He sealed the lid on the plastic bin. "Just in case it's a zombie snake."

"I don't think that snake is going anywhere. Leave it here. And I'll put it in my trunk before I head out to see the conservation officer. I'm sure he'll be interested. Plus, he'll know what to do with it."

"Gimme your keys. I'll put it in your trunk. I don't want to leave it out here in case there's more dumpster diving. Wouldn't that be a shock if someone stole it and opened it to find a big dead snake," he said, snickering.

Delanie tossed him her keys and went inside to gather her stuff for her afternoon meeting. Enough with the snakes. She was ready to go back to workman's comp and cheating husband cases.

THE PRIVATE EYE found a parking spot in the office park in Henrico County. Her brother, Steve, Smoky Bear hat in hand, stood at the reception desk waiting for her.

"'Bout time," he said.

"I still have three minutes," she said, rolling her eyes.

"We're here to see Al Cortez," Steve said to the receptionist who tapped on the keyboard.

"One moment please," the male receptionist said. He pressed some buttons on his phone. "He'll be here in a moment." The young man busied himself with a call.

A guy in khaki stepped out of a side office. "Hey, bud," the conservation officer said, extending his hand to Steve. "It's good to see you."

"You, too. Thanks for meeting with us on short notice. This is my sister, Delanie. She's a private investigator on the southside. This is Al Cortez. We worked together a few years back on a joint task force."

"Nice to meet you." The officer shook her hand. "Follow me. We can talk in the conference room right around the corner.

Delanie followed the two men who launched into a conversation about the best fishing spots in the area. She passed on the fish talk and trailed them down a gray carpeted hallway.

The conservation officer stopped at an oak door in a long narrow hallway. He held the door to the conference room for his guests. When the door shut, he became all business. "Have a seat. Ms. Fitzgerald. What did you come across that would be of interest to Game and Inland Fisheries?"

Delanie settled in a faux leather chair that squeaked when she moved. She planted her feet firmly on the floor to keep the wheels from moving and to minimize the noise when she fidgeted.

"Last week, the owner of a reptile store near our office died of an apparent heart attack, and his daughter asked my partner and me to look into some bank statements for the business that she couldn't reconcile. We did some research and found that the owner's son has a backroom with some contraband animals." She pulled a fairly substantial folder of research from her bag and pushed it across the table to Officer Cortez.

"He told you this?" He made notes on a yellow legal pad.

"No. When the father had the heart attack, he fell and broke several terrariums in the store. The daughter said she found two dead tarantulas on the day her father died."

"And?" The conservation officer paused.

"Then later, I heard a noise in our office which is a few doors down in the strip mall. I heard it for several days, and this week, we found a bright yellow and white reticulated python in our kitchen area. That sucker was over ten feet long. Maybe close to eleven or twelve," she said.

"What did you do?" He picked up her folder and started skimming through the pages.

"Besides scream?" She frowned at him. "I called the guy at Snakes and Scales, and he and his friend picked it up. They carried it across the parking lot back to the store. He said that it had been missing since the day his dad died."

"You can prove that the snakes and reptiles are illegal?" He looked at Steve.

"I have video clips. One is of a distributor in Northern Virginia. My partner traced some of the mystery payments to that business." Delanie squirmed in her chair. Remembering the squeakiness of the faux leather, she stopped. Then she fished through her purse and pulled out her phone to show him the videos.

After the last video played, he scratched his black buzz cut and said, "I need copies of these."

She passed him a thumb drive with Falcon Investigations emblazoned in red on the side. "But wait, there's more. This morning, my partner and I heard a ruckus in the alley behind our building."

"Can you describe the ruckus?" Officer Cortez asked.

"There was a lot of noise around the dumpster, and then we heard two gunshots. We found a dumpster diver in the back. The snake lunged at him. He dodged it and then put several bullet holes in it and the tarmac."

"He shot it?" the agent asked, raising his voice slightly.

"Yes. The gunshots stunned us. We're not used to gunfire at the office. Then we discovered the guy and the snake in the alley."

"Did you get the guy's name?" he asked.

She hesitated. Delanie could have kicked herself for not getting the dumpster diver's name. She knew Steve would give her a hard time about it later. "No. The gunshots and the snake rattled us, but I think my partner captured his truck's license plate when he left. It's on here."

"What happened to the snake?" Officer Cortez asked.

"It's in a container in the trunk of my car. Would you like it?"

His face lit up, and he jumped out of his seat. "Where are you parked?"

"This way." She led the two law enforcement officers to her black Mustang. Delanie clicked the key fob, and Officer Cortez pulled the container out of the trunk.

"I'd like for my colleagues to examine it. Do you have some time to wait?" He carried the plastic bin back in the building. This time, the Fitzgeralds followed him down a warren of hallways to a white tiled room that looked like a science lab.

Officer Cortez put the container on the metal table and stepped out.

"It's not alive, is it?" Steve asked.

"No. It has several chunks missing where the dumpster diver shot it. It twitched for a while, but it was dead when Duncan loaded it. Snakes make Duncan nervous, so he taped the container shut."

"Just thought I'd check. I didn't see any holes poked in the lid. What kind of snake was it?"

"Google id'ed it as a Gaboon viper. We'll see what Mr. Cortez and his friends say. If it's that, it's poisonous."

"Did you mention this to the Snakes and Scales guy?" he asked.

"No. Conveniently, it happened right before this meeting."

Officer Cortez and three colleagues filed in the room. They donned gloves that look like they planned to weld something. One stripped off the tape and opened the container. They carefully removed the snake from the trash bag and stretched it across the worktable. Curving the snake, they wound the tail back toward his head.

"This is a Gaboon viper," the older technician said. "It's known for having long fangs and more venom than other snakes. It's originally from Africa." He stretched the snake to its full length and held up the head for the group to see the fangs.

"Who knows you have this?" Officer Cortez asked.

"The people here, my partner, and the dumpster diver," she replied. "I'm sure the reptile store owner is aware that it's missing."

"Let's keep it that way. We're going to examine the snake and your video evidence. Are you available if we have any more questions?" Officer Cortez asked.

"Of course." She handed him a business card. "Thank you for your help and taking this off my hands. I wasn't sure what to do with it." The men poked, prodded, and took all kinds of measurements.

Officer Cortez and Steve shook hands. Delanie and her brother retraced their steps to the parking lot.

"Thanks for coming down here today." She and her brother stopped beside her Mustang.

"I'm glad you didn't have a live snake in that container." He grinned.

"What's next with the Montgomery investigation? Will anything change because of the poisonous snakes?"

"Explain what you're thinking." Steve checked his watch.

"My theory is that Ken Montgomery was attacked by one of the snakes, and it caused his nervous system to shut down. He fell into the glass cases, breaking them and freeing the inhabitants. The tarantulas didn't survive, but both snakes made a break for their freedom. Did they do a full autopsy on him? Can't they tell that he had venom in his system versus a run of the mill heart attack?"

"I'm not sure if the full autopsy has been completed. I'll check with the detective. I think they were leaning toward his existing heart condition. The daughter and the son both told the police and EMTs that he had multiple health problems," Steve said.

"I don't know whether or not he knew about the dangerous snakes. If he didn't, maybe he had let his guard down and wasn't expecting what he found in the terrarium. Ken Montgomery knew enough about snakes to handle them carefully. His daughter said that he was always trying to educate future reptile owners. So, my guess is that it wasn't a deliberate setup to kill him. I think it was an accident, but there is the issue of the illegal import of these species."

"I'm sure the state conservation officers will want to investigate further especially with the evidence you provided. And that outcome could lead to charges. I suggest that you and your partner steer clear of the pet shop for a little while."

"Let me know if you hear anything." Delanie climbed into the Mustang. "See ya."

He saluted with two fingers.

She backed out and told the radio to "Call Duncan."

After his quirky voice mail message, she said, "Dunc, I turned the Gaboon viper carcass over to the conservation officers. I've got a lot to fill you in on, and I'm not sure what to do about Tina. Call me when you can talk. I have a hunch."

16

DELANIE ENJOYED A QUIET MORNING IN THE OFFICE. ALL CASES EXCEPT Tina's were closed, and she had caught up on all her billing and reporting. Pushing the sense of panic about not having upcoming jobs confirmed and waiting in the wings out of her thoughts, she spent the morning planning her Friends-giving dinner. The list of guests grew daily. She figured she could squeeze seating for twenty in if she lined up long tables from the dining area in her bungalow through the archway and into the living room.

Delanie's phone chimed a customized ringtone. She clicked the button. "Hey girl. I was thinking about our Friends-giving. What's up?"

"Not much. Checking in to see if you picked your color palette yet for the party." her best friend, Paisley Ford said.

Delanie hesitated. "Fall colors, I guess."

"Good. I'll work on the centerpieces. Do you have tablecloths and napkins?"

"No. I plan on using six foot tables. The rectangular ones. I might have a black tablecloth packed away from last year's Halloween party. Oh wait, it may have spiders on it."

"That won't do. I'll see what I can pull together. Anything else I should know about?" Paisley asked.

"I finished my investigation at Freeda's. We caught the bad drag queen."

"Ooooh, Freeda's," Paisley cooed. "I haven't been there in years. We should do a girls' day brunch. Let's call Robin and her sister. Cassidy at the salon will want in. Can you get us good seats for the show?"

"I'm sure. I'd love to see the whole show from the other side of the stage. I only saw snippets from the back. I was working."

"This will be so much fun. Gotta run. My next appointment is here. Let me know the date for our girls' night out. Can't wait."

"Bye." Delanie clicked off. She jotted a note to call Deke about brunch reservations.

A tapping sound interrupted her planning. At least it was not that spooky sliding noise. Delanie made her way to the lobby. Tina Montgomery knocked on the glass.

"Hi, Tina." Delanie unlocked the door. "What brings you over?"

"I wanted to pop in and tell you what I found," she said, slightly breathless.

"Come in. Could I get you something to drink?"

"No. I'm good. I made a quick stop at the store to drop off some checks." She paused and took a deep breath. "I'm on bereavement leave from work to help Glen get things organized at the store, so I have more time to pour over the books and go through files. You know, to keep an eye on things."

"I'm sorry that you're having to go through this. Let's talk in the kitchen where we can sit down."

The woman followed Delanie down the dark hallway. "I heard about the snake you all found."

"Snakes plural. We were surprised by both of them. I'm glad your brother and friend could come and take one of them away. I'm not really into reptiles, and it scared the crap out of me. The second snake didn't fare as well as the first one." Delanie wrinkled her nose.

"I hear ya. I don't like going in the store by myself. We have to lock the lids on some of the cases because a few of them are good escape artists. I'm always creeped out when there's an empty case." Tina paused and drew a deep breath. She closed her eyes.

She leaned forward. "Tina, are you okay?"

"I'm fine. It's a lot to process. Anyway, I went back over the books from the past two years. I found nineteen instances of money coming in and going out from undefined sources. Here's the list and the account numbers. Maybe you all can work your magic on these. I appreciate all the help. My gut tells me that this was Glen's doing and not my dad's." Tina's voice trailed off as she looked down at her fingernails.

"I'll make sure that Duncan gets this."

"When do you think he will have an update?" Tina asked.

"I haven't seen him today, but I'll check in with him this afternoon and get you a more concrete answer."

"I have to be going." Tina stood and straightened her pink sweater with a basket of three kittens on the front.

Delanie led her back through the empty reception area and locked the door after she exited. She texted Duncan. *Are you coming in? We need to talk.*

A few minutes later, her phone dinged with, *Nothing good ever follows that phrase. Be there soon.* He added a smiley emoji for good measure.

Duncan and Margaret rolled in about an hour later. Margaret, more chipper than most days, ran from room to room, sniffing and snorting.

"She's in a perky mood."

"I gave her a bath this morning. She went limp on me, and I had to carry her upstairs and put her in the tub. She's a chunk of dead weight when she doesn't want to do something. But she does like the after-bath treats."

"I'm glad you both survived." Delanie followed Duncan to his office.

He flipped on two laptops and dropped in his chair. "So, what's going on around here?"

"Tina stopped in this morning. She found more instances of undocumented payments from the last couple of years. She has a hunch that it's Glen's doing."

Duncan reclined in his chair and propped his feet on the corner of the desk on a stack of folders, providing a view of his mismatched socks, one blue and one yellow and orange.

"You making a statement?" She pointed to his feet.

"No. I haven't done laundry in a while. Plus, who wants to be boxed in with matching socks?"

"Good answer." Delanie grinned.

"How did it go yesterday with Game and Inland Fisheries?"

"I gave them copies of all our notes and your videos. They were giddy to examine the snake."

Duncan raised his eyebrows.

"Steve said that there would probably be some kind of investigation. We should probably lie low for a while. And there is my dilemma. What do we do about Tina? We promised her an update."

"And when has a warning from law enforcement ever stopped you before?" he asked with a wink.

"True." Delanie looked down at the floor and her shoes. She had had this pair for about five years, and she was thinking about a much needed shoe shopping trip when she realized Duncan was waiting for her to continue. She cleared her throat and added, "I feel we owe her an update, but I don't want to jeopardize anything the conservation officers are planning. How long do you think it will take for them to act?"

"Well, since deadly snakes were on the loose, the authorities might expedite the process. How about if we give Tina an update on the payments. I'll see what I can find on the new ones. That would give her the information she wants without tipping off anything. Plus, I need a day or two to look over the new stuff she brought."

"That works. I have a weird feeling about this one. I don't think she's involved in the reptile smuggling side of the business, but I'm not sure what to think about Glen and his buddies. Was Ken's death an accident or was it something more malicious, made to look like an accident? We could be talking murder on top of all the illegal contraband. I really hope it was nothing nefarious."

Duncan let out a heavy sigh. "Let's go with our plan on the updates of the accounting register. And if something's going to happen with law enforcement, we'll wait and see. I'm sure we'll hear about it. I'm going to work on those new transactions."

"Tina's case is the only thing I have going on right now. So, maybe a little down time will be relaxing." She headed to her office.

"You? Relaxed? Do you even know how?" Duncan yelled behind her.

She puttered around her office and cleaned her desk. Bored with the administrative part of the job, she packed up to go shoe shopping. Her phone interrupted her getaway.

"Hi, Chaz. What can I do for you?"

"I wanted to talk to you about something weird that I need your help on. Can you come by sometime this week?"

"Do you have time this afternoon?" she asked, wondering what was weird to Chaz.

"Sure. I've got another debate on Sunday afternoon that I'm prepping for, but today would be good. How about three-thirty? I'm at the club."

"See you then." Just when it got boring, Chaz was there to save the day.

"Hey, Dunc. I'm going to grab lunch and go downtown to see what Chaz wants. He said he has something weird that he needs help with."

Duncan laughed. "You know that could be anything. Chaz is in a different time zone than the rest of us. Let me know what it is. He's usually very entertaining."

"He's definitely that." She tried not to giggle.

"Hey, I've made some progress on Tina's stuff. A couple of these numbers are for a reptile distributor in Las Vegas. Some are for Little

Arnie, a fish place in San Diego, and a good number of them are for the place in Belize. There are about four entries that I need to do some more work on. Hopefully, I'll have something by the time I see you next."

"Depending on what Chaz wants, I should be in tomorrow. I hope he's not signing me up to canvas neighborhoods or to do fundraisers for him."

"Nah, he's got enough dancers for that. He and his team are all over the news all the time. If the mayoral thing doesn't work out, he's still getting tons of free publicity for his club."

DELANIE PULLED into the side lot of the Treasure Chest and locked her car. Only a few open slots remained. Late lunch or early happy hour? She spotted Marco at the side door and waved. The service entrance would spare her a walk through the busy club.

"Hey, Marco. How are things? I have an appointment this after-noon with Chaz."

"Doin' well. It's good to see you. This place has been busy since the campaign started. I guess everyone wants to get close to the boss or see what his den of iniquity looks like. Come on back." He held the heavy, metal door for her. Music thumped around her. The pulsing bass gave her a slight headache.

She followed Marco through a warren of hallways to Chaz's office. Thankfully, the music faded as they walked.

"Hey, boss. Delanie's here," said Marco, who looked like he played football in a former life.

"Come on in. Can I get you anything to drink?"

"No thanks. How's the campaign going?" she asked.

"Good. I mean well. There's a debate on Sunday, and Petra and some of her folks will be helping me prep for. I'm one of the remaining candidates. I think this town is surprised that I've hung in this long. They're about to find out that I'm in this for real."

"You're always full of surprises, and from your lot out front, it looks like business is good." He was taking this campaign seriously. That still surprised her.

"Yep. Everyone wants to get a look at the taboo club of one of the mayoral candidates." Chaz winked and flashed a toothy grin.

"What can I help you with?" She sat in the guest chair across from Chaz's large, black lacquered desk.

"We've noticed something odd outside lately. Usually in the early morning hours. Something weird is going on around two or three. You know the Poe statue on the corner? Someone has been digging around its base. More than once. I'm having Steve extend our surveillance cameras to that side of the parking lot. Something's fishy. I want you to do some digging of your own and figure this out for me."

He reached for an envelope on his desk. "Here, this should cover about a week's worth of research. And I'll have my guy Steve send you any footage that he finds."

"Okay." She pulled out a contract from her bag and passed it to him.

He signed it with a flourish and handed it back.

"Duncan and I will get right on it. Do well on Sunday!"

Delanie hiked around the cinder block building that housed the Treasure Chest and covered a large portion of the corner of 15th and Main Streets, the area famous for being the previous site of the *Southern Literary Messenger*, where Edgar Allan Poe worked in the eighteen hundreds. Delanie often wondered what Poe would think of Chaz's establishment dominating the neighborhood now.

At the corner of the lot on a postage-stamp sized plot of grass, a large cement base supported a bronze statue of the famous author and poet. Poe, in a stoic, standing pose, watched over traffic on Main Street. Around the base, people had left mementos. Delanie spotted candles, books, small ravens, and a bobblehead of Poe.

She stepped around the base. Someone had been digging at the back of the statue. Loose dirt and sod had been shoved haphazardly in several holes. It did not look like there was any damage to the statue.

Delanie read the plaque and snapped several pictures with her phone. She made sure to capture pictures of the tributes. Leaning over, she picked up a small placard, signed, "The Raven." Another was a letter in a plastic bag with a poem handwritten on a piece of cardboard. The poem's creator was Lila Greene. Delanie carefully put the items back at the statue's base.

Checking her watch, she retrieved her car and headed to the Library of Virginia. Pulling into the underground parking deck, she took the elevator to the lobby. Delanie spent the rest of the afternoon wandering through the stacks looking at everything should could find about the *Southern Literary Messenger* and the Poe statue.

She made photocopies of pictures and articles of anything related to Poe. The *Southern Literary Messenger's* building had been destroyed in 1915, but parts of it were preserved and repurposed as the shrine in the garden at the Poe Museum. She made a mental note to stop by the Poe Museum soon to see what they could tell her about the statue.

Delanie's neck and back ached from pouring over the books and articles for the last few hours. Stretching to get the kinks out, she returned the materials to the kiosk. Delanie had learned a lot about Poe's home in Richmond, but she still was not sure why someone would want to dig around the base of the statue. It did not look like there was anything there to steal like copper wiring or building materials. The base was a stone and cement structure. But yet there were multiple holes. The metal statue was probably the only thing of value nearby. The mementos had only sentimental value to the fans who left them as tribute.

Before she exited the library's underground parking deck, she texted Chaz. *Can I talk to your guys who spotted the holes around the statue?*

A few seconds later, her phone dinged with his response, *Call Marco. He noticed it first.*

After a quick text to the head bouncer at the Treasure Chest, Delanie circled back to Main Street. She spotted Marco waiting for her by the back door.

Pulling up next to the cement steps, she pushed the button to lower the driver's side window. He leaned down and said, "Back so soon. You just can't stay away from us."

"I know. I'm hooked. Thanks for taking the time to talk to me. I know you're busy."

"Not a problem. Wanna head over to the statue?"

"Want a lift?"

"I won't fit in your little racecar. I'll walk."

"Gimme a second, and I'll join you." Delanie parked in an open spot and trotted over to where Marco waited. They walked around the building to the edge of the parking lot. Traffic hummed along on the surrounding streets.

"When did you first notice the digging?"

"About a week ago. It's happened twice that I know of. It's always after the club is closed."

"Any idea why?"

"No. There's nothing over there. The stuff they leave at the base isn't worth anything. And it disappears after a while. I'm not sure who takes it. The guys we saw aren't taggers either. There's no sign of graffiti." Marco watched traffic zoom by on Main Street.

Delanie circled the base of the statue. "It seems like all the digging is on the back corner. I need to find out why. Call me if you see the mystery guys again. Even if it's early in the morning."

"Yup." Marco did another lap around the base of the statue. "It's weird, even for around here."

A remote TV truck from a local affiliate had pulled into the lot. A guy in a navy blue jacket set up a tripod and camera nearby.

"Looks like you have company," she said.

"It's an everyday thing lately. I need to tell Chaz. He likes to make himself available for all interviews. Excuse me." He pulled out his phone and jogged back to the club.

Chaz was definitely getting his fifteen minutes of fame from this. Delanie paused and found a spot off-camera where she could hang out and watch what happened next.

Seconds later, Chaz, Marco, and Petra filed out of the club's front doors and walked toward the cameras like moths to a flame.

Chaz spoke to the cameraman as a svelte reporter climbed out of the truck, adjusted her short skirt, and headed for the club's owner.

Delanie moved closer to hear. Petra and Marco stood across from her near the main entrance. Petra made sure she had eye contact with Chaz.

The reporter patted Chaz on the arm, centered herself, and said, "This is Noreen Nurelli with Channel 12's Politics in the City. I'm here with local entrepreneur turned mayoral candidate, Chaz Smith. Mr. Smith, one of your fellow candidates, Ron Jenkins, gave a statement about you this afternoon, and he mentioned your incarcerations and your facial tattoo. Would you care to comment?"

Delanie saw Petra's face darken. She stared at Chaz, but he did not seem to notice the change in her countenance.

"Well, I didn't hear the comment in its entirety. But, like many of us, I sowed my wild oats in my teen years. And I did a lot of things I'm not proud of. My run-ins with the law occurred during my rebellious years as a juvenile, and I did my time and learned my lesson. I've been a successful Richmond business owner for almost twenty years."

"What about the arrests as an adult? Mr. Jenkins feels that you can't represent Richmond well if you have had so many issues with the law. He cited an entire list of times the police have been called to your club." She held up her phone for him to see her notes.

"Well, Noreen. Mr. Jenkins is mixing up things that need to be kept separate. My juvenile records were expunged when I turned eighteen and completed all my community service. I've had a few parking and traffic tickets over the years, but who hasn't? I was arrested last year for the mayor's murder, but my wonderful P. I. over there, Delanie Fitzgerald, helped me clear my name."

The camera and its bright light swung to Delanie and almost blinded her. She was sure she had a deer in the headlights look as she reluctantly waved.

"I run a night club – a gentlemen's club. We sell alcohol, and sometimes people drink too much and don't behave like they would at home. I'd like to thank Richmond's finest for always answering the call when we have an issue that needs law enforcement. I think the citizens would prefer that we let law enforcement handle the problems rather than looking the other way."

Noreen smiled at the camera and asked, "What about Mr. Jenkins's charges that your security is rough on the rowdy folks?"

"Again, I didn't hear what Mr. Jenkins said."

"Here," she said, holding her phone for him to see. Chaz paused to watch the short clip. He frowned and returned his composure as he looked at the camera.

"Our clientele is not made up of choirboys. Sometimes, my guys have to be firm with our clients who want to break the rules. We always act within the confines of the law. And we appreciate Richmond PD's assistance when it's needed." Chaz smiled at the camera and the young reporter who leaned in closer.

"What about your tattoo? Your opponent wants to know if it's a symbol of something," shed asked, batting her false eyelashes.

Petra stepped closer to Chaz. He touched the blue teardrop tattoo under his eye.

"This? I just liked the stylistic design. When my buddy from high school died about twenty years ago, I got it in his honor."

The lovely Noreen beamed at Chaz. "Thank you so much, Mr. Smith, for clarifying your opponent's charges and for talking with us about all of this. I'm glad we could get your side of the story and provide it to our viewers, so they can make good decisions based on good information. This is Noreen Nurelli, live at the Treasure Chest with mayoral candidate, Chaz Smith."

"And clear," the cameraman said.

"I appreciate it, Chaz. Call me if you have any other stories," Noreen said, shaking his hand and standing a little too close to the candidate.

"Thank you, Noreen. You know you'll be first on my list." He flashed his trademark Chaz smile and turned toward Marco and Petra.

When the news crew left, Chaz's team returned to the club. Delanie made her way back to her Mustang. Her phone dinged with five texts from people who had seen her on the news or on the internet.

17

DELANIE ROLLED OUT OF BED AND STRETCHED. THE SUN STREAMED IN from the side window. Eighteen minutes after ten. She did not mean to sleep that late, but she had stayed up until the wee hours searching for anything related to the Poe statue on the internet.

After a jolt of espresso, Delanie showered, dressed, and headed downtown to the Virginia Museum of History and Culture to explore their library. She hoped they would have things like letters and journals that would help her get a better picture of past events. The nice librarian directed her to their local collection, and Delanie found a long oak table where she could spread out.

Her stomach growled around two-thirty to remind her that it was past her normal lunch time. She gathered her notes and returned all the borrowed resources.

Delanie walked across the grounds to the Virginia Museum of Fine Arts next door and grabbed a salad. She found a seat facing the wall-sized glass windows that overlooked a water garden with a red Chihuly glass exhibit. The museum cafe buzzed with activity, but the view of the water and glass instilled a few moments of serenity.

Wishing she had time to explore the galleries, she glanced at her Fitbit and cleared her trash. Delanie decided to make one more stop at the Valentine Museum. She headed toward Cary Street and the museum that specialized in Richmond city history.

A docent with kind eyes and a tight silver bun steered her to the catalogue for the reference material. After her computer search, she found several articles and photos of the statue and its unveiling.

She added copies to her collection of notes about Poe's life in Richmond and the statue that honors him. At the back of an old folder, she uncovered a yellowed copy of an op ed piece that listed local objections to the statue. A contingent of old Richmond society folks felt that it was not appropriate to honor the author. They cited examples from Poe's past based on stories from Rufus Grishwold's less than flattering biography and the mysterious circumstances surrounding the author's death in Baltimore. The gist was that influencers of the day felt the statue was inappropriate and that the writer should not be recognized.

Delanie photocopied the article and dropped it in her folder. The museum staff at the reference desk who had been rather quiet, shuffled papers and restacked books. Glancing at her phone, she realized it was almost closing time. Delanie gathered her things and hurried to her car.

The last rays of the sun bounced off the taller buildings in the city's financial district, creating a shadowy effect. As she drove west, the skyscrapers turned into the tall pines and oaks of the suburbs, and the sun slipped behind the trees and turned the sky to an orangey pink swirl.

About twenty minutes later, she pulled into the parking lot near the darkened storefront of Snakes and Scales. The stores on that side of the shopping center looked closed. The front door of the reptile store had been propped open with two large plastic bins. Delanie cruised past but did not see anyone. She had her pick of open spaces in front of her office.

Snagging her regular parking spot, Delanie caught a glimpse of three men exiting the pet store with boxes and pet carriers. She turned to get a better look at about the time a fourth guy in a hoodie

traipsed around the end unit of the row of stores. Grabbing her
things, she climbed out for a better view.

The three guys loaded the stuff in a minivan. The fourth guy who
might have been Glen, stepped back from the vehicle and wiped his
hands on his pants.

Delanie trotted across the parking lot, and the men stopped and
looked up as she approached.

"Hey, Glen. How are you?" she asked, waving at the men.

He stepped back and looked at his feet. She sidled up next to the
van where she could get a better look at the contents. "How are things
going? I appreciate y'all coming over to get that boa constrictor that
was in our office."

"Lucy is a reticulated python." He looked at his feet. "It was no big
deal."

"Oh, sorry. I'm not current on my snake species. What are y'all
doing?"

"Uh, packing for a show tomorrow," Glen said, still looking at his
feet.

Doing a quick inventory, she counted fifteen boxes and bins with
air holes in the back of the van. She could not see what was in the
middle section of the vehicles.

"Well, good luck. I've got to run." She turned and jogged toward
her office.

Delanie unlocked the office door slowly, so she could spy on what
the guys were doing. She whipped out her phone and captured the
van and the cars parked near Snakes and Scales on video. The other
guys climbed into separate cars, and when Glen drove off in the van,
she texted Duncan. Her phone dinged with his response before she
managed to get to her desk.

I saw them taking boxes out this afternoon, too, he replied.

Interesting. She added a snake emoji.

Removing evidence???

Who knows? It looks fishy.

Deep down, she knew Glen was sneaking stuff out of the of his store. She needed to call Tina to see if she knew what her brother was doing with the inventory.

Delanie rummaged through the piles of files on her desk for the Snakes and Scales folder. She flipped through it to find Tina's contact information.

After a few rings, a breathless Tina said, "Hello."

"Hi, Tina. This is Delanie Fitzgerald. I hope I didn't disturb you."

"Oh, no. The cats and I are watching *Vera* on BritBox. What's up?"

"When Snakes and Scales does presentations how many reptiles usually go along?"

"Two or three of the mild tempered ones. Why?" It sounded like Tina was eating something as she talked.

"Just curious. I saw Glen and some of his friends loading a few bins in a minivan tonight. I wanted to make sure everything was okay. When I talked to him, he said they were going to a show."

"Oh, shows are different. If they're selling at a show, they may take eight or ten snakes and lizards. They don't take too many if they have to stay in a hotel. It's awkward when you have to explain what's in all the boxes with air holes. Sometimes, they'll stay with other dealers or sleep in the car. Most of the time, Glen does events he can drive to and from in one day. I haven't checked the store calendar lately, so I'm not sure where he was going. Shows are a big money maker for the store."

Delanie shivered unconsciously. She couldn't imagine sleeping in a van with a bunch of snakes. And not one packed to the gills with containers.

When she realized she hadn't replied, she said, "Thanks so much. I was curious. Take care. I'll see you soon."

"I have to go by the store tomorrow, so I'll find out where they went. See ya."

Delanie grabbed her laptop and navigated to the Snakes and Scales's website. After a few clicks, she found their events page. Nothing listed for the rest of the month. Something dodgy was going on at the snake store. Maybe Duncan could get some information about the other three men from the license plates she caught on tape.

Before she called it a night, Delanie pulled out her Poe folder. She flipped through her contacts and found Marco's number. After a few rings, she heard, "Hey, Delanie. What's up?" Loud conversations in the background made it difficult to hear him. She did not know anything about Marco outside of his security work that he did for Chaz. She hoped she was not interrupting dinner or his private life.

"Hey, Marco. I wanted to see if you recognized any of the diggers as Treasure Chest clients."

"Let me step outside. I'm at the club, and it's noisy." After a few seconds, he continued, "That's better. I don't think so. My guys have chased the guys off several times in the last month. None of 'em look familiar. I'll make sure security posts copies of their photos at the front door. My guys will be on the lookout if they try to come inside."

"Anything else unusual about them?"

"The whole thing is weird. I thought they were vandals at first, but they don't tag anything. We've spotted two or three guys each time. One is kinda old, and they always run off as my guys approach. It's not kids," he said with his voice trailing off.

"Call or text me if you think of anything else or if they come back."

"Will do." And the line went dead.

What was so interesting about an old statue that would cause them to come back multiple times and risk being caught with shovels? This made no sense.

18

DELANIE RUBBED THE KINK IN HER NECK. SHE STAYED UP LATE LAST night organizing her notes about the history of the statue, erected as a joint effort by the public library and the Richmond Poe Society. The groups, including school children, raised money to have the statue cast, and then they donated it to the city.

The project came to fruition with the statue's dedication in 1913. The statue still stands on the street corner in front of the *Southern Literary Messenger* even though the building was torn down last century.

She poured herself a second cup of coffee and doused it with enough milk to turn it a light beige.

Delanie could not find the significance of 1913. It was not an anniversary year of his birth or death. It seemed arbitrary. Usually, there is something to be commemorated with a statue's dedication. Puzzling.

She created a spreadsheet of her notes and her list of unanswered questions. Checking the internet for the Poe Museum's hours, Delanie decided to head downtown to see if she could get some of her questions answered by the experts.

Any more info on the snake accounts? She texted Duncan.

Nope. Still a mystery.

Going to the Poe Museum.

As she was heading out the door, her phone binged again with a text from Duncan. *Nevermore! You in tomorrow?*

She tapped in her response, *Bright and early,* and dropped the phone in her purse.

The sun had heated the inside of the car, and it felt toasty on a chilly fall morning. She cranked up the radio to her favorite eighties station. She did not care that the genre fell into the oldies category. The music was from her favorite era, and when a Vibes song came on, she caught her breath. It reminded her of the case where a tell-all author hired her to find Johnny Velvet, the Vibes's lead singer. She solved the mystery and bruised her heart in the process. Thoughts of Johnny Velvet living incognito in rural Amelia County, Virginia as farmer, John Bailey, still made her smile. She wondered what he was up to these days after he high-tailed it out of town with cold feet, ending their budding relationship.

Delanie revved the Mustang's engine and merged onto Route 288 on her way downtown. About a half hour later, she exited the Downtown Expressway and wended her way through the maze of one-way streets to Main Street. She scored parking in the tiny lot next to the Poe Museum under a large oak tree.

Stepping gingerly around the tree's roots, she made her way to the front of the Old Stone House, home to the Poe Museum. The antique, wooden door creaked when she lifted the metal latch. The door opened into the magical gift shop full of Poe gadgets, books, and T-shirts. The wooden floor creaked when she moved around the displays. Delanie browsed until the clerk finished with the couple ahead of her.

"Welcome," the young woman with long black hair said. "How may I help you?"

"I'd like a ticket for the tour and galleries."

"That's eight dollars, and the tour will begin here in about fifteen minutes in case you'd like to do a little shopping or browse the Enchanted Garden."

Delanie could not pass up a shopping excursion. Before the tour started, she managed to find two T-shirts, postcards, stickers, and a Poe bobblehead for Duncan.

A woman in period flowing skirts that rustled as she moved, waved her arms and said, "The Poe tour is about to begin. If you'll gather over here, please." The couple who were ahead of Delanie in line and another pair with a small child stepped through the back door from the gardens.

"Hello, everyone and welcome. I'm Mary Ellen, and I'll be your guide today. She led them to the front room of the little house and explained the importance of the artifacts.

When she talked about Poe's early life in Richmond, Delanie pulled out a small notebook and pen from her oversized purse. She jotted notes as the group explored the rooms and then made their way across the gardens to the other buildings on the property.

Delanie's favorite artifact was Poe's desk. She stood in the room facing it for several minutes when Mary Ellen paused to let the guests explore. For some reason, the desk captured her attention and drew her closer. She imagined the famous author and poet hunched over it, penning works that are still popular today. She wondered if in his youth he could imagine the historical and literary significance his writings would have on future generations.

Mary Ellen interrupted Delanie's daydream when she said, "If you all will follow me, we have one more building where we have a special exhibit of memorabilia based on films of Poe's work, and then we'll have time to explore the gardens.

Delanie filed in with the other visitors as they made their way to a long brick building. Inside the room, displays of book covers and movie posters highlighted Poe's contribution to the genres of mystery and suspense. Delanie jotted down the titles that were not familiar to her.

The group perused all of the popular culture displays and then exited to the garden area, which was surrounded by buildings on the three sides and a tall brick wall with shards of glass on the top.

"What's with all the glass on the wall?" one of the men asked as he examined the bricks.

"It's a nineteenth century security system," Mary Ellen said with a smile. "It kept animals and people from scaling the wall. Poe mentions this technique in his short story, 'William Wilson.'" She paused and pointed to the back of the garden. "And if you'll step over here, we have the Poe Shrine. The materials came from the building that housed the *Southern Literary Messenger* where Poe worked in Richmond," Two black cats darted across the lawn.

"Kitty cats," the little boy squealed.

"Yes," Mary Ellen replied. "That's Edgar and Pluto, the museum cats. They're our ambassadors."

The little boy scampered off toward the cats.

"And that's the end of our tour. Thank you so much for your time. Does anyone have any questions I can answer?" Mary Ellen asked.

A dark-haired woman in the back cleared her throat and asked, "Uh, yes. Are there any buildings related to Poe that are still standing in the city?"

"While many of the key buildings no longer exist, there are a few Poe sites in and around the city. His mother Elizabeth is buried at St. John's Church. His dorm room is on display at the University of Virginia in Charlottesville. The Elmira Shelton house on Grace Street was the home of his teenage sweetheart. And the Adam Craig House is also on Grace Street. It was the girlhood home of Jane Stith Craig Stanard, Poe's friend's mother who encouraged him to write. Also, on Grace Street, the Talavera House still stands. Poe visited there before his death in 1849."

"Does 1813 have any significance in Poe's life?" Delanie asked.

The tour guide paused a minute. Delanie hoped she did not think she was trying to stump her.

"There was never any documented birth or baptismal record, but most historians agree that he was born in 1809. For a time, Poe told some people he was born in 1813. We're not sure why or what brought that about."

"Interesting. Thank you," Delanie said, scribbling in her notebook. A charge of excitement ran through her. She wondered if that was why the statue was dedicated in 1913. It was the best explanation she had so far. "Can you tell me any details about the Poe statue or point me to any references?"

"Erected in the early 1900s, the Poe statue stands on the site of the *Southern Literary Messenger*. It's popular with tourists because of the influence he had on so many literary genres over the years. All kinds of people take selfies and leave tokens of appreciation at the statue. On any given day, you'll see flowers, candles, books, and other mementos around the base."

"Do you know of any books written about the statue?" Delanie asked.

"There's one in the gift shop. There are also books about the places in Richmond, Baltimore, and other cities that Poe frequented."

The woman next to Delanie nodded.

Mary Ellen continued, "Thank you all for coming today. I'll hang out here in the gift shop a little longer if you have any more questions."

"I do have one more question." Delanie stepped forward. "What happens to all the mementos that are left at the statue? I was over there last week, and there were quite a few."

"We have an intern here who goes over once a week and collects the items for preservation. We're going to do an exhibit here," Mary Ellen said.

"Thank you so much for answering all my questions." The older woman smiled and turned toward the cashier.

The small group in the gift shop dissipated, and Delanie browsed the book collection near the side door.

She paid for a book on the history of the statue and a collection of Poe's stories. She made her way to the car, excited to get back and see what information the little history book contained.

Delanie zipped through a drive-thru for lunch in a bag and returned home to spread her Poe Museum purchases on the kitchen table. She finished off her French fries and poured over the books.

She spent the next hour reading the thin blue book by Rosalind

Martin-Black, a librarian and amateur historian who called herself a history sleuth. The grainy, black and white pictures of the dedication were the most interesting to the private investigator. She wondered who else came out that day to see the unveiling of the statue besides the named dignitaries like the mayor, councilmen, and several local bankers. A group of school children filled one of the photos. It looked like a fairly large crowd attended the ceremony.

Delanie finished skimming the Poe statue book and flipped through the appendix to see the footnotes. A tiny reference to one of the photo credits caught her attention. It mentioned that the mayor laid the cornerstone that day, and a mason sealed it in the foundation. She made a note in her spreadsheet.

Martin-Black's book was published in 1982. She wondered if the author was still in the area. When she Googled the author's name and the book title, a local publisher that specialized in history and biography popped up. Another link led her to a website for the author, who had lived in Richmond for most of her life. On the contact page, she filled in her information. If she did not get a response, she would get Duncan to track down Mrs. Martin-Black, who taught as an adjunct professor at Randolph-Macon College.

Delanie flipped through the book again, looking for pictures of the cornerstone. Not having any success, she Googled the term, and hundreds of images of cornerstones appeared. Some were literally stones with a date of dedication. Others were hollowed out and contained mementos or time capsules. A jolt of excitement ran through her. She had to find out if the Poe statue had a time capsule. That could be what the diggers were after.

She scanned the book again without uncovering any new information. Turning to Google, she poked around the internet well after the sun set. Darkness creeped in her tiny bungalow. She flipped on the overhead lights, grabbed an iced tea, and put popcorn in the microwave.

Between bites, she searched for any information on the statue. Too much time had passed, so there was no hope of finding someone present at the dedication. She wondered if there were any diaries or notes left from anyone in attendance. If she could get names, she could check the Library of Virginia or the Valentine Museum again. She yawned and stacked her notes next to her laptop.

Delanie peeked at her phone. With nothing even mildly exciting to respond to, she retreated to her bedroom to watch television. The glamorous life of a private investigator.

19

THE NEXT MORNING, DELANIE AWOKE WHEN THE SUN STREAMED INTO her bedroom. She had fallen asleep in her clothes, and the TV had long ago slipped into sleep mode. She rose and did a few yoga poses. After a quick shower and strong coffee, she gathered her things and headed to the office.

No sign of Duncan or Margaret anywhere in the office suite. She grabbed a Coke and retreated to her desk. Skimming through the Valentine Museum's online resources, she did not see anything related to the statue, but she did find a contact number.

After several rings, a southern voice welcomed her to the Valentine Museum in the heart of Richmond.

"Hi. My name is Delanie Fitzgerald, and I'm doing some research on the Poe Statue downtown. Do you have any resources there who could help me? I'm specifically looking for information about the cornerstone."

"Let me connect you with one of our archivists. One moment, please."

After a few minutes of on-hold music, Delanie heard, "Hello. This is Anton Phelps."

"Mr. Phelps, I'm Delanie Fitzgerald, and I'm doing some research on the Poe Statue. Do you have any resources in your collection specific to its cornerstone?"

"That's interesting. I don't think I've had a request like that before. Let me see what I can find." He tapped on his keyboard.

"I'm afraid I don't have too much. I have some information on the sculptor, Phillip McKenzie. There are a couple of articles about the dedication. I could make copies of these and send them to you."

"That would be wonderful. Thank you so much." Delanie provided him with her contact information and disconnected. She Googled the *Richmond Times-Dispatch* and dug around on their contacts page until she found a number for someone in archives.

After several rings and two transfers, Delanie's connected. "Hello. Archives. This is Tristan."

"I was curious to see if you all had stories and pictures in your archives of the dedication of the Poe Statue in 1913." She heard him type something.

"Yes. I have a big article on the dedication, and there's a follow up in the next morning's paper."

"How would I get copies of those?" she asked.

"You can pay by credit card, and I can email copies to you, or you can order them and pick them up at our Grace Street office."

"I'd like to get copies emailed to me." She fumbled through her purse for her office credit card. After exchanging the account and contact information, Delanie hung up and sank into her chair. Maybe there would be a tidbit of something that would lead her to a reason for the digging.

Before she could continue any more searches, she heard the back door open. "Delanie," Duncan yelled.

"In my office. I'm looking into Chaz's latest request."

"More oppo research?" He poked his head through the doorway. Margaret dropped in, too. She found a nice spot in the corner for a snooze.

"No. His guys have noticed people digging around the Poe statue on the corner of his lot. He asked us to look into it. I haven't been able to locate anything definitive, but I did uncover that the statue has a cornerstone. I'm checking out some leads to see if it contains a time capsule. Otherwise, it doesn't make sense why anyone is digging around the base of a hundred-year-old statue. Think any helpful information would be on the part of the big bad web that you prowl around?"

"Could be, especially if there are any conspiracy theories or urban legends attached to it. I'll do some searching. Who knows what I'll find? Send me what you've got so far," he said.

"I'm waiting on copies from the Valentine Museum and the newspaper. We'll see if any of that helps. Chaz is having his guy, Steve, put up additional cameras. He said that they've seen these guys several times. It seems like it's more than random graffiti or vandalism. And I'm dying to know what they're looking for."

Duncan and Margaret disappeared into his office, and Delanie straightened the items on her desk. She struck gold in her email box. Author Rosalind Martin-Black responded to her query. She would love to meet and chat about the book. Grabbing her phone, she dialed the number before the woman changed her mind.

After introductions and chitchat, the women agreed to meet at Sacred Grounds, the coffee shop near VCU's main campus tomorrow afternoon. Reviewing her spreadsheet of questions, she added a few more and printed it for the meeting.

Her phone chimed with a new email alert. The archivist at the Valentine had sent the information he promised. Delanie read through it carefully and jotted down all the names mentioned. Most of the information detailed the life and work of sculptor Phillip McKenzie. She finished her drink and Googled random words related to the statue.

Today was be her lucky day for leads. She found a blog post that detailed the contents of several time capsules in the area. Delanie printed the article and reviewed the types of things saved during building and monument dedications. The Richmond Library's cornerstone contained a stone from the Cape Henry Lighthouse and the will of wealthy Maymont heiress, Sally May Dooley. The one for the Virginia

Museum of History and Culture contained a piece of wood from the *Merrimac* and wood from the grave of Stonewall Jackson. A lot of the time capsules contained things like copies of newspapers, historic souvenirs, and other trinkets. She dashed off an email to the blogger who wrote the article about three years ago. Maybe he would respond, too.

She called the Valentine Museum again and asked for Anton Phelps. After listening to his formal recording, she left a voice mail with her question about Richmond cornerstones.

"Hey, Dunc. Have you had lunch yet?"

"I haven't had breakfast yet. What are you thinking about?"

"Chinese?"

"That works. Give me a minute. I'll meet you at the front door."

ON THE WALK back across the parking lot with takeout containers filled with their lunch leftovers, Duncan and Delanie noticed the crowd of cars around Snakes and Scales. Business must be doing well. Or there were a lot of curious lookie-loos.

Duncan stopped by the kitchen to share his leftovers with Margaret.

"Hey, Dunc, did you ever send Tina any info on your account research?"

"Yesterday."

"I wasn't sure if we owed her an update or not. I talked to her briefly about Glen moving boxes out of the store. She said that he took snakes to demos and shows. The store seems to be doing well if the parking lot is any indication."

Duncan raised his eyebrows. "Maybe it's a snake club. Regardless, something's going on." He shrugged his shoulders and retreated to his office. His brown and white dog shadow followed as soon as she realized her guy and the food were gone.

Delanie sunk into in her office chair. The newspaper archivist had filled her order for the clipping requests. She read through them twice and added all the names mentioned from the 1913 article to her spreadsheet.

The article had a couple of sentences about the time capsule. The author described the contents as coins, a picture of the author, postcards, a map of Richmond, and a copy of "The Raven." Delanie scribbled down the details. Okay, what in that list was important to thieves today?

Her phone rang, interrupting her thoughts. "Delanie Fitzgerald, please. This is Dr. Anton Phelps."

"Dr. Phelps, thank you for calling me back. I'm the one doing research on time capsules and building cornerstones in Richmond."

"Oh, yes. I remember talking with you. What else can I help you with?"

"Could you tell me the significance or the value of items that people choose to include in cornerstones?" Delanie asked.

"It varies. More modern ones tend to have things that relate to the event. It's a time capsule to commemorate something. And I guess it was kind of the same with the older ones. Folks typically included coins, maps, souvenirs, and documents from the era."

"Are they ever opened?"

"Sometimes. It's usually if there's a big anniversary or another type of celebration. A couple of times statues were moved or buildings torn down, and the cornerstone or time capsule was found. I can't think of an expert in that area off hand. You may try the newspaper archives or online history websites if you have a specific cornerstone in mind. Niche topics appear on blogs a lot. It's interesting to see what things people from the past thought were important for those in the future," Dr. Phelps said.

"Thank you so much for your time." Delanie jotted down ideas that his conversation sparked. There had to be some reason someone was interested in this particular statue. And the fact that they had been back multiple times made it less random.

Tires squealed out front and four or five doors slammed. Delanie rushed to the lobby to see what was going on. No crash, so it did not sound like a car accident.

"Hey, Duncan. You may want to come and see this," she yelled after peeking out the front door.

Duncan, with his bulldog bringing up the rear, strolled into the lobby. "What's up?"

"There's a lot of action at Snakes and Scales today."

They stepped out on the sidewalk. Two dark SUVs, several Game and Inland Fisheries vehicles, and several Chesterfield and Virginia State Police cruisers had parked at all angles around the store. A tactical truck pulled in and blocked the main exit, while a yellow fire engine blocked the other exit.

"I guess they took your tip seriously," he said.

The excitement did not phase Margaret. She plopped down on the cement and found a spot for a nap.

More police vehicles arrived. The officers, some in tactical gear, entered the store. Then the police in the parking lot waved three white vans around the fire engine. All other traffic was detoured around the back of the shopping center.

Duncan and Delanie sat on the curb watching law enforcement go in and out of the building for what seemed like hours. She thought she saw her brother in a crowd of state troopers and other law enforcement officers.

Then, officers escorted Glen and Justin out of the store in handcuffs. They put them in the backs of separate cruisers and drove off. Duncan videoed the action while Margaret snored.

Two TV vans arrived and set up for live camera shots. Videographers from competing networks set up tripods and cameras near the curb, facing the pet store.

By now, a crowd had started to gather on the perimeter as conservation officers and others carried crates and plastic bins out of the store. They looked like a line of ants toting food back to the anthill. Conservation officers finally closed the doors of three white vans that sped off, caravanning behind each other.

Then as quickly as they arrived, the emergency vehicles left the property. Someone in a beige uniform taped a sign on the door.

"Well, that doesn't happen every day." Duncan stood and dusted off his jeans, and Margaret looked up with one eye open to see if she was missing anything.

"I wonder if Tina knows. And can the store survive this? They took a lot of their reptiles. Do you think they know about the ones Glen snuck out under the cover of darkness?"

Duncan shrugged. "I'm going to walk over in a few minutes to see what the sign says."

As the crowd dissipated and the camera crews left, Delanie returned to her office.

A few minutes later, she heard Duncan enter through the front. He stuck his head in her office. "The sign is a health department warning. It said that the business is closed until further notice."

"Wow. Tina has been through a lot in the last few weeks. This is probably stress that she doesn't need." She looked up from her laptop. "Temporary or permanent closure?"

"Dunno. But it can't be good. They obviously had a lot of banned reptiles. Let me know if you talk to your brother."

Delanie picked up her cell. She clicked the contact for Steve.

"Hey, D. What's up?" her brother asked.

"Saw you over in my neck of the woods today. How're things?"

"Yep. A joint team of state and local law enforcement raided Snakes and Scales. Other officers descended on EEK Distributors about the same time in Northern Virginia. Your videos were helpful for shutting down these guys."

"The other night, I saw Glen and his buddies taking crates out to a minivan. He said that they were going to a show. You might not have gotten everything."

"They're raiding their residences and a storage unit, too," her brother added.

Delanie shivered at the thought of poisonous snakes in a storage unit. "Thanks. Duncan said there was a health department sign on the door."

"They're shut down for now. Not sure what will happen while the cases are pending. Any more snakes at your place?" he asked.

"No. Just the two we found. Tina, the sister, said that three terrariums broke when her dad had his heart attack. They found the dead spiders, and we found two snakes. That's probably the extent of it. Or at least, I hope so." She blew a stray curl off her forehead. "I don't think I can take another snake surprise."

"Not sure if the guys will be charged with manslaughter in the elder Montgomery's death. The Commonwealth's Attorney is still weighing the options. We'll have to see what happens. If they knowingly put poisonous snakes in a cage, that might be considered more than an accident. Plus, they racked up quite a few charges for the possession of banned species."

"I'm hoping that Mr. Montgomery's death was a horrible accident. I'd hate to think someone caused it on purpose. Call me if you find anything else."

She heard an "uh-huh" from her brother and then he clicked off the call.

State and local law enforcement had conducted multiple raids based on Falcon Investigations' information, kindling a feeling of pride for Delanie. However, today's police activity did not bode well for Snakes and Scales. In an instant, the natural death of the owner had shifted to a manslaughter investigation and a slew of other charges.

20

THE NEXT AFTERNOON, DELANIE PARKED IN THE DECK ACROSS FROM
Monroe Park and walked around the sidewalk to the Sacred Grounds,
a coffee shop that featured eclectic artwork by VCU students. Delanie
looked around the store. Not seeing anyone who might be Rosalind
Martin-Black, she ordered an iced coffee and found a table near the
door.

The fluorescent orange, wooden chair squeaked when she drug it
across the cement floor. A few minutes later, an older woman with
shoulder-length silver hair breezed in the front door and looked
around. Delanie waved, and the author stepped over to her table. Her
bangle bracelets on both arms jingled like windchimes as she
approached.

"Delanie? Hi, I'm Rosalind. Let me get something to drink, and
we'll chat." She shifted her oversized Michael Kors handbag to her
other shoulder.

Rosalind returned with a steaming mug of coffee.

Delanie said, "Thanks so much for meeting me here. I enjoyed
your book. I found a copy last week at the Poe Museum."

"I'm glad you liked it. I fell in love with Poe in college, and I've
written a couple of books on things related to him. Don't you the love

that museum? I love their Unhappy Hours in the summer. And the two museum cats. They're adorable."

"The Enchanted Garden is my favorite."

Rosalind spooned sugar into her coffee, blew on the steam, and took a sip. "So, what are you interested in. I pulled out some of my research last night ahead of our meeting." She set her purse in the empty, lime green chair beside her.

"The time capsule in the base of the statue. I read online that it contained some coins, a map, and other mementos of the day. What can you tell me about it?"

"Well, the libraries, several school groups, and the Poe Society banded together to fund the statue. There was a big turnout for the dedication. The mayor at the time was George Ainslie. I think they collected things they thought would be interesting to future generations and things that were important mementos that represented the city and Poe."

"Anything that would be of monetary value today?"

"Doubtful. The contents are usually more sentimental. The historical significance is usually the value." The author took a sip of her coffee and stirred in another spoonful of sugar.

"Any idea where it's located since the statue doesn't really have a physical cornerstone?" Delanie asked.

"I'm guessing it's part of the base because they put the items in a metal box, and it was sealed in during the dedication. I think they pulled out one of the blocks and cemented it back when they put the time capsule inside. That's interesting. I never thought much about it. Are you a Poe scholar?"

"Not officially. Just a fan. I'm a private investigator. A property owner near the statue hired me to find out why someone was digging around the base of the statue."

"Someone was defacing the monument?" Rosalind's voice rose an octave.

"His bouncer noticed several people there in the wee hours one morning. They found holes in the ground at the back of the statue. I don't think there was any damage to the statue."

"That reminds me of something." Rosalind rummaged through her bag again. She pulled out a folder and flipped through several, loose pages. "Here. This is a picture of the dedication. I think you're right. The time capsule is probably at the back of the statue. This is the group standing in an arc around the side and back during the dedication day. That would make sense. But what would someone want with a time capsule? Do you think it's a prank? Or some kind of internet challenge?"

"I'm not sure. It wasn't an isolated event. Security noticed people out by the statue several times after the club closed. They're adults. It doesn't look like a teen prank," Delanie said.

"Very interesting. I can't think of anything else to tell you. But I'll go home and look through my files again. If I spot anything, I'll call you. I'm curious about all of this."

"Thank you so much for your help."

"Not a problem. I always enjoy talking about Poe." Rosalind drained the last few drops from her mug. "Just let me know what you find. I love knowing how a good mystery ends."

"Will do." Delanie shook the woman's hand. "It was very nice to meet you."

"Do you have a card?" the author asked.

Delanie passed a business card across the table, and Rosalind dropped it in her purse and rose.

After Rosalind left, Delanie cleared the table and walked across the green space of Monroe Park to retrieve her car. The brisk afternoon felt good after the steamy temperatures of July and August. A steady stream of VCU students in constant motion on the paths radiating to different parts of the campus filled the park. Delanie had fond memories of goofing off, playing Frisbee, and sunbathing in the park when she was a student here. The park had recently been renovated, and the overhaul made it a central hub of the academic campus. Shaking off the urge to linger in the park, Delanie made a beeline for the parking deck.

~

DELANIE TOOK the spot next to Duncan's Camaro. She glanced over her shoulder at the darkened pet store across the parking lot. She hated to see it shuttered, but she was still angry that Glen did not warn anyone about the two escaped snakes. Shaking off the negative feelings, she headed for her office.

Hearing voices inside, she followed the sounds to the kitchen. Tina Montgomery sat with her back to the door. Duncan sat across from her, and of course, Margaret waited patiently at Duncan's feet in case there were snacks.

"Oh, hi, Delanie. Tina stopped by to give us an update," he said.

"It's nice to see you. Can I get you anything?" When the other woman shook her head, Delanie pulled out the chair closest to her and sat. She dropped her messenger bag on the floor at her feet. Margaret waddled over to greet her.

"Like I was telling Duncan, the police raided the store yesterday and took a lot of the inventory. Glen and his friend, Justin, have been selling exotic, really exotic reptiles. And they raided their homes and a storage unit that I didn't know Glen had."

"That python scared me to death. That was the last thing I expected to find in our office kitchen. And that viper in the dumpster jarred everyone when that guy started shooting at it." Delanie leaned over and patted Margaret's boxy head for comfort.

"I'm sorry. I had no idea what Glen was doing. And I find it hard to believe that my dad knew about it either. He wouldn't have tolerated it in his store. Animals and their well being were always a priority for him. He tried to educate prospective buyers about the needs of snakes and reptiles. Any pet is a commitment, but some of these species need extra care and attention." Her voice trailed off as she looked down at her hands and nails that had been chewed to the quick.

It seemed odd to the Delanie that Ken Montgomery could be in the store every day and not notice exotic species. Maybe Tina did not want to think that her dad was a party to the lucrative, illicit transactions. Or maybe she was working on her own alibi.

"Are you okay?" Delanie asked.

"I've got to talk to the estate lawyer this afternoon. They left some of the animals in the store, so I have to figure out how to take care of them. I'm not sure how long Glen will be in custody. And I have to figure out how to bail him out."

Delanie flipped through her contacts. "I have names of some bail bondsmen in the area if you want me to send them to you. The first on my list is Free Bird Bail Bonds. Some of my clients have called them. They come highly recommended."

Tina smiled a half-smile. "Thanks. That will be helpful. I wouldn't know where to start." She coughed and continued, "I'm not sure if we'll be able to reopen the store. I thought it was a mess before, but this takes the cake. Nothing like a little more stress on top of a lot of stress," she said with a heavy sigh. All the air inside her seemed to escape, and she leaned on the table like a deflated balloon.

"I'm sorry that you've had all this thrust on you. Did your dad have any other pet store owners or contacts you could call for advice?"

"That's a thought. A lot of the store owners help each other out if they don't have inventory or someone was looking for something special. Dad had a loose network of friends that he could call. I've got to contact the health department and the police to see when I can get back in the building." She played with a button on her sweater. After a long pause, she said, "I wanted to stop by and thank you for your help. I'm kinda relieved that it's over. Maybe the best thing would be to close the shop. It's so full of memories for me now, and a lot of them are sad. I'd kind of like to move on."

Delanie thought about what would happen to Glen if Tina closed the store. Before she could comment, Tina stood. "Thanks for helping me get to the bottom of this. I'm sorry that you all got surprised by the snakes."

"I'll walk you out," Duncan said.

A few minutes later, he and Margaret returned to the kitchen. "Well, that wraps up another one."

"I hope she can liquidate the store and move on to something else. Her heart's not in the reptile store," Delanie said.

"Wonder what's next for her brother after the raid? It can't be good."

"I assume he could do some time. There's got to be some penalty for reckless endangerment. Steve said that he'll be charged with trafficking banned species. And he could also be charged with manslaughter in his dad's death, especially if law enforcement throws the book at him."

Duncan shrugged. "Normally, I'm happy when we finish a case. This one makes me feel a little bummed."

"I know. I've been in a funk since the raid, but we had to alert authorities. There was not one, but two dangerous snakes on the lam. I can't believe Glen knew they were loose, and he didn't do anything. He could at least have come clean and put out a warning. The whole thing still gives me the willies." She slung her bag over her shoulder in a huff.

Delanie settled in her office to check emails. None about new cases. But an email from Titan 51 caught her attention.

Titan 51, who did not give his real name, blogged about quirky, historical events that were often linked to conspiracy theories. His rambling email was as mysterious as the digging at the Poe statue. Delanie read it twice, and she still was not sure what he was saying. He rambled on about Poe's death and conspiracies to ruin the author's reputation. A few sounded plausible and then the email took a turn toward the paranormal. Delanie rubbed her eyes and stared out the window.

Curious, she opened her internet browser and scanned Titan 51's blog archives for anything related to Poe. Disappointed at not finding anything on the Richmond statute, she searched further until she found a piece about the controversies surrounding the author's death in Baltimore.

At least the post was better written than the email. Titan 51 imagined Poe's last days in Baltimore. He proposed that the author, found in the streets in someone else's clothes, had been abducted. At the time, it was popular for operatives to approach men, get them drunk, and kidnap them. When they woke up, they would be on a boat in international waters – on a navy ship, where they were forced to serve. Titan 51 suggested that as a possible explanation for Poe's predicament.

The blogger surmised that Poe was able to escape his captors, but somehow, he was injured and never recovered. Delanie followed the theory until the last paragraph where the post changed tone. Titan 51, not the first person to suggest that Poe had been involved in a conscription kidnapping, bragged that he was the first to suggest that it was really an alien abduction. He concluded that he felt alien contact would explain some of the themes in Poe's works. He had also written a short story about it and included a link to it. Delanie printed both and added them to her files. She sighed. The post was just a vehicle to promote the blogger's short story.

All the theories were giving her a headache. When she did not find anything else interesting, Delanie packed up and headed out for a change of scenery.

AFTER AN AFTERNOON of running errands and cleaning house, Delanie slipped into a T-shirt and yoga pants to binge watch episodes of *Bosch*. Midway through the third episode of the new season, her phone rang.

"Hey, Delanie. This is Marco. Sorry to bother you so late, but the diggers are back. Steve noticed them on camera. We're watching to see what they're going to do. Can you come down?"

She glanced at the time on her DVR, twelve-thirty-eight.

Delanie sighed and hoped he did not hear her. "Sure. I'll be right there." She found her tennis shoes and put on a trench coat over her lounging outfit. Maybe no one would notice. She did not have the time or energy to change clothes.

Making good time with the combination of light traffic and her fast car, she pulled into Chaz's side lot and texted Marco that she had arrived.

Her phone dinged with a response. *Meet me at the side door.*

A few minutes later, the head of security held the door for her. The club's music pulsed and throbbed to the point where communication was difficult as she followed him down a narrow hallway. He led her back to the security office and shut the door. The metal door muffled the music slightly.

Steve, Chaz's security guy, sat looking at a bank of screens. He enlarged the view from one camera on the screen in front of him.

"Whatcha got?" Marco asked.

"There are three of them, and they're still out there. One is walking around, keeping watch. The other two are digging around the base of the statue. They've been at it off and on for about an hour. They don't seem worried that someone will notice."

"I think they're after the time capsule," Delanie said.

"Huh?" Steve grunted.

"When they dedicated the statue, they included a time capsule of mementos for future generations."

Steve raised one eyebrow and squinted. "They're here kinda early tonight." He took a swig of his bottled water. "I've always spotted them after the club closed."

"Do you have any clear shots of their faces?

"I'll see if I can get some for you." Steve clicked the keys and panned through the different views.

"We could take a walk with a few of our guys to see what's going on. Let me go round up the guys," Marco said.

Delanie fidgeted in her seat, and Steve returned to his bank of monitors. Marco and two men the size of linebackers filled the small space near the door. Like Marco, both men were dressed in black jeans and T-shirts. "Delanie, this is Rikko and Tony. They're going around the far side of the building. Delanie and I will go around the other way. Hopefully, we'll look nonchalant like we're out for a walk or looking for our cars. Let's see what these clowns are up to."

Trying to quell the apprehension that bubbled up, Delanie took a couple of deep breaths and followed Marco out the door. They strolled through the parking lot toward the outer rows. No one was on their side of the statue. She wondered what Rikko and Tony could see from their vantage point.

Marco and Delanie edged closer to the grassy area when a shrill whistle cut through the night sounds of the city. Delanie jumped. Marco scooted around the statue as the two diggers bolted.

Rikko and Tony gave chase across the street. Horns blared as they cut across four lanes of traffic and darted down an alley. They heard a car start nearby and peel out of the parking lot.

Marco sauntered back to where Delanie stood, looking at the holes around the base of the statue. The men had dropped two shovels and a pick. "The smaller guy, the lookout, tore off in an old Toyota 4Runner. He was sitting in the vehicle over there. We'll see if Tony or Rikko had any better luck."

The wind blew, causing Delanie to shiver. She pulled her trench coat tighter around her as they waited.

After what seemed like hours, Rikko and Tony trotted across the street when the light changed.

"Sorry, boss," Tony said. "I chased the tall one, and Rikko had the older one. But we lost 'em."

"For an old dude, he could run," Rikko added. "They darted down an alley and over a fence. I think they caught a ride with somebody."

"The lookout tore out of the parking lot after you took off. He was sitting in an old Toyota. Hopefully, Steve can work his magic and get the plates," Marco said.

They stared at the base of the statue as Delanie touched the stone above where the men had dug. "I talked to a woman who wrote a book about the statue. She thinks the time capsule was sealed up in the back at one of the corners. It looks like they're focusing on the base with all these gopher holes. I wonder if they thought something was buried here?" she asked.

Marco shrugged and picked up the abandoned tools and tossed them over his shoulder. "Let's go see what Steve's got."

The tiny band followed him through the parking lot to the security office. Rikko and Tony disappeared inside the club. Marco put the shovels and pick in the corner and pulled an outdated office chair next to Steve for Delanie.

"We're back," Marco said. Let's see what you captured on your candid cameras."

He moved the feed back about an hour and increased the view. They watched the older Toyota SUV pull in near the statue. The thin guy in a dark hoodie and the older one climbed out and pulled tools from the cargo area. Then they slipped on yellow emergency vests, and the skinny one pulled an orange traffic cone out. The third guy remained in the SUV and rolled down the window. His arm dangled outside with a lit cigarette.

The two men in the safety vests dropped the tools behind the statue and circled the base. They stopped at the back corner. Then one put the traffic cone in the parking space nearest the statue. The other guy walked back and forth, in and out of the camera shot. Then the digging started. Delanie wondered if the vests were supposed to make them look like utility workers. The third guy got out of the truck once and circled the statue. After some chatter that Chaz's team could not discern on the security tape, he returned to his vehicle.

The other two men would dig for a while and then check the dirt in the hole. Then they would move on and dig in a new spot. They repeated the process for about twenty minutes. Then the thin one traded his shovel for the pick. He slid his hands around the blocks at the bottom corner. Then he tapped the pick where the cement sealed the blocks together.

Delanie scooted closer to the bank of TV screens to get a better look at the men. The younger one continued to tap along the block's perimeter. A shrill whistle rang out. Delanie watched Chaz's bouncers tear after the guys. Then the SUV gunned its engine and sped off.

"This is the fourth time they've been out there. The other times, they dug holes on the sides but refilled them before they left. They're getting braver. This is the first time they showed up while people were still out and about on the street." Steve's chair squeaked when he leaned forward.

"It looks like they brought props this time. Can you zero in on the Toyota to get a plate?" Delanie asked.

He backed the footage up a few frames and paused the feed. Then he zoomed in and jotted down the license plate. Steve handed her a sticky note.

"Thanks. Could you make me a copy of the footage, too?" she asked.

"You on Dropbox?" he asked.

She nodded and fished out a business card with her email on it. "Use this address."

"He tapped on the keyboard and said, "Done. You should have it."

"Thanks. If they come back, call me. And where did you hide your cameras in a parking lot to get such good angles?"

Steve grinned. "I have my ways...One's on the telephone pole near the street, and the other is on a light pole on the other side."

"Well guys, I'm going to call it a night. Thanks for the adventure. Let me know if you see anything else weird around the statue. And tell Chaz I said hello," Delanie said.

Marco rose and held the door for her. "Will do. I'll walk you out."

Marco escorted her to her car and made sure it started before he jogged back to the club where the night's festivities were in full swing.

Tomorrow, she'd get Duncan on the camera footage and the license plate. He should be able to trace it in no time.

Delanie turned up the radio to keep her awake on the drive home. Her only goal for the near future was to crawl in bed and warm up her frozen fingers and toes.

21

DELANIE DODGED CARS DURING THE LUNCHTIME RUSH AND DARTED through a drive-thru for tacos.

At the office, she found Duncan with his feet propped up on the conference room table. He looked comfortable with his laptop on his stomach. She was not sure if he was napping or working on something. Margaret snored like a moose from under the table.

"Hey," she said. He jumped. "Sorry. Didn't mean to startle you. I brought lunch." Margaret looked up and sniffed the air.

"Thanks. Tacos, Margaret?" The bulldog stood, circled the table, and snorted in agreement.

Delanie spread the food on the table and pulled her laptop out of her messenger bag. "I'm going to send you the footage of the statue diggers. Steve, at the Treasure Chest, got a license plate off the lookout vehicle." She handed him the sticky note with the number.

"Easy peasy." He stuffed the rest of his first soft taco in his mouth. His fingers clicked on his keyboard for a few minutes. "Here it is. It's a 2004 gray Toyota 4Runner, registered to a Peter J. Mills, Jr. at 15815 Tinsbury Place. Let's see." He tapped more keys. "It's a subdivision off of Route 301. And the home owner is listed as Martha M. Mills.

According to Google Maps, it's a smallish blue two story on the corner." His voice faded as he tapped more keys.

"Thanks. There were three guys. Ol' Pete was the lookout."

Duncan handed Margaret part of his taco and wiped his hands on his jeans. "Let's see who Peter J. Mills, Jr. is."

Delanie read emails and cruised the internet while Duncan tapped on his laptop.

"Ding. Ding. Ding. Here's what I found so far," Duncan said.

Delanie opened a blank page and prepped to take notes. "Hit me."

"Martha Mills owns the house. According to tax records, she and her husband owned it for twenty-two years. The husband disappeared off the title in 2015. Pete works as an assistant manager at a Wawa gas station. We already know about the SUV. Let's see what I can find from social media. Hmmm. Not much on his Facebook page. He posted some party pictures about a month ago."

"Can you send me copies? Maybe I can see if any of his drinking buddies are his digging buddies."

Delanie opened the photos he sent and looked through the Treasure Chest video to see if anyone matched.

Duncan spoke and made her jump. "You're into it, huh? There's also a 2014 white Sonata registered to his mom at that address. Pete doesn't have much of a social media presence. Hey, I had a thought."

Delanie waited patiently while Duncan clicked away on his keyboard.

He said, "A-ha!" This time, Delanie and Margaret jumped. "I knew that sounded familiar. Remember when you asked me to look at the plates on cars outside of Snakes and Scales? You know the night they were moving boxes out of the store. That 4Runner was one of the vehicles near the store. It belongs to Pete Mills, and he has some connection to Glen's store."

Delanie furrowed her brown and jotted notes in her file. She was not sure if it was a coincidence or whether it had anything to do with either case, but the information might be a puzzle piece later that connects to something else. She learned years ago to never discard anything. A fragment of information just might be the key to a case's resolution.

"Good to know. Not sure where it will lead, but I wrote it down. I'll do a drive-by of the residence to see what I can see. Any idea which Wawa he works at?"

"Nope," Duncan said.

She grabbed her burner cell phone and Googled numbers for the gas station chain. Noting several near his home, she picked one and called.

When the line connected, she said, "Hi, I'm Amy Nelson, and I was in the store the other day, and I talked with one of your staff, Pete Mills. Is he there by chance?"

It sounded like the person dropped the phone. "Sorry. No. Pete doesn't work here. Can someone else help you?"

"No thanks," Delanie said as the voice clicked off.

She found another store number and dialed again. "Hi, I'm Amy Nelson. I stopped in the store last week, and Peter Mills helped me. Could I by chance talk with him?"

The male voice replied, "He's off today. He'll be back tomorrow around six. Can I help you?"

"I'll stop by tomorrow." She ended the call. "I found which one he works at. I'm going to do a drive-by this afternoon, and maybe I'll pop by the gas station tomorrow for coffee."

"Let me know if you need me to do anything," Duncan said as he returned to his laptop.

"Will do." She picked up the taco wrappers and napkins. "See you later. I'm going to do some snooping."

About thirty minutes later, she parked the Mustang around the corner from the Mills's residence in front of a neighbor's house that was for sale. She hoped that if anyone noticed her, they would think she was looking at the property. The location provided the perfect spying spot for the Mills's house. Putting on Duncan's magic cap with the camera, she grabbed a clipboard in case she needed cover. She pulled out her Nikon with the zoom lens and set it on the passenger seat.

She scanned all the neighbors' houses. Most of the driveways were empty, and she did not see anyone outside this afternoon. Everyone must be at school or work. The Mills's house, a two story with wooden planks, could use some paint. Overgrown bushes bookended a small cement stoop with crooked metal railings. Stray sprigs of grass popped up in the cracks of the sidewalk and the asphalt driveway. No curb appeal.

About the time Delanie was about to call it quits on her stakeout, a dark SUV sped down the street in her direction. The driver pulled into the Mills's driveway and screeched the brakes. Pete slammed the driver's side door and bounded up the three front steps. She snapped several pictures as he disappeared in the house after slamming that door, too.

She grabbed her phone and texted Duncan. *Got any phone numbers for Pete Mills?*

Drumming her fingers on the steering wheel, she watched the house where nothing happened. It felt like time crawled – even though it was minutes before her phone dinged with the text, *Home 438-9903 Cell 212-9833.*

Delanie replied to Duncan's text with a couple of smiley face emojis.

A blue Honda Civic pulled into the driveway behind the 4Runner. She snapped pictures of a tall, thin guy in a gray hoodie who stepped out of the smaller car. He rang the bell and entered when Pete swung the door open. Delanie watched for a little while, and when nothing else happened, she drove out of the subdivision and found a parking lot on the main road where she stopped to make a call.

Pulling out her burner phone, she dialed Pete's home number. It rang and rang. A voice mail with a woman's voice told her she had reached the Mills's residence. Delanie disconnected and called the cell number.

After three or four rings, she heard a gruff, "What?"

"This is Amy Hudson, and I'm conducting a short survey. Would you be interested in answering a few questions?"

"No. You're bothering me. Don't call again." The line went dead.

Friendly sort. She put all of her spying props on the passenger seat and headed home to compare the Treasure Chest video with her photos.

Delanie settled in at her kitchen table with her laptop about a half-hour later and started a file on the Poe statue diggers. Her plan was to visit Pete's job tomorrow and tail him when he left.

She pulled the Civic's license plate number from one of her photos and texted Duncan for another search. So far, she had information on one of the three guys who had an interest in the Poe statue. She was pretty sure the blue Honda Civic guy was one of the guys that Marco's security guys chased. Why were these guys so interested in the statue?

Nothing else from her notes or the pictures jumped out at her. She put everything back in her work bag and rummaged through the kitchen to see what she could throw together for dinner. Delanie realized she probably needed to do a grocery store run this week. Dinner was part of a leftover takeout salad and an ice cream sandwich with a side of mindless, reality TV.

A little after two-thirty, Delanie's phone dinged and jarred her out of a dream about Duncan playing football. She shook off the groggy feeling and the weird dream and checked her burner phone. *Blue Civic belongs to Jamie Jones.* She texted Duncan a thumbs up emoji, turned off the TV, and headed to bed.

In bed, Delanie tossed and turned for what seemed like hours. She replayed all the details that she knew about the Poe diggers. What could they be after? Her thoughts muddled together, and she fell into a fitful sleep.

22

DELANIE ADJUSTED HER PURPLE THIGH-HIGH BOOTS AND HELD THE DOOR at Freeda's for Paisley.

Her friend ran her fingers through her blond ringlets and straightened her Supergirl cape. Deke came through for them with a front row table for the Howl-o-ween drag show. It was Paisley's idea to wear superhero costumes when she saw the costume contest poster on the website. Delanie reluctantly resurrected her Batgirl outfit from RVACon. Duncan would be so proud.

"Hi, Deke. It's Delanie and Paisley," she said, not sure he could recognize her with the full purple mask.

"Of course. You all look great. I'm glad you could join us on this side of the stage. The gals will be thrilled that you're back. They miss you."

Delanie smiled under the costume. "Thanks for setting us up with tickets. We have three more joining us. Oh, this is my friend, Paisley Ford."

"Nice to meet you. You all are at table one. We'll send the rest of your party in when they arrive."

By the time they found their seats and ordered Freeda's famous pink cocktails from Alejandro, Robin and her sister Trish arrived sans costumes. A few minutes later, Paisley's coworker, Cassidy, plopped into the empty seat next to her boss. She sported a full Harley Quinn jester costume.

"Thanks so much for inviting me." Cassidy adjusted her headpiece. "This is going to be a hoot. And these seats are amazing."

"Everybody, this is Cassidy. Cassidy, meet Delanie, Robin, and Trish," Paisley said, pointing at everyone at the table. "Does everyone have singles for tips? If not, I brought a bunch from the shop."

Alejandro dropped off a plate of appetizers and a cheese board as the stage lights flashed and the music blared through the speakers, making conversation difficult. Paisley snapped some photos of the group. Not an empty seat anywhere.

The lights pulsed, and Kiki Jubilee took the stage to a montage of Aretha Franklin songs. At the end, the crowd whooped, and arms with dollar bills flew in the air. Kiki blew kisses and collected her tips.

Tara Byte came out next in her lime green showgirl costume and lip synched to "It's Not Easy Being Green." She switched places with Paige Turner and Kiki Jubilee, who sashayed on stage for a duet of "Ebony and Ivory." At the end, Kiki said, "Whooo hooo. I spy my friend Delanie with my little eye. You look good, girl. Where's Batman?"

A spotlight focused on Delanie's table, and Batgirl waved. Cassidy stood on her chair and whooped. Between her and Kiki, they whipped the crowd into a cheering frenzy.

Paisley poked Delanie in the ribs, "This is so much fun!"

The evening flew by as act after act was better than the previous one. Tara Byte did a great Cher rendition with her aquamarine necklace in its rightful place. It sparkled every time the stage lights hit it.

Deke introduced Anna Conda, and she sang "Happy Birthday" as Marilyn Monroe for all the celebrations in the audience. Ginger Snap relieved her of her microphone and did a medley of "red" songs. She pointed to Delanie when she lip synched Prince's "Little Red Corvette."

And no one in the audience was seated when the entertainers did a medley of Queen songs.

When the applause died down, Kiki stormed the stage and yelled, "Hey, y'all. It's Halloween. Anybody feelin' freaky?" The crowd's roar echoed through the dining area as "Monster Mash" pulsated through the speakers.

All of the queens paraded in the audience and selected a costumed partner. Kiki grabbed Delanie's arm and kissed her on the cheek. Then she led her on stage for the march. Delanie felt the beads of sweat on her forehead from the multitude of stage lights. At the end of the song, they all held hands and took a grand bow.

As the guests returned to their seats, the queens collected the last round of tips, and Deke invited each table on stage for a group picture.

Delanie had not had this much fun in a long time. It was nice to be able to stop by and visit Freeda's and not be spying for work. She had a special place picked out in her office for the group picture.

Cassidy and Paisley left sharing the costume prize of one hundred dollars and tickets to a future Sunday brunch. And even in her Batgirl boots, Delanie was still several inches shorter than all the queens. Best Halloween ever.

23

THE NEXT MORNING, DELANIE DRAGGED HERSELF OUT OF BED AT NINE-thirty. The coffeemaker took too long to make her mood better, so she jumped in the shower. The hot, pulsating water, and steaming caffeine made her feel more human. A piece of buttered toast helped, too. She flipped through her notes again. Why were two millennials interested in the contents of a time capsule in an old statue. And who was the older third guy.

Jotting "Jaime Jones" in her notes, she tapped her pen on the table. Delanie had time to swing by the office before she planned to stake out Pete Mills's job.

She grabbed a pair of jeans, navy sweater, and her tennis shoes. She spent a few minutes in the bathroom pulling her long, red curls in a ponytail and swiping on some lipstick and mascara. Her phone interrupted her beauty routine, such as it was.

"Delanie, this is Rosalind Martin-Black. I hope I didn't catch you at a bad time."

"No, it's good to hear from you."

"After we talked, I went back through my book notes. I'm kind of a packrat. I was curious about the time capsule after you mentioned it. I found some notes from years back when I talked with some folks who had relatives at the dedication. I can confirm the items you listed were in the box that was sealed in the base of the statue. There were also things like magazines and photos included. I'm going to email you a couple of articles and a list of names who were involved in the dedication. I hope this helps," the author said.

"Thank you so much for your time. I look forward to seeing what you uncovered."

"Call me any time. I love talking about Poe and our city's history. And don't forget to let me know what you all find. I'd love to know how this ends."

"Of course. Thanks again for all of your help. It's been invaluable."

"Bye now. We'll chat soon," the woman said with a lilt in her voice.

~

DELANIE FELT MUCH BETTER after her workout. She had settled into her office desk and unpacked all her notes by the time Duncan and Margaret wandered in.

"Working on Chaz's case?" he asked.

She nodded. "The author of the statue book sent me a list of names of people involved with the dedication. Not sure if it'll lead me to anything, but I thought I'd look through the names. A long time has passed."

"I found a few things on your Jaime Jones. I'll send you a file in a minute."

"Thanks," she said to Duncan's back. He and his sidekick made a beeline for the kitchen.

Delanie printed Rosalind's information and updated her notes with Duncan's new finds. According to his secret places on the internet, Jaime Jones, aged twenty-three, worked at his father's pawnshop on Midlothian Turnpike. The blue Civic was registered to the elder Jones. And Jaime's last known address is his father's home at 1967

Neptune Drive near Robius Road. She Googled the address to find a picture of a brick split level.

Gathering up her things, Delanie yelled, "Duncan, I'm going to go spy. I'll be in tomorrow. Call me if you need me."

She heard a muffled, "Be safe" from the back of the office suite.

Delanie pulled into the Wawa on Route 1 after a drive to the other part of the county. She cruised around the building and parked on the side, farthest from the gas pumps and the store. Spotting Pete Mills's 4Runner beside the privacy fence, she settled in to watch the door.

At four minutes after two, the building's black, metal door opened, and a guy dashed out. Delanie barely had time to start the engine before Pete hopped into his SUV and hightailed it out of the lot. She followed from a car length behind, dodging customers headed to the gas pumps. She had to floor it to keep up. A few minutes later, he turned into his subdivision. He drove fast and skidded to a stop in the driveway.

Slamming the front door, he disappeared inside. She was about to check out Jaime Jones's address, when his blue Civic sped around the corner and squealed tires on the driveway behind the SUV. He grabbed a case of beer and a bag from the passenger seat and jogged to the front porch. Pete, wearing jeans and no shirt, opened the door and admitted his friend.

Since she knew where Jaime was, she decided to go peek at his house. After punching in the address in the GPS, Delanie followed the directions to a house in a middle-class neighborhood between the mall and the Bon Air historic district.

White numbers on a black, plastic mailbox matched the address. No cars sat in the driveway. In this neighborhood, kids played in front yards and driveways. She parked down the street and grabbed a lanyard and a clipboard from her spy box in the trunk. Hoping no one looked too closely at the lanyard, Delanie flipped it over, so they would not see that was a backstage pass from a concert.

She picked the house across the street from Jaime's and knocked on the front door. An elderly woman in a flowery housecoat opened the door but stood behind the glass storm door. "May I help you?"

"Yes, ma'am. I'm Nicky McDonald, and I'm validating census information for Chesterfield County. Could you tell me how many live at your residence?"

"Two. My husband Elrod and I, and our two cats, Mamby and Pamby, if you're counting pets. We're the Crawfords."

"Awwwww. I bet your cats are adorable." Delanie smiled and scribbled pretend notes on her clipboard. "Thank you so much. I have two adults for this address. Do you know your neighbors?" she asked, looking at the Jones's house. "I knocked on the door and nobody answered."

"They're never home. Jim Jones lives there. His wife Rosemary died a few years back. He lives there with his son Jaime and that big dog that barks all night. It scares my cats. And I saw the son once with a big snake in the front yard. Lord knows what else he has in that house. It's all gone to pot since the wife died. Rosemary would never have tolerated that boy's behavior."

"So just Mr. Jones and his son. And the dog? And possibly a snake?"

The elderly woman nodded and sighed. Delanie made another note on her clipboard. As she turned to leave, the woman said, "I wish Jim's son would move out. He plays loud music and hangs around the house with his friends when he's not working."

"Where does he work?"

"Jim owns Midlo Pawn, and his son works there sometimes. Not enough if you ask me. He plays that awful music too loud. He's obnoxious when his dad isn't here. If my children had been that rude, they wouldn't have made it to his age. In my day, people were more respectful. And don't get me started on those stupid video games." She let out another heavy sigh.

"Thank you so much for all the information. I appreciate it," Delanie said.

The woman smiled and shut the front door. Delanie saw the

curtains move in the front window. Mrs. Crawford must be the nosy neighborhood watch, a PI's dream.

Delanie jumped in her car and zoomed down Midlothian Turnpike. As she moved from Chesterfield County into southside Richmond, the stores switched from big box retailers to smaller, Mom and Pop places in strip malls. Many of the establishments sported signs in Spanish. Spotting the one for the pawnshop in a block of stores that had seen better days, Delanie made a quick turn and found a parking place where she could watch the front door.

The store lights were on, and a red neon sign blinked "PEN" every few seconds. She spotted guitars, tools, and a drum set in the front window that also advertised "We Buy Gold" and "Specializing in Heirlooms" on yellowed poster board signs.

The door swung open and two guys stepped out on the sidewalk. They chatted and climbed in an older blue Chevy truck. A few minutes later, a tall, man, probably in his late fifties, stepped out on the sidewalk and lit a cigarette. He wore a navy golf shirt with Midlo Pawn embroidered on the front. Delanie reached for her camera and snapped pictures of him in front of the store. Maybe Jaime's father was the older, third guy?

Delanie backed out of the parking spot and told the car, "Call Duncan."

After a couple of rings and Duncan's voice mail, she said, "Hey, Dunc. I have pictures of Jaime Jones's home and work. There is an older guy at the pawnshop. Could you see what you can find on James Jones and Midlo Pawn. See you tomorrow."

She called her friend Paisley Ford. After a few rings, she heard, "Hey girl. What's up?"

"Same old stuff. But we're closing cases. Do you have time this week to grab dinner?"

"How about tonight?" Paisley asked. "We can talk about your latest adventures and your Friends-giving. I have some ideas for table decorations. How about six-thirty tonight? We could meet at Mexico on Hull Street."

"Sounds like a plan. See you then." Delanie ended the call.

DELANIE SEARCHED the internet for information on the Jones family and the pawnshop. On its Facebook page, she saw an ad for its historic collectibles. She printed it and added the page to her collection of seemingly unrelated information.

Glancing at the clock on the stove, she dashed to her room to find something to wear other than a sweater and jeans. Paisley, a hair stylist and fashion plate, always looked like she stepped out of a magazine shoot. Delanie settled on skinny jeans with a black camisole with an oversized, tan cardigan. She rounded out the outfit with her brown boots and bangle bracelets that matched her chunky necklace and earrings. She fluffed her hair and added more makeup than normal.

A little before six-thirty, a hostess seated Delanie near a plate glass window. She perused the menu and checked email. Paisley drifted in about twenty minutes later.

"Sorry," she said, breathlessly. "I had a last-minute walk-in, and it took longer than I expected. Did you order?"

"Just iced tea. How are things?"

"The shop's busy. Even with the addition of Cassidy, my new stylist. I guess that's a good problem to have." Paisley picked up the menu and flipped through the laminated pages.

The waitress returned to freshen Delanie's iced tea and drop off more chips. "May I get you something to drink?"

"A margarita, please. A big one. And I know what I want if you're ready to order."

After jotting down their requests, the waitress returned to the kitchen.

"So how are things with you? Anybody new in your life that I don't know about since Halloween?" Paisley batted her long eyelashes.

"Work's busy. And that's a good thing. Nope. Nobody new. Every once in a while, I go out with Eric, but it's usually dinner or some kind of sporting event."

"The FBI agent?"

Delanie nodded as she scooped salsa with a tortilla chip. "He works a lot too, and he's always assigned to some case somewhere far from here. It's nothing serious. He's fun to hang out with when he's in town. I don't see it being long term." She fiddled with her earring.

Before Delanie could change the subject, Paisley smiled a half-smile and turned her head. "So, what gave you the idea for a Friends-giving?"

"We always head off to other places for the holidays. I thought it would be fun to get together one weekend and have dinner. We haven't had a party in a long time, and I need to catch up with people. Plus, if folks aren't celebrating with families, it'll give them a chance to hang out and eat turkey."

"You know the guys are going to wanna watch football." Paisley pulled the chip basket closer to her side of the table.

"I don't care. It'll be fun to catch up. I'll get a turkey and some of the sides at Publix, and then folks can bring stuff if they want."

"Will Eric be there?" she said in her sing-song voice.

"If he's not working."

"Good. I'd love to meet him, even if he isn't long term" she said with a wink. "What about Robbie?"

"He said he would if he didn't have to work, too."

"It'll be nice to see him again. It's been a long time. Is he seeing anyone?" Paisley asked, straightening the napkin in her lap. She had had a crush on Delanie's wilder brother since elementary school. He always thought of her as his kid sister's annoying gal pal, but that did not stop her friend from flirting.

"He's always dating someone, but I gave up learning their names a long time ago. They're never around long."

The waitress returned and put the hot plates on the table. Delanie dug into her chicken taco salad, while Paisley nibbled on a soft taco. Between bites, she said, "I can bring a pecan pie and my green bean casserole. Who else is coming?"

"Robin, her sister and brother-in-law, you, me, Eric, Duncan and

Evie, maybe Chaz, my new friend Lamar, and Deke. You know people will bring people."

"Of course. Can I bring Will?"

"Sure, but who's Will? I thought you were dating that guy in investments."

Paisley wrinkled her nose and pushed her plate toward the middle of the table. "That was last summer. He was nice and smart, but he smothered me. I am not checking in constantly with a boyfriend. Who has time for that? He'd Facetime or SnapChat me four or five times a day. It got old. I work for a living. It felt like he always wanted to know what I was doing. Anyway, I met Will through one of my clients. He's does social media marketing for some big insurance company, and he's funny. You'll like him. He's not clingy."

Delanie nodded. It was often hard to keep up with Paisley's love life. Before she could respond, her friend said, "Chaz, really? Do you think he has a chance at being Richmond's next mayor?"

"I guess as good as any. The election is next week. He's got a campaign machine going at his club. He hired a publicist, and she's fierce. Oh, you're going to like this. He's also going to open an all-male review in Goochland. That should jazz up the nightlife on the West End."

"We're definitely going to his new place. And you should be able to score us a really good table there, too. Chaz likes you." Paisley wiggled her eyebrows.

"Just friends," Delanie said. "He grows on you after a while."

"It'd be kind of cool to have the next mayor of Richmond at your holiday dinner. Do you have enough chairs? What am I thinking? Do you have enough plates and silverware for everyone?"

"Of course. I have my mom's china and flatware. It's cream colored, so it'll work with the fall theme. I can get folding chairs if I need them. We'll be okay with seating."

"You might be able to be domesticated yet. Have you learned to cook anything? Who am I kidding? How many nights do you eat out?"

"Does take-out count?" Delanie asked.

Her friend laughed as the waitress put the check on the table. "Can I get you all anything else?"

"No, we're fine." Delanie grabbed the check.

"You got it last time."

"But you cut my hair and didn't charge me."

"What are friends for. Let me get the tip." Paisley's blond corkscrew curls bounced as she moved her head and rooted through her purse for her wallet.

They chatted long after the waitress returned Delanie's credit card and continued their conversation in the parking lot for another twenty minutes.

On the drive home, Delanie reached to change the radio channel when a commercial came on that made her pause. It was an ad for a jewelry store that specialized in heirlooms and historical pieces. If the jewelry store in the commercial and the snake store had an online business and backroom, she wondered if the pawnshop had one, too.

Once at home, Delanie switched into a T-shirt and yoga pants and crawled into bed with her tablet and a notebook. She flipped on the TV and found an 80s movie marathon of John Houston films to keep her company.

Clicking around on the internet, she found Midlo Pawn's website. One could buy all kinds of trinkets and baubles online. She scoured the site and looked at their jewelry, coins, stamps, books, and historical souvenirs. Presidential campaign buttons, old coins, Civil War buttons, and early editions of books, many autographed, dominated the most popular list. She wondered if any of the items had provenance. Where did the Joneses get their stock?

24

DELANIE'S PHONE RANG WHILE SHE STOOD IN LINE AT THE DRY cleaners. "Hi, Dunc. What's up?"

"You coming into the office today? I found some stuff on your pawnshop guys."

"How about if I pick up lunch and meet you there? Burgers okay?"

"Sure. Get a plain cheeseburger for Margaret. She chased a squirrel down the street this morning, and we're both recovering from the romp."

After a quick run through a drive-thru, Delanie pulled into a spot in front of Falcon Investigations. Snakes and Scales, with its notice still taped to the door, stood abandoned across the noticeably empty parking lot. It did not feel the same with it closed.

"Duncan!" she yelled from the hallway. "Lunch is here."

Margaret galloped down the hall, followed by her favorite guy.

Once they were seated in the conference room, he pulled wrapped food out of the bags and dug into his burger.

"Thanks. I missed breakfast." He tore a cheeseburger into small bits and put it on the paper wrapper on the floor for Margaret, who wolfed it down.

Delanie grabbed the yellow wrapper before Margaret inhaled that, too. "What did you find?"

Duncan wiped his hands on his jeans and tossed the wrappers in the trash. "I need my laptop." Margaret looked around for French fries. Not finding any more food, she settled under the table on high alert for anything that dropped.

He returned and plopped down in the chair across from her. Delanie admired all the geeky stickers on his laptop lid.

"Okay, Midlo Pawn is owned by James Jones. He owns the house on Neptune Drive. There was a wife listed ten years ago on the tax records, but her name disappeared in 2008. The father drives a red 2000 Volvo S70."

"I talked to one of the neighbors about the son. She complained that he hung around the house too much, playing video games and blasting loud music. The Midlo Pawn has an online business. Lots of coins, stamps, and books. I wondered if the pawn business in Central Virginia was that good. They have a lot of pricey inventory on their site."

"Yet their lifestyle is middle of the road. Nothing flashy." Duncan said, "Using my superpowers, I was able to nose around on his server. There's not much traffic or transactions on their public website. Actually, it hasn't been updated in about three months. You'd think a point of sale site would have more activity. But wait. There's more. I did find another site when I was poking around the dark corners of the internet."

"A second site?"

"Yep. You need special browsers to access it, and a lot of the transactions are done in bit coin. The stuff on this site was a tad sketchy. He goes by NightHistory on this site. He posts stuff like rare coins or first editions. It's a no-questions-asked kind of place."

"Interesting. I'd like to get a look inside his pawnshop, but I'm not sure if he'd recognize me from that night at the Treasure Chest."

"Huh?"

"Marco called me one night. He said that the guys who had been digging around the base of the statue were back. We went out to check it out with some of his security guys. Pete was the lookout. The other two ran, and Marco's guys gave chase. It was dark, but they might have seen me. How about you go with me? If we pose as a couple and I change my look, then maybe we can chat him up about a gift for your dad who's a history buff."

"I'll be Kirk, the boyfriend. Who's a computer programmer and collects high-end comic book memorabilia, and you can be Melanie my girlfriend who's a librarian with a penchant for history, graphic novels, and superheroes."

Delanie wiped off the table. "Okay, but I don't think we need detailed dossiers for this gig. Give me a few minutes. I have some wigs in my office. I think it's a blond kind of day."

She slipped in her office and pulled out a wig from her credenza. In front of the bathroom mirror, she tucked her red curls under the wig and applied a lot of heavy makeup. She would have to send Tara Byte a picture of her new Malibu Barbie look.

On her way back to the conference room, she remembered Duncan's magic hat with its hidden camera. She turned around and headed to the office to grab it. The hat would keep the wig in place since she did not use duct tape like the queens.

"You about ready?" she called to Duncan.

He came out of his office with a bomber jacket over his T-shirt. "Yup. Kirk reporting for duty." He clicked Margaret's leash to her collar, and Delanie followed them out to his Camaro.

Street parking in front of the pawnshop was scarce, so Duncan circled the block. He found an unpaved lot behind the strip mall. They hiked around the building with Margaret sniffing every bit of trash she encountered.

Delanie pulled on the dirty glass door. A sharp electronic squeal sounded when they entered. She reached up and turned on the camera in her cap.

"Hey, folks," the tall, thin man said from behind the glass counter that ran the length of the store. Every inch of space was covered in things that seemed to be loosely grouped by what they were. The cluttered look reminded Delanie of that hoarding reality TV show.

Layers of dust covered most of the wares. She wondered how he kept the inventory organized. It did not look like there was a huge demand for most of the stuff.

"What can I do for you?" he asked.

Duncan cleared his throat. "Hi. My girlfriend, Melanie, and I are looking for a birthday present for my dad. I was hoping to find a cool book or something Civil War related. He's a reenactor, and I'd love to get him something authentic."

"I have quite the collection. All our books are over there." Then the man pointed to a sagging shelf crammed with hardback books and an old set of encyclopedias.

Duncan blew the dust off and flipped through some of the books.

"If you don't find what you're looking for there, I have antique postcards up here and some Civil War stuff in this case. I also have lots of jewelry. Interested in that? Get your girl something pretty."

Delanie batted her eyes and made a beeline for the jewelry. "Oh, honey. There are some pretty rings here, but nothing that your dad would like. But my birthday is coming up soon. I like that big, purple one right there." She tapped the dirty glass cabinet.

Duncan pretended to look at the rings before he wandered to another counter under a 1980s security camera. "I'm thinking something from the Civil War. What do you have besides minié balls and buttons?"

"What did you have in mind? I may be able to call around and get it if I don't have it," the man said.

"I'm thinking like a good Civil War relic that his buddies wouldn't have. Got anything belonging to anyone famous?" Duncan asked.

"Not here. But I do in my private collection. I've got a lot of daguerreotypes and photos. I have a locket that once belonged to Varina Davis. And I have a key to the Lee family house." Delanie stared at the tall man. A scraggly beard, with more gray than brown, outlined his gaunt face. His hooded eyes gave him a lethargic look.

"I've got a Stonewall Jackson pocket watch, too," he added.

"How much for the pocket watch?" Duncan leaned over the glass cabinet. Margaret got bored and sat on his foot.

"It's authentic, so I couldn't let it go for less than three thousand."

"What kind of documentation comes with it?" Duncan asked.

The older man's brow furrowed. "It's as is."

"Let me think about it. I want to get him a good gift, but that's a bit steep in the price department."

Delanie walked slowly up the aisle next to the glass case, making sure to capture the contents. She did a lap of the store.

"Well, honey, what do you want to do?" Delanie sidled up to Duncan and grabbed his arm.

"Three thousand is a lot. Maybe we could think on it. Do you have a card?" Duncan asked.

The man pulled out a bent business card from his shirt pocket and pushed it across the case to Duncan.

"How about we go back and look at that Civil War knife that guy on Route 1 had?"

"Okay," she said in a singsong voice.

The store owner did not try to coax them back with another offer.

Once inside Duncan's yellow car, Delanie turned off the camera. She left the wig on in case the man was watching from the store. "The inventory looks kind of stale."

Duncan checked to see if Margaret had settled in the back seat. "I think they make most of their money online, where the buyers don't care whether its authentic or not. I doubt they had anything controversial or of questionable origin in the store. They're inspected by police from time to time."

"Let's go back and look through his websites. Maybe there's a clue there. Do you think his stuff is fake?"

"Dunno. But it also might be hot. On the dark web, there is a huge market for stolen art and relics. Collectors want real things, and they don't care if they're stolen. There are lots of people who buy this kind of stuff just to say they have it. And most of the time, no one else asks any questions."

Delanie raised her eyebrows. "I'm sure there's a lot of counterfeit stuff out there, too. If you tell a good story, you can always find someone who'll fall for the snake oil." When they were far enough from the pawnshop, she pulled off the hat and wig and fluffed her curls.

Duncan gunned the yellow car's engine and roared down Midlothian Turnpike. "Let's go see if we can tell if what they have online is stolen or fake."

25

DELANIE DROPPED HER MESSENGER BAG AND KEYS ON THE TABLE, KICKED off her shoes in the living room, and jumped into bed with her clothes on. She and Duncan had finished at the office about twenty minutes ago. They spent hours pouring over James Jones's site on the dark web. They inventoried the high dollar items and did as much research as they could on them. With the help of a relic hunters' site that Duncan found, they determined that at least twenty items had been stolen at one time from either small museums or private collections. They could not tell whether the Joneses stole the items or whether they were just trafficking them. Either way, the business was not on the up and up.

The pocket watch he mentioned had been stolen from an antique store in Fredericksburg, Virginia. And the Varina Davis locket was missing from a Daughters of the Confederacy collection in Alabama. The dusty pawnshop must be the front for the online relic business.

She rolled over and the next thing she remembered was her phone buzzing across the nightstand. She wiped the sleep out of her eyes and reached for the phone. Sun streaming in through the curtains did not indicate what time it was. But her phone did – seven-thirty in the morning.

"Hi, Chaz." She tried not to sound as groggy as she felt.

"Hey. It's election day. I didn't wake you, did I?"

"No, it's okay. I'm excited for you."

"I was hoping you could come down to campaign central some-time this afternoon or evening. Polls close at seven tonight, so the results should come in after that. Bring your pal Duncan if he's available. I appreciate all of your help. We're going to celebrate tonight. No matter what happens."

"Sounds good. I'll see what he's up to today."

"Great. And tell all your Richmond friends to get out and vote. Team Chaz!"

"Will do." She clicked off and rolled over for a couple more hours of sleep.

AFTER TWO ESPRESSOS and a hot shower, Delanie felt more human and ready to deal with Chaz. She found Margaret and Duncan in the conference room finishing off tuna sandwiches and watching all the local news channels on the big screen.

"What's up?" She sat in a chair across from Duncan.

"Your boy's been on all the stations today. Earlier, they showed him and his entourage at the polls. I'm sure that was exciting for the folks at his polling place. Quite a show."

Delanie smiled. "He invited us to come by campaign central this afternoon. He said they're having a party regardless of the election outcome."

Duncan looked sheepish. "I can't. Evie and I have a date. And I'd rather not take her to the Treasure Chest."

"Not a problem. I'll explain that you're tied up. I'll go."

"You know there's a chance he could win this thing," he said.

"I think he really wants it. He's been pulling some of his stunts, but they haven't been over the top. I think his publicist has been keeping him on a short leash, and he's trying to appeal to the respectable masses. It should make for an interesting evening."

"It might be kind of cool being the mayor's go-to folks for research. I'm okay with it as long as he keeps paying us," Duncan said with a smirk.

"Find anything else on the Civil War items?"

"Just a couple more that were reported stolen. But none of the thefts are recent."

"Isn't it brazen to offer stolen items for sale?" she asked.

"It's buried deep in the dark web. He probably thinks that the owners won't be looking there. Plus, the reward may outweigh the risk. And some guys do it for the thrill. Or he might just be the middleman."

She pulled out her laptop and woke it up. "Rosalind Martin-Black, the author, sent me a list of people who were at the dedication of the statue. I'm going to see what I can find on the history sites. I'll send you the list. Not sure if any of them will turn up in the dark places you hang out."

Delanie emailed him the list and became engrossed in her search. She found tidbits on local history and genealogy sites about the mayor and a couple of the council members present at the statue's dedication.

Duncan yelled, "Shazam!"

Delanie jumped and stared at him. "What?"

"I searched the names on your list and found something interesting. There's a story on a conspiracy site about your statue. And the Joneses may have come across this too since they're all over the dark web. Right before the statue's unveiling, a jewelry shop owed by a Mr. Thomas P. Keller was burgled. He reported a bunch of things missing, but the most curious was a very valuable 1849 O Liberty coin. Here's where it gets sketchy. It's rumored that Mr. Keller, one of the guys present at the statue's dedication, had something to do the with robbery in order to collect the insurance money for the missing items. The police never recovered the stolen items. One of his relatives told the blogger who wrote the article that it was family lore that Keller had put the coin in a time capsule of the Poe statue to get rid of the evidence."

Delanie sat up straight in her chair. "Do you think the legend has any truth to it?"

"It seems to fit with what they're doing. If they read it, it could explain why they're so interested in that particular time capsule." Duncan scrolled through the article on his screen.

"How do we catch them in the act? I don't think they've been back since Marco's guys chased them off."

Duncan shrugged. "You either wait for them to make the next move, or you think of something to force their hand."

"Definitely the latter. I think we need to do something. But let me give it some thought. Right now, I have to pack up and go home to find something to wear to Chaz's shindig. I'm sure I'll be overdressed for a strip club celebration."

AROUND SIX-THIRTY, Delanie locked the Mustang and texted Marco. Her phone dinged with, *Meet me at the back door.*

By the time she climbed the cement steps, Marco had opened the door. "Hi. Chaz will be glad to see you. He's a bundle of energy today." Marco sported a black #TeamChaz T-shirt with his standard black jeans and leather boots.

Delanie smiled. "I can imagine. It's a big day. Nice T-shirt."

"We all got one. Come on back," he said.

Delanie followed him down a hallway next to the club. Lights and music pulsated from the pirate-themed club. Marco held the conference room door for her.

"Hey, look who it is," Chaz yelled as he lifted her off the ground with a bear hug. Then he grabbed a red #TeamChaz ball cap of the table and plunked it on her head. Everyone in the room had either a hat or a campaign button.

"Hi, Chaz," she said when she was back on firm ground. "It's good to see you. How are you?"

"Results will be coming in after seven. I'm a little antsy. Help yourself to food and drinks. We're having a party here tonight. So enjoy!"

Chaz buzzed around the room like he had had one too many espressos.

"She scanned the conference room. Marco stood quietly near the door. Chaz's publicist, Petra, in a sleek navy-blue suit, stood next to the bar with two men in dark suits. The taller of the two was Chaz's lawyer, Rick Dixon. Other friends mingled or sat in the overstuffed conference room chairs that had been pushed back against the walls. A large flat screen TV, tuned to a local station, hung muted on the far wall.

Delanie put a few hors d'oeuvre on a gold plate. She picked at a stuffed mushroom and sampled the crab dip. A couple at the bar immediately sucked her into their conversation. They introduced themselves as Justin Collins, the beer distributor, and Kathy Ray, Chaz's caterer. Kathy spent the next twenty minutes excitedly detailing her duties as caterer for a large swath of Richmond's party-goers. And not to be outdone, Justin interjected random facts about being a top beer guy for the mid-Atlantic region. Delanie listened politely about the beer and food consumption at Central Virginia restaurants and clubs.

Thankfully, Chaz interrupted the chatter when he stood in a chair. "Shhhhh! Everyone. It's after seven, so all the polling places are closed. He clicked the sound button on the remote and climbed down from the chair. The guests huddled around the TV as the local anchors interrupted *Wheel of Fortune*.

The talking heads mentioned the mayoral race and showed pictures of the four candidates. Then they showed clips of all of them voting in their own districts with voice-overs of why they were the best candidates. The male newscaster said that they would interrupt regular programming when there were results. In the meantime, a red ticker would scroll across the bottom of the screen with updates.

All conversation ceased and all eyes were glued to the TV. Steve, the surveillance guy, popped in and whispered something to Marco and exited as quickly as he appeared. Marco cleared his throat and said in his deep baritone voice, "Camera crews are setting up in the parking lot."

Chaz was in his element. He slicked back his blond hair and adjusted the collar on his red silky shirt. Chaz always wore clothes from the hipster generation, a demographic he had aged out of years ago. Petra stepped over and put her hand on his shoulder. She said something to him and handed him a mint. He took several deep breaths and turned toward the TV.

Delanie's palms were sweaty as the red ticker announced the preliminary counts from all the precincts. At ten minutes after seven, Chaz was leading the other candidates. Tossing her plate and plastic utensils in the trash, she grabbed a Coke and sat down next to the beer distributor. As the hour wore on, Elrod Meekins, Christine Addison, and Chaz bounced in and out of first place. Ron Jenkins lagged behind the others in last place.

Delanie had never seen Chaz this nervous, even when he was accused of murdering the last mayor. He was stoic much of the time he was arrested and thrown into jail. He alternated between pacing the floor and checking his phone.

By seven-thirty, Chaz and Christine Addison kept changing first and second places every time the results crawled across the screen. The gentlemen's club owner could hardly contain himself. Rick Dixon moved over and stood beside Chaz and Petra. He put his hand on his client's shoulder and whispered something in his ear. It did not calm Chaz for long. He continued to buzz around the room.

The group chatted through *Wheel of Fortune* and *Jeopardy*. When some police procedural started at eight o'clock, the newscasters interrupted with updates.

"Shhh! Shhhh! Shhhh!" Chaz commanded as he blasted the TV's volume.

The female newscaster said, "The race is too close to call. Only eighty-four votes separate the leader, Christine Addison, from second place, Charles Wellington Smith, III. Stay tuned. We'll be back in the next hour with updates."

The male newscaster commented, "Yes, this one is a nail-biter. We've got ourselves a horse race between retired school principal

Addison and gentlemen's club owner, Smith. Stay tuned. We'll bring you all the latest information."

Chaz lowered the volume and headed to the bar for a Diet Coke. Petra and Rick bookended him and guided him toward the table. The rest of the room huddled in small groups with an eye on the TV.

The two talking heads on the local news interrupted every hour for an update that the race was too close to call. Finally, minutes before the eleven o'clock news, the channel put up a teaser about the mayoral race. The room fell silent. Everyone stared at the television set.

After updates about a robbery in the Fan and a car crash in Midlothian, the male newscaster announced that Christine Addison was the new mayor of Richmond. She beat local businessman, Charles Wellington Smith by one hundred and sixty-nine votes. The mood in the room deflated, and everyone looked at Chaz.

He paused for a minute and then raised both arms and fist pumped the room. "Nobody thought it would ever be this close. We did a damn good job, folks. We almost won this thing. We outperformed everyone's expectations!"

The room cheered. When the roar died down, Rick Dixon asked, "Are you going to request a recount?"

"Nah," Chaz said. "Christine will make a wonderful mayor. I got to know her quite well through all this, and she's what Richmond deserves. I'm going to get my jacket and head out to the parking lot to give my concession speech. I'd appreciate it if you'd join me."

The group, still sporting #TeamChaz gear, paraded out to the parking lot behind Chaz and his staff. The candidate found his mark behind the lights and the cameras on tripods. All the local TV stations had cameras next to those from out of town stations and a gaggle of print reporters, who were vying to get closer to the action. He turned slightly, so that the Treasure Chest's neon sign featured prominently in the shot.

"Thank you all for coming and for all of your support. We fought a long, hard campaign. I want to thank my team for all of the time and energy they put into this endeavor. I wouldn't be here without you all. I think Richmond elected a wonderful mayor in Christine Addison, and I wish her the best. And I will do what I can to support her. Congratulations, Christine. You'll be a great mayor."

The reporters called "Chaz, Chaz, over here" and peppered him with questions for the next half hour. Finally, Chaz threw his hand in the air. "Thanks, everyone. You've been great. Come see me at the Treasure Chest." He turned, and his entourage followed him back inside to the main stage. The music and lights no longer pulsated. Someone had set up a banquet table with balloons and confetti.

Steve handed Chaz a microphone. "Thank you all for your support. Please eat and drink up. It's a party. Second place isn't too bad for a strip club owner who everyone dismissed early on." The group cheered. Hundreds of clientele and guests filled plates and glasses.

Delanie wended her way through the noisy crowd to get to Chaz. "Thank you so much for inviting me. I need to head out soon. I'm sorry that you didn't win," she said, close to his ear.

"I'm good. I never thought I would do this well. Thanks for all of your help." He hugged her. When he turned to chat with other well-wishers, Delanie headed home.

Her phone dinged.

Heard your boy came in second, Duncan texted.

Bittersweet, she responded.

Delanie put the car in gear. It had been a long night, but she still needed to see if she could prod the diggers back into action.

26

THE NEXT AFTERNOON, DELANIE WAS TIRED OF WAITING FOR SOMETHING to happen. She gathered her things and headed for her car. She decided to do a drive-by of Pete Mills's property to see what she could see.

About twenty minutes later, she found a spot down the street where she had a good view of Pete's front door. His SUV sat in the driveway with Jaime Jones's car parked behind it. It must be game time for the dynamic duo.

When nothing exciting happened in the quiet neighborhood, she fished out her burner phone and dialed Pete's cell.

After a few rings, a gruff, "What?" answered her call.

"Mr. Mills? This is Joyce Taylor, and I'm conducting a short survey about your TV and movie preferences. Do you have a few minutes to answer a very short survey? You could win a $25 Amazon card."

"Porn. That's my favorite. Did I win the gift card? Cause I'll buy more porn. And you're interrupting our game. Stop bothering me." He clicked off.

Delanie started the car and drove to the Jones's house. Maybe she could find something there while the two younger guys were preoccupied with their video games.

About thirty minutes later and a stop for an iced tea, Delanie pulled into the street where Jaime Jones lived with his father. The house looked empty. No cars in any of the nearby driveways either. She parked several houses down in front of the yard with the for sale sign and settled in to watch.

A school bus passed by, along with several other cars. She counted things in the nearby yards to pass the time. Stakeouts were her least favorite part of the job.

As she grabbed her phone to check email, an older red Volvo putted down the street and pulled into the Jones's driveway. The car knocked and gurgled after the man shut the engine off. Stepping out, he left the driver's door open.

He walked to the curb and checked the mailbox. He stuffed the contents under his arm and returned to his car, grabbing a backpack and several boxes from the front seat. He kicked the car door shut and headed for the porch. He disappeared into the house a few minutes later.

Delanie caught a glimpse of movement at the neighbor's house. She thought she saw Mrs. Crawford's curtains move in the front window.

Delanie settled in to see what else would happen. A neighbor two doors down arrived home and checked his mail. Delanie felt creaky and wanted to stretch.

At about the time she was thinking about bagging the stakeout, Jim Jones exited the house from the side door with three cardboard boxes. She slipped her keys and phone in her jeans pockets and stole out of the Mustang. Her quarry had turned the corner to the back-yard, so she jogged down the driveway.

She tiptoed around the side of the house, listening for any sound of footsteps approaching. At the corner, she paused and then peeked around for a quick glimpse.

The elder Jones sat his boxes on the ground and unlocked three locks on a back door. He pushed the door open and picked up his boxes and retreated inside. He wanted to keep something secure with all those locks.

A few minutes later, Jim Jones stepped out of the door, looked behind him, and turned toward Delanie. She ducked around the corner. Her heart pounded. She hoped he did not see her. She waited. Every second that passed felt like minutes.

When he did not appear, she took a glance at the backyard. Reaching for his phone, James Jones paced around the patchy grass area near the door. Delanie caught only snippets of his conversation. He waved his free arm around a lot and punctuated his key points with fist pumps. It looked intense. He forgot to close the door.

In case he turned the corner suddenly, she ducked behind a large oak tree. She hoped he did not notice her movement. As she caught her breath, she waited and listened.

Footsteps approached, so she made herself as small as she could behind the trunk. Jim Jones opened his car door and threw a box inside. The he started the car that sputtered and jerked. The car belched a small, gray cloud when the man backed out of the driveway.

Her heart pounded. She took several deep breaths to calm down enough to take advantage of James Jones's absence.

Delanie ran around the back of the house. The door to the storage area still hung open. Flipping on her flashlight app, she scanned the room.

Large metal shelves lined three walls from the floor to the ceiling. Rooting around, she found a stack of paintings wrapped in bubble wrap. Plastic bins of wrapped jewelry boxes and boxes of old books filled the first two shelves. Dust mites tickled Delanie's nose.

Each shelf contained boxes and bins of things that looked like antiques. She tried to peek inside containers and not disturb anything. She tiptoed from shelf to shelf.

Delanie turned and stubbed her toe on a white R2D2-looking thing that made a sloshing sound. Suppressing a yelp, she recognized it as a dehumidifier. Delanie gulped in a deep breath and continued to explore the remaining shelving units. The one in the back had three shelves full of large wooden boxes. She lifted the lid on the first one to find what looked like a large partitioned jewelry box filled with coins in cardboard mounts. She took pictures of her finds.

The door moved and creaked. She turned in a panic as the door opened slowly. Spotting an empty space in the back, Delanie found a corner to hide as best she could. She extinguished the light on her phone and held her breath. She strained to listen for any approaching noise.

Was Jim Jones back? How was she going to explain her presence on his property? What if she got trapped inside the storage area?

27

Delanie's heart leapt in her throat. She counted to one hundred by fives. After a deep cleansing breath, she listened. The wooden door slowly creaked and inched open. Hide or attack? Her pulse beat in her temples.

Delanie froze, listening for footsteps or anyone turning the door handle or locks. Her fear was that he had returned and remembered that he had left the door unlocked.

The only sound was her heartbeat pounding in her ears. Adrenaline flushed through her. She tried to think of an excuse to explain why she was trespassing in the pawnshop owner's storage room. Nothing plausible came to mind.

Delanie willed her heart rate to calm down. She had to focus and be ready to confront whomever was outside that door. She listened for what felt like ages. Nothing moved, and she did not hear anything over the slight hum of the dehumidifier.

She waited another ten minutes and then a few minutes more. Nothing happened. To kill time, Delanie decided to check out the last set of shelves and then see if the coast was clear. That might give whomever it was time to go somewhere else.

She clicked on her flashlight application. Poking through the last few boxes, she took pictures of heirloom jewelry in small velvet bags. Mostly brooches and earrings. There were two small dinner purses with intricate beaded designs on the sides. The beads looked like real pearls. She carefully put everything back in the larger box. Delanie snapped more photos and gingerly stepped around the dehumidifier on the floor.

All was still silent outside. Maybe it was time to peek out. As she crept toward the door, it moved again and creaked. She froze with nowhere to hide. She hid her phone to douse the light.

She strained to hear anything. Eerily quiet. And the door stayed put.

Then she heard someone yell, "Cooper, Cooper. Where are you?" It sounded like a female voice. Good. Not one of the Joneses.

She took a deep breath and stepped toward the door. Her eyes adjusted to the darkness with only a faint outline of light around the frame. The door creaked again, and bright light rushed in through the crack.

Then she saw something long and tan that made a sniffing noise. She aimed her flashlight app at the door and spotted a dog nose protruding through the door's opening.

She let out a sigh of relief that echoed in the storage area. A large golden retriever sniffed around the door.

"Cooper. Cooper, get back in your yard. Come here, boy. Do you want a treat?"

At the magic word, the nose disappeared, and Delanie heard galloping.

Deciding not to press her luck further after being exposed by Cooper, she waited a bit and then slipped out of the storage area and shut the door.

She crept around the side of the house and walked briskly to her car. She did not feel safe until she slammed the driver's door and started the engine. She checked that the doors were locked and then sped out of the neighborhood.

When Delanie felt calmer, she did a drive-thru for comfort food and an early dinner. She headed home to peruse the photos from today's snooping session at the Joneses. Duncan would love her Cooper story.

THE WHOLE JEWELRY store robbery bothered Delanie. She spent the next morning at the office researching the business, Thomas P. Keller, and his family. The family store sat on a block of Broad Street in the downtown area. According to online city maps, it had been a boarding house in the 1800s that had been replaced by an apothecary and later a restaurant. The first instance of the Keller jewelry store was three blocks down and on the other side of the main thorough-fare. The wooden structures had been torn down to make way for more modern buildings in the early twentieth century. The Keller jewelry store had been one of the first tenants of the modernized stores. Delanie jotted the address in her notes. According to Google Maps, a shoe store currently occupied the site.

She trekked into the kitchenette for a mug of coffee, hoping the caffeine and sugar would ward off the fog of sitting at her computer so long.

The last drips of coffee landed in her mug, and the machine gurgled. She blew on the steam and returned to her office to review her notes on the Kellers.

Delanie filled up several pages on the history of the jewelry store from a family genealogy page that listed quite a few generations. She printed the names and Googled the ones that were born after World War II. Maybe with any luck she could find some living relatives.

The jeweler, Thomas Keller, had three sons and a daughter. She let out a squeal when she found Chip Marshall, a son of the Keller daughter. According to the application that Delanie used to find people, Marshall lived in Richmond's West End and worked as a realtor.

She left a voice mail for him, hoping that he would respond. Her stomach growled to let her know that it was past the normal lunch hour. She packed her things and did a drive-thru run for a chicken sandwich and a frozen lemonade.

Without anything else pressing on her calendar, she decided to do a drive-by downtown to get a look at where the Keller store once stood. Maybe it would spark an idea or two about today's mystery of the Poe statue.

After getting stuck in traffic before the tollbooth, she finally exited the Downtown Expressway and cruised down Broad Street, making sure to stay clear of the Pulse bus lanes. Delanie found a one hour parking lot near the block where the jewelry store once stood.

She grabbed her bag and walked around the corner to the store's front. She pulled out a copy of an old photo she found online. Some of the original architecture around the front door and the three windows on the second level were the only traces of the previous store. The bricks had been painted a bright blue to match the new LED sign for the sneaker store.

Opening the glass door, Delanie stepped inside as a shrill sound announced her entrance. Two guys behind the counter looked up. "Hey," the taller one said. "If we can help you with something, let us know."

She smiled. "I'm Delanie, and I have a weird question. I'm researching the history of the jewelry store that inhabited this building in the early 1900s." She held up the picture of Keller's for the men to see. "I was curious to see if there was anything left here from the jewelry store days."

The taller of the two men laughed. "That was a long time ago. I'm Dannell Taylor, and this is my brother DeShawn. When we opened this store five years ago, we leased the first floor. The second has been converted to an apartment."

"When we moved in, we found lots of clothing racks, hangers, and a box of 1970s ties, but that was about it. The place has been a couple of different stores before we moved in. There weren't any safes or jewelry cases or any hidden jewels to be found," DeShawn said. "There's a room in the back without windows. It's kinda small and boxy. It might have been some kind of vault or something. Too bad we didn't find any jewelry. We use the room now as a breakroom."

"Thanks for your time. I wanted to see if anything remained from the jewelry store's former life."

"It would have been nice to find a bag of forgotten jewels or gold," DeShawn said laughing. "Feel free to walk around. If you change your mind and need new kicks, let me know."

Delanie wandered to the front window and snapped a picture. She held up the black and white photos again of a bygone era.

"Thanks," Delanie said as she waved at the Taylor brothers. She stopped to take another photo of the front of the store on her way out.

Her phone rang and a number she did not recognize popped up.

"Hello. Delanie? This is Chip Marshall returning your call."

"Mr. Marshall, I'm doing research on your family's jewelry store from the early part of the last century, and I was wondering if you had a few minutes to talk."

"I'm closing up a house right now after a showing. I'm free after three. I'm in the Chesterfield area near Hull Street Road."

"How about three o'clock at the Starbucks at Hancock Village?" she asked.

"How about three-thirty at the one next to Panera that's further east?" he countered.

"Sounds good. Thank you for your taking the time to talk to me. See you soon." Delanie returned to the suburbs and found a parking spot in front of the busy shops about fifteen minutes ahead of her appointment with the realtor.

After ordering an iced white chocolate latte and snagging the only empty table. She sat with her back to the wall, so that she could see out the large window and watch the door.

About twenty minutes later, a short man in a white dress shirt and khakis entered and looked around. She checked her phone for a photo match from his website. He looked like an older version of the picture.

Delanie waved, and he walked over and set his briefcase in the empty chair.

"Hi, I'm Chip Marshall. Delanie?" He extended his hand. "I'm going to get some coffee. I'll be back in a minute."

When he returned to the table with his drink, he put his briefcase on the floor. "What can I help you with?" He stirred his steaming coffee.

"I'm doing some research on your family's jewelry store. Actually, I'm researching the contents of the time capsule from the Poe Statue and that led me to your grandfather's story," she said.

"Oh, the famous heist." He settled back in the metal chair. "There's lots of legend and family lore about that."

"I'd appreciate any information that you can share."

He took a sip of his coffee and paused. "There are family tales and conspiracy theories. I take it you've been on the internet?"

She nodded. He paused and then smiled with no other response. Delanie wondered what his reaction would be.

"The story went viral on the internet. I get calls from time to time for interviews from bloggers. Anyway, there was a theft. My grandfather used to tell the story at all family gatherings. He and his assistant opened the store that fateful morning to find some glass cases shattered and valuables missing. Back then, they left valuables in the cases overnight. The security was a lot different."

"So, what were the family theories?" Delanie asked.

"When I was small, the kids were always sent off to another room. We'd eavesdrop on the adult conversations. My grandfather got the insurance money eventually, but the business never really recovered, and he had to shut down the store. There was always talk when he wasn't around that cast a shadow on his innocence. My relatives hinted that he might have been in on the planning of the whole thing. The police always thought it was an inside job, but no one was ever charged. And the police never recovered any of the items. And as far as I know, the stuff has never turned up anywhere else either. I mean like it wasn't in my mother's jewelry box or anything."

"What's your theory?" Delanie asked.

"My grandfather was what we'd call a grifter today. He was always looking for easy money or ways to get things from other people." The realtor snickered.

"I read a story online that claims your grandfather hid the stolen items in the time capsule in the statue." Delanie took a long sip of her iced coffee.

"I read that, too. Not sure if it's true or not. But if so, that would finally solve the mystery of what happened to the loot." He glanced down at his phone.

"According to Rosalind Martin-Black's book, your grandfather was at the Poe statue dedication." Delanie pulled the book from her purse and found the page with the black and white picture of dignitaries around the statue on dedication day.

He stared at the picture and then flipped through the pages. "That one is definitely my grandfather." He tapped the image of a short man in the dark suit and fedora. "I'll look through my parents' photos when I get home. Give me your email, and I'll let you know what I find."

"Thank you." She fished a Falcon Investigations card out of the bottom of her purse. "There were no family stories about ever finding out if the rumors were true?"

"No. Not that I know of. My mother thought it was all gossip. I guess they were always a little afraid that he had engineered the robbery," Chip Marshall said.

"I'll let you know if I find anything more. I appreciate your time."

"Not a problem. And if you ever decide to buy a home, let me know. I'm going to head out. I have calls to make. But let me know if you find the stolen items. I'd love to know how the story turned out. I always thought he had something to do with it." Chip Marshall rose and picked up his briefcase.

At home, Delanie updated her notes with today's finds. Then she spent the rest of the evening searching for anything related to the Keller burglary on the internet.

She texted Duncan to see if he could find any other information about Thomas Keller. If there is more out there, her partner would find it. And maybe some truths were buried among the theories and wild conspiracies.

28

DELANIE'S PHONE RANG AS SHE STOOD IN LINE AT THE POST OFFICE.

"Hey, Delanie. This is Chip Marshall. I went home after we talked and went through some old boxes in the attic. You made me curious about my grandfather and his possible involvement in the sordid tale." He continued before she could comment, "I found a couple of things I'd like to show you. Do you have some time this week?"

"How about this afternoon or tomorrow morning?" she asked.

"This afternoon is good. Same place. How about three?" Chip, always the negotiator.

"See you then." Delanie had enough time to finish her errands and meet the realtor to see what he had to share. She hoped it was something definitive about the missing items from so long ago. Otherwise, her leads were drying up.

The coffee shop stood empty except for two baristas when Delanie arrived, so she ordered a peach tea and found a table near the door.

By the time she had skimmed through her email, the realtor wandered in. He took off his fancy sunglasses and nodded at her. He ordered coffee and joined her.

"Thanks for meeting me." He put his briefcase on the table,

snapped the latches, and pulled out several items. "I hadn't thought about my grandfather and the robbery in years. You piqued my interest with your questions. I went home and dug through the attic. I found some old boxes, filled with stuff my mother had collected through the years. She came up during the Depression era, so she kept everything. Anyway, there were several boxes full of my grandfather's appointment books. Here's one from 1913 and another from when the jewelry store went under in the twenties."

Delanie flipped through the yellowed pages of the small leather book that detailed Keller's schedule for the fateful year of the burglary.

"I also found my mom's diaries. This one was about the time of the scandal." He handed her a small red, leather-bound book. The spine had cracked, and the attached ribbon had frayed into a fuzzy pompom.

Delanie opened the diary to a page in the middle and glanced at the neat, loopy handwriting that had started to fade. "May I make a copy of these?"

He fished through his briefcase again. "Already thought of that. My assistant took care of that for me this morning." He handed her two clipped stacks of photocopies. After she took them, his hand lingered in midair, waiting for the calendar and diary.

She handed over the originals.

"I read through a lot of them until the wee hours. It was a new perspective of my family for me. I still don't know what to think. My mother doesn't believe that her dad was involved. She was daddy's little girl, and he could do no wrong in her eyes. I'm still on the fence. There's definitely room for suspicion," Chip Marshall said.

"Thank you so much for sharing these. I'll go through them and see what I can find."

"Keep me posted on what you uncover." He rose, put on his sunglasses, and snapped his briefcase shut. "Gotta run. Houses to sell. Good luck with the investigation."

Delanie grabbed her tea and drove to the nearby Rockwood Park. She found a quiet spot near the nature center and the hiking trails.

Rolling down the windows, she read through Chip's photocopies, making notes and marking items of interest. She read through the documents twice as twilight fast approached. The breeze caused her to shiver. Starting the car, she put on the heat to knock off the evening chill.

Most of Thomas Keller's calendar detailed appointments with clients and vendors. She spotted some patterns and wanted to think about it some more. The diary was an interesting read, mostly about day-to-day things that a young woman thought about. It was light and cheery with memories about parties, beaus, and school. It turned darker after the jewelry store heist. The daughter, Elizabeth, blamed the crooks for causing her family's world to turn upside down. People whispered and rumors flew. They did not get as many social invitations as they had in the past, and her favorite boyfriend said he could not see her any more. Elizabeth knew it was because everyone thought her father was in on the theft. She devoted pages to declaring his innocence without much substance to back up her claims.

The diary ends abruptly after she wrote about a church picnic where some of the older women whispered about Elizabeth and her family. It ended on a rant about how so-called family friends whispered about her father and his scandal. Delanie wondered if there was another book that documented the rest of the story.

Not wanting to go home, she told the car to call Duncan.

After a couple of rings, he said, "Hey."

"Hey back at you. What are you up to?"

"Nothing. Margaret and I are just watching a marathon of *The Twilight Zone*. What's up?"

"Chip Marshall, a descendant of Thomas Keller, the jeweler, found some family mementos. I read through them, and I think I see some patterns. I was just wondering if you had some time to help me go through it. I think I need someone to talk it out with."

"Yeah, sure. Have you eaten?"

"Nope."

"Margaret and I will pick up a pizza and meet you at the office in a few."

"Sounds good. See ya." She backed out of the parking lot under the thick canopy of trees and chased the last bits of sunset down Hull Street Road.

After pizza and hours of pouring over all the names in Chip's family documents, Delanie and Duncan created a spreadsheet of anyone mentioned.

"Cool spiderweb," she said, after Duncan graphed the data.

"These dots are all the people, so we can see who Thomas Keller connected with most. I can convert it to a graph by date if we want to look for patterns. He seems to meet with friends and jewelry distributors on a regular basis. And he had a lot of civic group meetings. Sometimes a visual helps."

"And don't forget the rotary club and the local business council." She reached for her notes on the case to see if any of the names matched the ones at the statue's dedication. "Hmmm. I was hoping that some of these folks would match the photos in the statue book. The only repeats are Thomas Keller and the mayor."

Duncan and Margaret looked at her. "This is a really cold case," he said.

"I was hoping to find some connections. That fizzled."

"I think you did a good job. Without having a smoking gun, our hunch is that Thomas Keller was involved with and profited from his store's burglary. And conspiracy theorists on the net think that he took the money and hid the loot in the time capsule."

"Yep. You're right. I think this case is beyond frigid, and we're not going to find anything definitive. So how can we force the diggers to make a move?"

"Up for an adventure?" he asked with a smirk.

"Always."

"Grab your burner phone and let's call the pawnshop. Maybe if he has an interested buyer, it will turn up the heat. Use your sexiest phone voice and ask him questions about historical items that you really really want."

Delanie fished out her burner phone and cleared her throat. She dialed the number for Jim Jones's store.

"Midlo Pawn," a man answered.

"Hi, my name is Melanie Johnson, and my boyfriend and I were in the store a while back looking for a gift. We talked to Jim Jones. Is he available?"

"I remember you. Tall blond with the guy with the chubby dog."

"Yes, Kirk and I were looking for something for his father's birthday. Our anniversary is coming up, and I was looking for something interesting for Kirk. He's an American literature professor, and I was hoping to find something that belonged to an author. Could you help me with something he would like?"

"I don't have much in the store. In my vaults, I have several first editions from people like Faulkner, Hemingway, and Mitchell. You interested in a book?"

"Maybe. Got anything by Poe?"

"I might. Give me tonight to check, and I'll call you back. This a good number?"

"Yes. Thanks," she said as he disconnected.

Duncan raised his eyebrows. "I hope he doesn't get suspicious and go to ground."

DELANIE'S PHONE rang in the middle of her reality TV binge. Realizing it was her burner phone, she rummaged through her purse for it before the call landed in voice mail.

"Hello. Melanie? This is Jim at Midlo Pawn. I went through my collections of first editions tonight. Unfortunately, I don't have anything by Poe. I do have a Hemingway and a Harper Lee first edition. I found a small framed photo of old Edgar. Let me know if you're interested in any of these. When do you need it by?"

"I have until the twentieth," she replied.

"Oh, then you can come by the store then. I was going to say we could meet tonight if you need to have it quickly."

"What kind of prices are we talking about?" she asked.

"The Hemingway is eight K, the Lee is three K, and the Poe picture is two."

"Two hundred for the picture?" she asked.

He laughed. "No, sweetie. Two thousand."

Delanie let out a low whistle. "I love him and all, but those are pretty steep. Do you have any wiggle room on the Poe?"

"Maybe. Wanna meet me tonight to see it? We could work something out."

"I don't want to waste your time. I need to be between three and five hundred."

"No, sweetheart. I can't go that low. Let me know if you change your mind. But you may want to be quick about it. This stuff tends to move quickly." He disconnected before she could reply.

Delanie scowled and texted Duncan. Nothing seemed to be shaking loose on this investigation. She would have to come up with something else to encourage these guys to make a move.

29

Delanie jumped out of the bed the next morning with an idea to prod the diggers to move. She grabbed her phone and dialed.

A groggy Duncan said, "Delanie? It's seven o'clock."

"Sorry. I think I figured out what to do about the pawnshop guys. After you've had your coffee, could you send them an email as a rich buyer and ask James if he has any coins with interesting stories. Tell him that you're big on conspiracy theories and urban lore. It's worth a try."

Duncan tapped on his keyboard for what seemed like an eternity. "There," he finally said. "I sent it. I'll let you know if he bites. But in the meantime, I'm going back to bed. See you later."

Already wide awake, Delanie grabbed a banana and her gym bag. She'd start her day there and then head to the office.

After her workout, she jumped in the car as her phone rang.

"Hey, Duncan. What's up?"

"It didn't take long to get a response from our friend James. He said he has a stamp that was originally stolen from Napoleon. It got passed around in France until some upstart of an American stole it and took it to Boston. Then he said he's got a coin that was found on Oak Island in Nova Scotia. There's a legend that there's a treasure buried there from the Knights Templar. The rumors suggest that the treasure could be gold, jewelry, or original Shakespearian manu-scripts."

"Interesting. Did he give you a price?"

"Yeah. The stamp is ten thousand, and he wants fifteen thousand for the Oak Island coin."

"The stolen antiquities market must be profitable these days. His quotes are pricey. Tell him you want an American coin with a cool story. Tell him you want something related to an author. Maybe that will stir up something."

"Okeydoke. Let's see what happens." Duncan clicked off.

First, creepy contraband reptiles and now stolen historic arti-facts. Delanie wanted to get these guys who were selling stolen antiquities.

Before she could think more about the pawnshop owner, her phone dinged with another email from Titan 51. He thanked her for providing him a lead on the Poe statue. He had attached a copy of his next blog post on theories about the cornerstone. Delanie rolled her eyes.

Turning on the radio in her car, she settled in the driver's seat to read his theory. The gist of his article was that the time capsule in the Poe statue served as a cover up for a jewelry store heist in the early 1900s. Titan 51 felt that the store owner coordinated the theft and later collected on the insurance money. No new leads. Just a rehash of what she had already found. At the end, he also talked about other surprise time capsules that were found when buildings were demol-ished. This post seemed better written than some of the others on his website.

Titan 51 did not offer any theories about whether the jewelry store owner or his family planned to retrieve the valuables. It sounded like it was a convenient way to get rid of evidence. She scanned to the end of his article looking for footnotes or credits. Nothing to substantiate his claims.

Disappointed that the blogger did not reveal anything new, she texted Duncan his handle and website address to see if he could uncover anything else. She was probably chasing leads that would not reveal anything, but she had to be sure.

Delanie threw her things in the passenger seat of her car and drove to the office.

Grabbing a water from the refrigerator, she sank into her chair. Finding her office credit card, she called the *Richmond Times-Dispatch* archives again for anything on the jewelry heist and Thomas P. Keller.

The nice archivist had quite a few articles to send her this time. While she waited for the email, she browsed online files at the Library of Virginia. Nothing new there either. Thomas P. Keller was the youngest of three sons who took over the store after his father and eldest brother's deaths. Thomas P. Keller had a penchant for get-rich quick schemes, and he ran the store into the ground in a few short years.

According to a magazine article she found, the store had a turn-around after a devastating burglary. The feel-good piece detailed store renovations and a bigger staff at the jewelry store.

Another article focused on the burglary. Criminals broke into the store and stole several valuable pieces in the inventory. No one was every charged with the theft. Curious about what else was stolen in the targeted theft, she made a note to see if she could find the insurance claim. This matched what Chip Marshall had told her.

Not finding anything else interesting, Delanie packed up. She would pick up dinner and review her notes again from the comfort of home.

An hour later, Delanie finished her take-out soup and salad and checked her phone. The newspaper's archivist came through with several articles. She woke up her laptop and perused the files.

After pouring over the stories, she rummaged through her cabinets for something chocolate. Not finding any candy, she raided the package of chocolate chips she was saving for a future batch of cookies.

The local reporters in the historic articles described the colorful past of Thomas P. Keller and his contemporaries. According to the paper, a diamond brooch purported to have stones from an Indian Maharaja, a valuable coin, and a pair of ruby and diamond earrings were stolen from the collection. The three items, were valued at over $650,000 in 1913.

She found an online calculator that would convert that amount into today's money, and she whistled when $16.5 million popped up on her screen. Nothing to sneeze at. In one article,

Delanie noticed that Thomas P. Keller praised his father's forethought to heavily insure the store's inventory.

The last article was a bankruptcy and liquidation notice for the store in 1923. The recovery after the robbery did not last long, she mused.

Her phone rang, interrupting her thoughts of Keller's poor business skills. "Eric FBI" popped up on her caller ID. She clicked the green button.

"Hey, what's going on? Busy?" he asked.

"No, just doing some research on a case that might involve a jewelry heist in 1913," she said.

"Cold case?"

"Icy. The insurance company paid off the claim. But it ties into a case that I'm working now. Where are you?" she asked.

"Doing an investigation in Kansas. It's really flat out here. You can see for miles. And it's nothing but fields."

"When will you be back in Richmond?" She picked up a few more chocolate chips.

"Hopefully, next week if all goes as planned."

"I'm having a Friends-giving next weekend. I hope you can come."

"You cooking?" he asked.

"No. What are you, chicken?"

"Just curious. I've never seen you cook before. Actually, you never have food in your house. I thought I was about to see a new side of you."

"Does that mean you're coming? I'm having most of it catered."

"Sounds good. What can I bring?"

"Wine or dessert unless you have a specialty dish. Let me know when you're back in town." He had grilled dinner for her once. She wondered if he had any hidden culinary skills.

"Will do. It's good to hear your voice. See you soon."

"Bye." She disconnected. It was good to hear from him. She wondered where their relationship was going. He was always busy with work, and if he was deep in an investigation, it could be weeks before he called or texted. It did not seem like dating when he was always somewhere else.

30

DELANIE'S ALARM CLOCK READ TWO FORTY-EIGHT WHEN SHE OPENED one eye to see what the buzzing noise was. Realizing it was her phone, she grabbed it. "Hello."

"Hey, Delanie. It's Marco. The diggers are back. We're watching them on the cameras. Steve said they just got here."

"Okay, I'm on my way. Let's not approach them. I'd like to catch them with the goods. I'll be there as soon as I can."

"Sounds like a plan. I'll call you if anything changes. Meet me at the side door as usual."

She threw on a sweatshirt and jeans and pulled her hair up into a messy ponytail. She gunned the Mustang's engine and made it downtown in record time.

Marco held the big, metal door for her. The cleanup crew mopped the floor, and all the chairs sat on top of the tables in the main room. She had never seen the stage with all the overhead lights on before. The brightness made her squint.

In the security office, Steve flipped from camera to camera on the bank of screens that dominated his desk. He zoomed in on the one on the light pole near the statue. The father and son duo, James and Jaime, dug around the base of the statue. James focused on the back corner, and Jaime concentrated on the corner closest to him. Both men wore reflective vests and hard hats. When Steve changed camera views, she spotted Pete in his SUV, parked for an easy getaway.

"They're still at it," Marco said as Steve nodded. The two other bouncers, Rikko and Tony, who looked almost like twins decked out in tight T-shirts, black jeans, and leather motorcycle boots, stood in the doorway.

Delanie nodded at the men, who watched silently from the back of the room. Steve zeroed in on the statue. James Jones left the camera frame and returned a few minutes later with a hatchet and a pick. Jaime dropped his shovel and joined his father at the statue's corner. The older man started chipping away at one of the blocks.

Delanie gasped. "It looks like they're trying to break through the base. That's where the time capsule is if the book I read is correct."

"Let's roll," Marco said. "Tony, you take the front. Rikko, be a ghost, and sneak up on the lookout. We don't want him to zoom off this time. I'll take the other side. When they get the statue open, we've got to stop them before they escape with whatever they came for. Delanie, you can stay here with Steve."

She cocked her head and cut her eyes at the head bouncer. "Okay, okay," Marco said. "But stay behind me. Chaz'll kill me if you get hurt."

They filed out and jogged down the hall. Once outside, the men found their places. Tony and Rikko disappeared into the alley behind the club. Marco pointed at his eyes with two fingers and then pointed toward Delanie. She nodded and followed behind the giant man. She had to jog to keep up with his pace.

Out front, there were few hiding places since the parking lot stood mostly empty. All the nearby clubs and restaurants had closed. She followed Marco around the Treasure Chest's perimeter. They were out in the open as they inched forward to the statue's front. Delanie hoped the pawnshop guys were paying attention to their work and not the surroundings.

One of the men yelled, "Found it. Come here and help me. It's stuck." Delanie heard some scraping noises and then a car door slam.

"It was true," one of the men said. "I'll be damned. Look at that."

Another voice said, "Just like the web guy said."

Then Delanie heard a scuffle and then a loud noise, closer to the back of the statue. Marco took off running and the scuffle got louder.

By the time Delanie rounded the corner, Tony was sitting on top of Jaime. He had his arms pulled behind his head. Marco kicked the hatchet out of reach and landed on James. The older man struggled for a minute or two, but he was no match for the head of security. Marco zip tied his wrists and pulled James to his feet.

"He put something in his pocket." Delanie pointed to James.

Meanwhile, Jaime decided to be a tough guy. He struggled and almost wiggled free from Tony's grasp. He tried to bite the security guard. After a missed swing and couple of kicks, Tony punched the younger man, and he went limp on the ground. As he was zip tying Jaime, Rikko came around the corner with Pete. He had both arms twisted in a painful position behind the younger man's back and above his head. Pete grimaced and whined. Tony appeared with several zip ties. A minute or two later, all three of the diggers had been subdued.

Marco caught his breath. "The old dude put something in his pants." He reached for the man's pockets and turned them inside out. Two coins fell on the ground and made a tinkling sound when they hit the asphalt.

Delanie scooped them up. One was silver colored with a woman's profile on the front. The second silver one featured a woman's head and a bunch of stars. It had 1893 at the bottom. The men had dumped the time capsule on the sidewalk. Delanie took pictures of the spilled contents and the two coins. She could see a map, postcards, and copy of *The Raven*. Scooping everything up, she put them in the metal box. She snapped a few more pictures of the damage.

Marco made a phone call and gave the club's address. "So, what are you clowns up to?"No one responded. James lay on his stomach on the grass, while Pete and Jaime sat on the curb away from each other. The two younger men stared at their shoes. Rikko and Tony stood guard.

"You can talk now, or you can tell the police when they get here. There's quite a lot of damage to this statue," Marco said.

Right on cue, two Richmond Police cruisers pulled into the lot with lights flashing. The red and blue lights bounced off the nearby buildings, creating a disco effect. Two officers climbed out and approached the motley crew encircling the statue of the Father of the American Mystery.

"Hey, Marco," the female officer said, approaching the group. "What's going on here." Two other police cars pulled in and parked at angles behind the first cruiser.

"Hey, Sergeant Martin. My guys caught these three digging around the statue here. And then they broke it and pulled out the time capsule. I found this one with two coins in his pocket." He nodded his head toward the older man.

Delanie stepped forward and handed the officer the time capsule.

"Well you've got them all wrapped up nice and neat for us, the only thing that's missing is a bow on top. You guys made it easy for us tonight," Sergeant Martin said.

She moved over to talk to the older man while other officers took the two younger guys in custody. Another officer took pictures of the scene and the broken box. He inventoried the items and put them in individual paper bags. Then he loaded all the tools into the back of his police car. The male officer searched all three men and inventoried the items in their pockets. James had a wallet, cigarette lighter, and an antique diamond brooch in his jacket pocket. More of the stolen loot?

When Sergeant Martin finished with the pawnshop owner, she approached Marco and Delanie. "Got camera footage of their antics?"

"Of course. Chaz likes cameras. This is Delanie. She's a private investigator. When we spotted these clowns digging last week, Chaz asked her to figure out why. Come with me and Steve'll get copies of the surveillance for you," Marco said.

"What were they after?" Sergeant Martin asked, crossing the parking lot.

"The older man, James Jones, owns Midlo Pawn. One of the younger guys is his son Jaime, and the other is a friend named Pete. The pawnshop has an online gig going on the dark web that deals in historical artifacts. My partner and I researched a lot of their offerings, and they were stolen from private collections or museums."

"But why the contents of the statue," the police sergeant asked as Marco held the metal door for them.

"The time capsule was installed when the statue was dedicated in 1913. Most of the contents were benign, but James found a tale on the dark web that it might contain some coins. He did some research and found that two had value, and I guess he wanted to add them to his inventory. There was a jewelry store heist in the early 1900s, and the coins and some jewelry were stolen. The hypothesis was that the store owner arranged the burglary to collect the insurance money because he was always strapped for cash. And he hid the evidence in the time capsule to keep it out of sight."

"Good job. I need your contact information. We may have more questions later," Sergeant Martin said.

Delanie handed her a business card. "No problem. I have copies of all my research."

After the police gathered what they needed, they hauled the three diggers off to the city jail.

Delanie said good night and drove home with the windows down. The cool November air helped her to stay awake. She'd have to call Rosalind and Chip tomorrow to give them an update on the time capsule and the contents. Sometimes, there is some truth to a legend, even conspiracy chatter on the dark web.

31

DELANIE PARKED BESIDE DUNCAN AND HURRIED INSIDE THE OFFICE with breakfast and coffee. "Morning!" she yelled when she closed the front glass door.

"We're back here. What'd ya bring?" he asked.

"Breakfast, but more importantly, I've got strong coffee." She dropped her things on the conference room table.

"By all means, we need to celebrate. We've had quite the productive month around here. Thanks to you. You busted up drag queen theft, we solved the case of the missing snakes, we solved the mystery of the time capsule, and Chaz almost became mayor."

Delanie unwrapped her breakfast burrito and took a couple of bites. "Business is really turning around for us." She reached for her coffee. "I appreciate all you do, too. You're the best resource for information."

"I hate to say it, but I think Chaz and his wacky cases are responsible for our good press." He licked his fingers.

"I got a call from Richmond PD, she said. "Officers raided the home of Pete Mills. They found a couple of poisonous snakes when they searched the house. Another Snakes and Scales client."

"Did they raid the Jones's house?" he asked.

"Yup and their pawnshop. I think they were keenly interested in the online business and all the hot artifacts. The Jones kid had a snake, too."

"They'll close a lot of stolen property cases with that one. They should give us a medal." Duncan balled up his wrapper.

"I don't know about any awards. I'm glad we closed the cases. Are you, Evie, and Margaret coming to my Friends-giving tomorrow?"

"What do you want us to bring? We're not going to have twenty people bringing potato salad, are we?" he asked.

"No. I told people different things. This'll be our pre-Thanksgiving dinner before we scatter and celebrate with our families. It'll be fun."

"Evie and I have been cooking a lot lately. We'll probably bring some vegetable dish. You need anything else for the party? Should we come early to set up?"

"Nope. We're good. Paisley's doing the decorating. I ordered ham, turkey, rolls, and Boston cream pie. Just come and enjoy. We'll have plenty of food. I'm not sure what to do today. It kinda feels a little boring now that all the drama has ended."

"Enjoy the quiet. It won't last long."

Right on cue, her business cell phone rang. "Falcon Investigations."

"Hi, lady. This is Kathy Meyers from Lion Insurance. I have a couple of insurance jobs I could use your help with."

"Be glad to help. Send over the details, and we'll get right to work for you," Delanie said.

"You're a peach. I'll get those to you momentarily. Thanks a bunch," Kathy said.

Delanie disconnected the call. She pulled her laptop from her messenger bag to see the cases Kathy had for her this time. She preferred workman's comp ones with no snakes.

～

THE NEXT MORNING, Delanie checked the turkey and ham warming in the oven. The doorbell rang. "It's open," she yelled.

The door rattled, but no one entered. When she investigated, Delanie found Paisley balancing several items and kicking the door with her foot. Her friend's hands were full of a large box, overnight bag, and two shopping bags. "Thanks. I've got more in the car."

"Moving in?" Delanie asked.

Paisley smirked and shook her head. After two trips, the women had all the food and decorations transported inside.

"I'm going to put my clothes in your room, okay?" Paisley asked.

Delanie nodded. "Thanks for all of your help," she said to the back of Paisley who was already headed for the master bedroom downstairs.

Paisley breezed in and started unpacking the boxes and bags. "Are the tables where you want them?"

"I was thinking we could put all the food and drinks on one table in the kitchen area, and everybody could fill plates buffet style. We could push my kitchen table against that wall and use it with another long table."

Paisley pulled out tablecloths in coordinating fall colors. She covered and smoothed and then rearranged some when the colors did not suit her taste. Sunflower centerpieces brightened each table. "Okay. I'm about ready for the place settings." Paisley pushed a corkscrew curl from her face.

"They're in here on the kitchen table." Delanie grabbed a stack of plates and took them to the living room. The PI spent the next thirty minutes ferrying plates and silverware to Paisley, who methodically arranged them on the long table. Delanie was sure that if she took a ruler to them that the place settings started at the exact same placement for each guest.

"The tables look stunning. You outdid yourself." Delanie hugged her friend.

"Thanks. I'm done here. I'm going to get dressed in your room. Will is going to be here soon," she said with a giggle.

Before Delanie could check on the food, the doorbell rang. FBI Special Agent Eric Ellington stood on her porch with a bottle of wine and a Ukrop's lemon chess pie.

"Hi. Come on in."

He handed her the dessert and kissed her on the cheek. "It's good to see you."

"It's been a while," she said, wistfully. "How was Kansas?"

"It looked about the same as it did in *The Wizard of Oz*."

"Make yourself at home. The remote is on the coffee table if you want to watch TV."

"What can I help with?" Eric asked.

"We're almost done. My stuff is warming, and we'll add food to the table as it arrives." She set the pie on the kitchen table. "We'll put drinks on the edge of this counter. How's work?" She moved an empty ice bucket out of the way.

"Busy. I've been travelling a lot. It's nice to be back in Virginia."

"Anything you can talk about?"

"The weather's nice in San Diego, and the barbeque was good in Memphis. The Kansas assignment finally ended. I'm glad we wrapped that up this week." He wandered into her living room and flipped the TV. He clicked until he found ESPN.

"You sound like a travel agent," she said from the kitchen. The doorbell rang and interrupted their conversation. "Could you get that?"

Delanie did not hear any conversation, and no one came inside. She dropped a dish towel next to the sink. She peeked around the front door and Eric. She gasped.

John Bailey stood on her porch with a bouquet of flowers.

Eric excused himself and returned to the living room when Delanie appeared at the door. John remained silent, and she stepped outside on the small porch. She pulled the door closed behind her. A cool breeze rustled the leaves left on the trees and caused her to shiver.

"Hi. What are you doing here?" Her heart fluttered, and she could feel the blood rushing to her face. She did not know whether to be pleased to see him or to fly off in a rage to let him know how much he had hurt her when he skipped town when they were seeing each other.

"I came to apologize, but I see that you're busy. My timing is never right," he said with a half-smile.

Delanie did not know what to think about his surprise appearance. Memories floated around her head like jetsam after a storm. A tell-all author had hired her last summer to investigate a rumor that Johnny Velvet from the 80s band the Vibes had faked his death and was living incognito in Virginia. When she was about to reveal that that was indeed true, John Bailey had hightailed it out of town and left his farm and her in the lurch and bruised her heart in the process.

It became apparent that Delanie should say something to break the awkward silence. "I don't know quite what to say. This is a surprise."

"I should have stayed and faced the music. It wasn't as bad as I thought it would be when that book came out. The publicity has died down. I'm sorry," he said, handing her the flowers.

"Thank you," she whispered. She took a deep breath. "Would you like to stay for lunch?" she asked as Duncan's car pulled in her driveway.

"Thanks, anyway. I have to head out. I wanted to stop by since I was back in town. I'll see you around."

John Bailey turned and trotted down the steps toward a blue truck parked at the street. Delanie stared, not quite sure how she felt.

Duncan, Evie, and Margaret made their way up the path to the porch. Duncan looked over his shoulder and then at Delanie. "Was that Johnny Velvet? He's back?" Evie did a double take, straining to see the former rock star.

Delanie nodded and held the door for her partner, his girlfriend, and his faithful sidekick.

A radio thumped and boomed. The noise stopped when Chaz

and Marco climbed out of the infamous gold Hummer, parked by the mailbox. That should keep her neighbors talking for a while.

Chaz trotted up the sidewalk with a case of bottles, and Marco had a pie. She put John's flowers in a vase and set them in the kitchen. Trying to cover up the shock of seeing John Bailey on her porch, she pushed thoughts of him and last summer out of her head and returned to her guests.

THESE ARE REAL…

Arena Football – I made up the Richmond Rowdies, but Richmond does have an arena football team called the Richmond Roughnecks, and they play each spring at the Richmond Coliseum.

Bon Air – This is an area of the city where Richmond residents went to escape the southern summer heat. Most of the Victorian homes in the village date back to the 1800s.

Bon Secours Redskins Training Camp – The Washington Redskins Football team hold training camp in late July/early August in Richmond with an eight-year deal with the city (spanning 2012-2020). The facility is located behind the Science Museum of Virginia.

Brandermill – Awarded the "Best Planned Community in America" in 1977, this was the first community of its kind in Chesterfield, Virginia. It surrounds the Swift Creek Reservoir and has a golf course.

Chesterfield County, Virginia – Formed in 1749 and named for the fourth Earl of Chesterfield, the county is south of the capital, Richmond. It is the third most populous county in the Commonwealth of Virginia.

Church Hill – This is an historic neighborhood in Richmond that overlooks the James River. St. John's Church, site of Patrick Henry's "Give me Liberty" speech and Chimborazo Park, the location of the famous Civil War hospital, are historic sites in the area. Chaz Smith has a townhouse here with a great view of the river.

Edgar Allan Poe – The famous author, poet, literary critic, and father of the modern mystery lived for a time in Richmond, Virginia. After his parents' deaths, he was taken in by wealthy Richmonder, John Allan. As a young man, he held a position at the *Southern Literary Messenger*. Poe's mother is buried at St. John's Church (made famous by Patrick' Henry's "Give me Liberty" speech). I took some liberties and built Chaz's Treasure Chest on the site of the *Southern Literary Messenger*. And there is a statue of Edgar Allan Poe in Richmond, but it's on the lawn of the Virginia State Capitol. I made up the one on Chaz's property to house the valuables in the fictitious time capsule.

The Fan – This is a neighborhood of about 85-blocks in Richmond. The streets are laid out in a fan shape. It boasts a variety of architectural designs, interesting shops, and unique restaurants. Freeda's is a figment of my imagination. Richmond does have a fabulous brunch drag show at Godfrey's on Grace Street. Their French toast is amazing.

Freebird Bail Bonds – Freebird Bail Bonds is a real company in Central Virginia. Many thanks to Harry Rosmarin and Michael Haskins, who spoke to my Sisters in Crime chapter about the ins and outs of bail bonds in Virginia.

Goochland County – Named for Sir William Gooch, Royal Lieutenant Governor, the county formed in 1728 and was originally part of Henrico County.

Henrico County – One of the eight original shires in Virginia, this county surrounds the city of Richmond (which was a part of it until 1842) on the east, west, and north sides.

Library of Virginia – This gem on Broad Street in Richmond, Virginia is part library, museum, and archives. Hundreds of resources are being digitized and are available online. They have a wealth of genealogy information. I uncovered hundreds of years of my family's history here, and the reference librarians are so helpful and generous with their time.

Maymont – This lovely park, mansion from the Gilded Age, and gardens are located in downtown Richmond near Byrd Park. Once the home to financier, James Dooley, the park has a wildlife rehabilitation area, Italian and Japanese gardens, and a petting zoo/nature center. I always visit the bears when we go to Maymont.

Merrimac – *The Merrimac* was a Union frigate that was captured, rebuilt, and renamed the *CSS Virginia* during the American Civil War. It battled the *USS Monitor* off the coast of Virginia in the first battle between ironclad naval vessels.

Midlothian – This is a town in Chesterfield County. It was originally a coal mining region and home to Virginia's first railroad. And the Urban Farmhouse Market and Café is a wonderful place to stop if you're visiting the Midlothian Library.

Monroe Park – This is the city of Richmond's oldest park. Located on the Virginia Commonwealth University campus, it's a hub for city residents and college students. Over the years, the site has been the site of rallies, fairs, and a camp for Civil War soldiers.

Poe Museum – The Old Stone House in Richmond, Virginia houses a vast collection of Edgar Allan Poe artifacts. The house is near his boyhood home and the *Southern Literary Messenger*, where Poe worked. The museum hosts "unhappy hours" in the garden. Edgar and Pluto are the real museum cats. Stop by and meet them.

Randolph-Macon College – This is a private, liberal arts college located near Ashland, Virginia. Ashland is a town in Hanover county, and it defines itself as "The Center of the Universe."

Richmond City Hall – Located in downtown Richmond on Broad Street, the skyscraper has an observation tower at the top. It's also located diagonally across the street from "Old" City Hall, the Victorian Gothic building, completed in 1894.

Richmond Coliseum – Built in the 1970s, the coliseum has been home to professional basketball, hockey, and wrestling, college basketball, arena football, arena auto racing, and numerous concerts and conventions. In 1972, parts of *Elvis on Tour* were filmed here.

Richmond Times-Dispatch – The newspaper serving Richmond and Central Virginia has the second highest circulation in the Commonwealth.

Rockwood Park – This is a 161-acre park in Chesterfield County that has walking trails, a nature center, dog park, and recreational facilities with tennis and pickleball courts.

Sears Catalog Homes – While there are several Sears Catalog homes in Hopewell, Virginia in the Crescent Hills neighborhood, I moved one to western Chesterfield County for Delanie's residence. The homes were ordered from the Sears and Roebuck catalog and were shipped by rail. Delanie's Yates model dates back to 1939. Gerry Fuss, my friend and long-time Chesterfield County resident, let me know that there are several Sears homes in the Bon Air area.

Shockoe Slip and Shockoe Bottom – Located in downtown Richmond, this area lies between the financial district and the James

River. A lot of the buildings are restored warehouses, and many of the streets and alleys have cobblestones. A lot of Richmond's nightlife is in this part of town. My short story, "Art Attack" in *Deadly Southern Charm* is set in a gallery in one of these warehouses.

Short Pump Town Center – This is an upscale mall on west Broad Street. The area used to be home to a tavern for travelers between Richmond and points west. Legend has it that the name came from a porch installed over the pump at the tavern. When it blocked the handle, it had to be altered to fit under the new room. After it was cut off, it was a "short pump."

Ukrop's – This family-owned grocery store, based in Virginia from 1937-2010, was famous for its exemplary service, Southern hospitality, baked goods, and prepared meals. They catered my holiday dinners for years, and their lemon chess pie was out of this world.

Valentine Museum – This museum in the heart of Clay Street is dedicated to the history of Richmond. Founded in 1898, it is also known for being Richmond's first museum. The museum property also includes the Wickham House.

VCU – Virginia Commonwealth University is a public, urban research university in Richmond, VA. Its hospital and graduate art programs are renowned. This is Delanie's alma mater.

Virginia Museum of History and Culture – Formerly the Virginia Historical Society, this museum and reference collection house a wide variety of artifacts from fossils to maps that tell of Virginia's history.

ACKNOWLEDGMENTS

Writing is a long process and often a solitary effort. But I'm glad I'm not alone. I want to thank my family and friends who provided all the wonderful support for this book – Stan Weidner for putting up with all my writing adventures, my parents who instilled in me a lifelong love of reading, Cortney Cain for her amazing feedback, Meagan and Jocelyn Cain, my social media subject matter experts, and Bill Cain for always keeping everyone entertained.

And I appreciate all the encouragement, love, and support from my Bethia UMC family.

Many thanks to Mark McBride and Eric Harris for all the information on exotic snakes and fish. Thank you to Rosemary Shomaker, Fiona Quinn, and Tina Glasneck for helping me with my drag show research. Bob Scott and Kristine Downing, I appreciate all the good ideas and advice. Darleen Kirkland, thanks for the story about the ghost fish.

I am so grateful for my talented Sisters in Crime, Guppy, Virginia is for Mysteries, Pens, Paws, and Claws, and James River Writer friends.

Your support is invaluable! Frances Aylor, Mary Burton, LynDee Walker, Teresa Inge, and Jayne Ormerod – I cannot thank you ladies enough!

Thanks to my critique group: Mary Miley, Rod Sterling, Susan Campbell, Frances Aylor, Sandie Warwick, Catherine Brennan, and Marjorie Bagby for all the great feedback. Deb Rolfe, you will be missed. Sandie, thanks for all the ideas for Chaz and his antics. #TeamChaz

Many thanks to the lunch crew, always my first focus group: Sandy Garrett, Melissa Harmon, Melissa Camp, Darrell Dyson, Justin Harmon, and Cindy Puller.

Joy Pfister and her wonderful crew at Studio FBJ are fabulous, and Lynda Bishop is an amazing editor. Fiona Jayde does a wonderful job on the artwork and covers, and Tina Glasneck makes sure everything is perfect and ready to go. I cannot thank you all enough for turning my words into a book.

And I am so grateful for my readers who follow Delanie, Duncan, Margaret, and Chaz's adventures.

CPSIA information can be obtained
at www.ICGtesting.com
Printed in the USA
FFHW011442051219
56487766-62296FF